KU-675-132

The Infamous Arrandales

Scandal is their destiny!

Meet the Arrandale family—dissolute, disreputable and defiant! This infamous family have scandal in their blood, and wherever they go their reputation will *always* precede them!

Don't miss any of the fabulous books in Sarah Mallory's dazzling new quartet!

The Chaperon's Seduction
Already available

Temptation of a Governess
Already available

Return of the Runaway
Available now

and look for the fourth and final sinfully scandalous story, coming soon!

Author Note

These days we think of surgeons as being at the top of the medical profession—skilled lifesavers, possibly even more important than general practitioners. In the eighteenth and nineteenth century things were very different. Doctors and physicians might be considered gentlemen, but surgeons worked with their hands, and rarely had any formal qualifications, so they were considered artisans, tradesmen. This is the world occupied by Raoul Doulevant, a Belgian surgeon who is proud of his skills but who knows he cannot be considered a suitable husband for the daughter of a marquess.

Cassie is an Arrandale, the errant granddaughter of the Dowager Marchioness of Hune. She is mentioned in the earlier books of this mini-series but never seen, having eloped and run off to France with her husband during the short-lived Peace of Amiens. Now, in 1803, the peace is at an end, Cassie is a widow and she wants to return to England.

This is the story of Cassie and Raoul's flight through France. It is dangerous, difficult, and as they learn more about each other they realise their worlds are just too far apart for them to find happiness together without momentous sacrifices on both sides.

Enjoy their journey!

RETURN
OF THE RUNAWAY

Sarah Mallory

All rights reserved including the right of reproduction in whole
or in part in any form. This edition is published by arrangement with
Harlequin Books S.A.

This is a work of fiction. Names, characters, places, locations and
incidents are purely fictional and bear no relationship to any real
life individuals, living or dead, or to any actual places, business
establishments, locations, events or incidents. Any resemblance is
entirely coincidental.

This book is sold subject to the condition that it shall not, by way of
trade or otherwise, be lent, resold, hired out or otherwise circulated
without the prior consent of the publisher in any form of binding or
cover other than that in which it is published and without a similar
condition including this condition being imposed on the subsequent
purchaser.

® and TM are trademarks owned and used by the trademark owner
and/or its licensee. Trademarks marked with ® are registered with the
United Kingdom Patent Office and/or the Office for Harmonisation in
the Internal Market and in other countries.

First published in Great Britain 2016
By Mills & Boon, an imprint of HarperCollins*Publishers*
1 London Bridge Street, London, SE1 9GF

Large Print edition 2016

© 2016 Sarah Mallory

ISBN: 978-0-263-26308-4

Our policy is to use papers that are natural, renewable and recyclable
products and made from wood grown in sustainable forests.
The logging and manufacturing processes conform to the legal
environmental regulations of the country of origin.

Printed and bound in Great Britain
by CPI Antony Rowe, Chippenham, Wiltshire

Sarah Mallory was born in the West Country and now lives on the beautiful Yorkshire moors. She has been writing for more than three decades—mainly historical romances set in the Georgian and Regency period. She has won several awards for her writing, most recently the Romantic Novelists' Association RoNA Rose Award in 2012 (for *The Dangerous Lord Darrington*) and 2013 (for *Beneath the Major's Scars*).

Visit the Author Profile page
at millsandboon.co.uk for more titles.

To Marianne—
from the proudest mum in the world.

Chapter One

Verdun, France—September 1803

The young lady in the room at the top of the house on the Rue Égalité was looking uncharacteristically sober in her dark-blue linen riding habit. Even the white shirt she wore beneath the close-fitting jacket bore only a modest frill around the neck. She had further added to the sobriety by sewing black ribbons to her straw bonnet and throwing a black lace shawl around her shoulders. Now she sat before the looking glass and regarded her reflection with a critical eye.

"'Lady Cassandra Witney is headstrong and impetuous,'" she stated, recalling a recent description of herself. Her critic had also described her as beautiful, but Cassie disregarded that. She propped her chin on her hand and gave a tiny huff of dissatisfaction. 'The problem with being headstrong and impetuous,' she told her image, 'is that it leads one to make mistakes. Marrying Gerald was most definitely a mistake.'

She turned and surveyed the little room. Accompanying Gerald to Verdun had been a mistake, too, but when the Treaty of Amiens had come to an end in May she had not been able to bring herself to abandon him and go home to England. That would have been to admit defeat and her spirit rebelled at that. Eloping with Gerald had been her choice, freely made, and she could almost hear Grandmama, the Dowager Marchioness of Hune, saying, 'You have made your bed, my girl, now you must lie in it.'

And lie in it she had, for more than a year, even though she had known after a few months of marriage that Gerald was not the kind, loving man she had first thought him.

A knock at the door interrupted her reverie. After a word with the servant she picked up her portmanteau and followed him down the stairs. A light travelling chaise was waiting at the door with Merimon, the courier she had hired, standing beside it. He was a small, sharp-faced individual and now he looked down his long narrow nose at the bag in her hand.

'*C'est tout?*'

'It is all I wish to take.'

Cassandra answered him in his own language, looking him in the eye. As the bag was strapped on to the chaise she reflected sadly that it was little enough to show for more than a year of married life. Merimon opened the door of the chaise and continued to address her in coarse French.

'Milady will enter, if you please, and I will accompany you on foot. My horse is waiting at the Porte St Paul.'

Cassie looked up. The September sun was already low in the sky.

'Surely it would have been better to set off at first light,' she observed.

Merimon looked pained.

'I explained it all to you, milady. I could not obtain a carriage any sooner. And this road, there is no shelter and the days can be very hot for the horses. This way we shall drive through the night, you will sleep and when you awake, *voilà*, we shall be in Reims.'

'I cannot sleep in *here*.' Cassie could not help it, she sniffed. How different it had been, travelling to France with Gerald. She had been so in love then, and so hopeful. Everything had been a delicious adventure. She pushed away the memories. There was no point in dwelling on the past. 'Very well, let us get on, then. The sooner this night is over the better.'

It was not far to the eastern gate, where Cassie knew her passport would be carefully checked. Verdun still maintained most of its medieval fortifications, along with an imposing citadel. It was one of the reasons the town had been chosen to hold the British tourists trapped in France when war was declared: the defences made it very difficult for enemies to get in, but it also made it impossible for the British to get out.

When they reached the city gate she gave her papers to Merimon, who presented them to the guard. The French officer studied them for a long moment before brushing past the courier and approaching the chaise. Cassie let down the window.

'You are leaving us, *madame*?'

'Yes. I came to Verdun with my husband when he was detained. He died a week since. There is no longer any reason for me to remain.' She added, with a touch of hauteur, 'The First Consul Bonaparte decreed that only English men of fighting age should be detained.'

The man inclined his head. 'As you say. And where do you go?'

'Rouen,' said Merimon, stepping up. 'We travel via Reims and Beauvais and hope to find passage on a ship from Rouen to Le Havre, from whence milady can sail to England.'

Cassie waited, tense and anxious while the *gendarme* stared at her. After what seemed like hours he cast a searching look inside the chaise, as if to assure himself that no prisoner was hiding on the floor. Finally he was satisfied. He stood back and handed the papers to Merimon before ordering the postilion to drive on. The courier loped ahead to where a small urchin was holding the reins of a long-tailed bay and as the chaise rattled through the gates he scrambled into the saddle and took up his position beside it.

Cassie stripped off her gloves, then removed her bonnet and rubbed her temples. Perhaps now she was leaving Verdun the dull ache in her head would ease. It had been a tense few days since Gerald's death, his so-called friends circling like vultures waiting to strike at the first sign of weakness. Well, that was behind her now. She was going home. Darkness was falling. Cassie settled back into one corner as the carriage rolled and bumped along the uneven road. She found herself hoping the roads in England were as good as she remembered, that she might not suffer this tooth-rattling buffeting for the whole of the journey.

The chaise began to slow suddenly and Cassie sat up. For some time they had been travelling through woodland with tall trees lining the road and making it as black as pitch inside the carriage. Now, however, pale moonlight illuminated the window and Cassie could see that they were in some sort of clearing. The ground was littered with tree stumps and lopped branches, as if the trees had only recently been felled and carried away. She leaned forward and looked out of the window, expecting to see the lights of an inn, but there was nothing, just the pewter-coloured landscape with the shadow of the woods like a black wall in every direction.

The carriage came to a halt. Merimon dismounted, tied his horse to a wheel and came up to open the door.

'Step out, milady. We take you no further.'

Cassie protested furiously as he grabbed her wrist and hauled her out of the carriage.

'How dare you treat me thus,' she raged at him. 'Your contract is to take me to Le Havre. You will not get the rest of your money if you do not do so.'

His coarse laugh sent a chill running through her.

'No? Since you have no friends in Le Havre, and no banker, you must be carrying your money with you. Is that not the truth?'

The chill turned to icy fear.

'Nonsense,' she said stoutly. 'I would not be so foolish as to—'

Another horrid laugh cut through her protests.

'But certainly you would. Give me your purse now and perhaps we will not hurt you quite so much.'

Cassie glanced behind her to see that the postilion had dismounted and hobbled his horses. He was now walking slowly towards her. If only she had not left her bonnet in the chaise she might have made use of the two very serviceable hatpins that were secured in it. As it was she had only her wits and her own meagre strength to rely on. She took a step away from Merimon who made no move to stop her. Why should he, when the postilion was blocking her retreat?

'I shall be missed,' she said. 'I have told friends I shall write to them from Rouen.'

'A week at least before they begin to worry, if they ever do.' Merimon gestured dismissively. 'No one cares what happens to you, apart from your husband, and he is dead. I cannot believe the English *détenus* will be in a hurry to tear themselves away from their pleasures.'

No, thought Cassandra, neither could she believe it. Gerald had ensured that all her friends there had been his cronies, selfish, greedy persons who only professed affection if it was to their advantage. She was alone here, she was going to have to fight and it was unlikely that she would win. Cassie tensed as Merimon drew a long knife from his belt. He gave her an evil grin.

'Well, milady, do we get your money before or after we have taken our pleasure?'

'Never, I should think.'

The sound of the deep, amused drawl had them all turning towards the carriage.

A stranger was untying the reins of Merimon's horse. The man was a little over average height, bare-headed, bearded and dressed in ragged homespun, but there was nothing of the peasant about his bearing. He carried himself like a soldier and his voice was that of one used to command.

'You will move away from the lady now, if you know what's good for you.'

'We have no quarrel with you, citizen,' called Merimon. 'Be on your way.'

'Oh, I do not think so.'

The stranger was walking towards them, leading the bay. With his untidy hair and thick beard his face was but little more than a dark shape in the moonlight, but Cassie saw the gleam of white as he grinned. For a long moment there was silence, tense and expectant, then everything exploded into action. With a howl of rage Merimon hurled himself at the stranger and at the same time Cassie saw the postilion bearing down upon her.

That was fortunate, she thought. Merimon was the bigger of the two and he had a knife. With the postilion she had a chance. Cassie tensed as he approached, his arms outstretched. His ugly, triumphant grin told her he thought she was petrified, but just as he launched himself forward she acted. In one smooth, fluid movement she stepped aside, turning, bending and scooping up a branch about the length and thickness of her own arm. Without a pause she gripped the branch with both hands and carried it with all her force against the back of the postilion's knees. He dropped to the ground with a howl.

'Nicely done, *mademoiselle*.' The stranger trotted up, mounted on the bay. He held out his hand to her. 'Well?' he said. 'Do you want to come with me, or would you prefer to take your chances here with these *scélérats*?'

Villains indeed, thought Cassie, quickly glancing about her. Merimon was on his knees, groggily shaking his head, and the postilion was already staggering to his feet. Swiftly she ran across to the stranger. She grasped his outstretched hand, placed one foot on his boot and allowed him to pull her up before him. He lifted her easily and settled her across his thighs before urging the horse to a canter.

Cassie had no fear of falling, the stranger's strong arms held her firmly before him. The choice, since she was sitting sideways, was to turn into the man or away and Cassie opted for the latter, twisting her body to look ahead. The black shawl had snagged on one arm of her riding habit and now it fluttered like a pennant over her shoulder. It must have flown into the rider's face because without a word he pulled it free, tossing it aside as they pounded away into the darkness of the trees. Cassie turned her head to watch it drift slowly to the ground behind them. Her only symbol of grieving for her husband, for her marriage. It was gone. She faced forward again, looking ahead into the darkness. Into the unknown future.

Chapter Two

They rode through the woods with only the thudding beat of the cantering horse to break the silence. Cassie made no attempt to speak. It was difficult to see through the gloom and she wanted her companion to concentrate his efforts on guiding them safely between the trees. Only when he slowed the horse to a walk did she break the silence.

'Do you know where we are going?'

She immediately berated herself for asking the question in English, but he answered her with only the faintest trace of an accent.

'At present I have no idea,' came the cheerful reply. 'Once we are clear of the trees and I can see the sky I shall be able to tell you.' He added, when she shifted before him, 'Would you like to get down? We should rest this nag for a while.'

He brought the horse to a stand and eased Cassie to the ground. It was only then she realised her legs would not hold her and grabbed the saddle for support.

The man jumped down beside her.

'Come, let us walk a little and your limbs will soon be restored.'

He put his arm around her shoulders and pulled her close. His clothes were rough and smelled of dirt and sweat, but Cassie was in no position yet to walk unaided so she allowed him to support her. His strength was comforting, but he puzzled her. His manner and his voice belonged to an educated man, yet he had the ragged appearance of a fugitive.

She said cautiously, 'I have not thanked you for coming to my rescue. What were you doing there?'

'I needed a horse.'

His calm answer surprised her into a laugh.

'That raises even more questions, *monsieur.*'

She thought he might fob her off, but he answered quite frankly.

'I was being pursued and ran into the woods for cover. I saw the horse tethered to the carriage wheel with no one to guard him, since your companions were too busy threatening you. I was very grateful for that and thought it would be churlish to ride off and leave you to your fate.'

'It would indeed.'

Cassie kept her voice calm, but she was beginning to wonder if she had jumped from the frying pan to the fire.

She made a slight move to free herself and immediately he released her. Reassured, she continued to keep pace with him, the horse clip-clopping behind them while the moon sailed overhead in the clear, ink-blue sky.

'So you *are* a fugitive,' she said, with some satisfaction. 'I thought as much.'

'And you are not afraid of me?'

Cassie's head went up.

'I am afraid of no one.' She realised how foolish her swift retort would sound, considering her current situation, and she added slowly, 'Not afraid. Cautious. As one should be of a stranger.'

'True, but we can remedy that.' He stopped and sketched a bow. 'I am Raoul Doulevant, at your service.'

He expected a reply and after a moment she said, 'I am Lady Cassandra Witney.'

'And you are English, which is why we are conversing in this barbaric tongue.'

'Then let us talk in French,' she replied, nettled.

'As you wish.' He caught her left hand. Neither of them was wearing gloves and his thumb rubbed across the plain gold band on her third finger.

'Ah. I addressed you as *mademoiselle* when we first met. My apologies, *madame*.'

She was shocked that his touch should feel so intimate and she drew her hand away. 'We should get on.'

When she began to walk again he fell into step beside her.

'Where is your husband?'

Cassie hesitated for a heartbeat's pause before she replied.

'At Verdun.'

'He is a *détenu*?'

Again she hesitated, not wanting to admit she was a widow. That she was alone and unprotected.

'Yes. That scoundrel you knocked down was the courier I hired to escort me back to England.'

'A bad choice, clearly.'

She felt the hot tears prickling at the back of

her eyes and blinked them away. This was no time for self-pity.

'And what of you?' she asked him, anxious to avoid more questions concerning her situation. 'Who is pursuing you?'

'Officers of the law. They think I am a deserter.'

'They *think* it? And is it not so?'

'No. I was discharged honourably from the navy six months ago.'

She said, a hint of censure in her voice, 'In the present circumstances, with the country at war, I would have thought any true Frenchman would wish to remain in the service of his country, *monsieur*.'

'Any true Frenchman might,' he retorted. 'But I am from Brussels. I grew up in the Southern Netherlands, under Austrian rule.'

'And yet your French is excellent.'

'My family came originally from a town near the French border and moved to Brussels when I was a babe, so I grew up learning the language. Then I moved to Paris and later joined the French Navy, so you see, for years I have spoken nothing else.'

* * *

The lady made no reply and Raoul asked himself bitterly why he put himself out to explain. What difference would it make to her? She was English and everyone knew they thought themselves superior to the rest of Europe. It was the very worst of bad fortune that he should have saddled himself with an English aristo!

'The horse is rested now,' he said shortly. 'I think we can ride again.'

He mounted and reached down for her, pulling her up before him. He tried not to think how small and feminine she was, how the faint trace of perfume reminded him of balmy summer days. She settled herself on the horse, her dark curls tickling his chin. When the horse stumbled in the dark she clutched at his sleeve and instinctively he wrapped one arm around her waist.

She gasped and said haughtily, 'Thank you, you do not need to hold me so tightly. I am in no danger of falling now.'

His jaw clenched. If she thought he had designs upon her she was much mistaken. Silently he released her and put both hands back on the reins, but it was impossible not to be aware of her for she was practically sitting on his lap. He thought ruefully that he would have enjoyed the situation, if she had been anything other than an Englishwoman.

They travelled on, alternatively walking and riding, but maintaining an awkward silence. Raoul concentrated on guiding their mount through the near darkness of the woods. At length he noticed that the trees were thinning and they emerged on to a wide track that stretched like a grey ribbon in the starry darkness. They dismounted and Raoul stared up at the sky. The moon had gone and the stars were dimming in the first light of dawn.

'Do you know where we are now?' she asked him.

'We have been travelling north.'

'The wrong direction.'

'That depends upon where one wishes to go, *madame*.'

Cassie bit her lip. She was in a foreign land, enemy country. This man had saved her from an immediate danger, but there was no reason why he should do more for her. Indeed, the alacrity with which he had released her when the horse had missed its step suggested he had no wish to help her further. Yet she needed help. Her encounter with Merimon had shown her that.

She asked politely, 'What is *your* destination, *monsieur*?'

'Brussels.'

'I want to get to England. Do you think it might be easier from there?' She added, trying not to sound anxious, 'I gave my passport to the courier.'

'Then you have no papers.'

'No.'

Suddenly she felt very vulnerable, alone in the middle of France with a stranger. A fugitive and she had only his word that he was not a villain. His next words sent a chill of fear through her blood.

'Do you have any money?'

Even in the gloom Raoul saw the look of apprehension flicker across the lady's face and it incensed him.

He said coldly, 'I am no thief, *madame*, I do not intend to steal from you.'

She came back at him with all the arrogance he had come to expect from the English, head up, eyes flashing.

'How do I know that? You stole the horse, after all.'

His lip curled, but it occurred to him that she had no other defence so he reined in an angry response. Instead he growled, 'Remember, *madame*, I could have left you to your fate with those two villains.'

'That is very true,' she acknowledged. 'I am obliged to you and I beg your pardon.' She drew in a long breath, 'And, yes, I do have a little money.'

Her stiff apology doused his anger immediately. He smiled.

'Then you have the advantage of me, *madame*, for I have not a sou.'

'Oh, I see. Let me give you something for rescuing me—'

He recoiled instantly.

'That is not necessary,' he said quickly. 'After all, I have this fine horse, do I not?'

'Yes, of course. He will carry you to Brussels, I am sure.' She paused. 'Is it far from here?'

He shrugged. 'Depending on just where we are, three or four days' travel, I would think. *You* would do better if you head for Reims, it is much closer and you will be able to buy your passage from there to the coast.'

'Thank you.' He watched her look at the sky, then up and down the track. 'So, Reims would be that way?'

She pointed in a southerly direction, trying to sound matter of fact, as if she was well accustomed to setting off alone, in the dark, along a little-used road through an alien land, but Raoul heard the note of anxiety in her voice.

She is not your concern.

'Yes,' he replied. 'If you keep to this track I have no doubt it will bring you to the Reims road. The sun will be coming up soon, you will have no difficulty finding your way.'

'Then I will bid you *adieu*, Monsieur Doulevant,' she said quietly. 'I thank you for your assistance and I hope you reach Brussels safely.'

She gave a little curtsy, suddenly looking so lost and woebegone that every protective instinct he had rose to the fore.

'Wait!'

Don't do this, man. You owe her nothing.

Raoul ignored the warning voice in his head.

'I will take you as far as Reims.'

The flash of relief he saw in her face was quickly replaced with suspicion.

'How do I know you will not strangle me for my money?'

He ground his teeth.

'If I strangle you, milady, it will be for your sharp tongue!'

Strangely, his words seemed to reassure her. She gave an imperious little nod.

'I accept your escort, sir, and I thank you.'

'It is my pleasure,' he replied with equal insincerity. 'Come, we will ride.'

As she allowed herself to be pulled once more on to the horse Cassie was relieved that she was not obliged to make the long walk alone. Her escort explained that they must not overtax their mount and they made slow progress. The road was deserted and they saw no one except a swineherd who was happy to sell Cassie his food sack in exchange for a handful of coins. The bag contained only wine and bread, but it was enough for two and at noon they rested in the shade of a tree to eat.

Cassie was hot and thirsty and when he handed her the flask she took a long draught. The wine

was very rough and she felt its effects immediately.

Her companion broke off a piece of bread and
held it out to her.

'So you left your husband in Verdun?'

'Yes.' Cassie was tempted to tell him her husband was dead, but she remembered Merimon's
taunt and decided it was safer to infer she had
a husband to protect her honour, even if he was
many miles away. 'Yes, he is at Verdun.'

She took the bread and nibbled at it as he surveyed her with his dark eyes.

'I am surprised he allowed you to travel alone.
You are very young to be married.'

Cassie straightened.

'I am old enough!'

One dark brow went up.

'How old?' he asked her. 'You do not look more
than eighteen.'

'I am nearly one-and-twenty and have been
married a full year.'

'*Vraiment?* Tsk, what were your parents about
to allow such a thing?'

'My parents died when I was a child.'

'Even worse, then, for your guardian to approve it.'

Cassie thought of Grandmama.

'She did not approve. We eloped.'

Cassie wondered why she had told him that. She was not proud of how she had behaved and the fact that it had all gone wrong just showed how foolish she had been. Falling in love had been a disaster and it was not a mistake she intended to make again. Glancing up at that moment, she thought she detected disapproval in those dark eyes. Well, let him disapprove. She cared not for his opinion, or for any man's. She scrambled to her feet and shook the crumbs from her skirts.

'Shall we continue?'

With a shrug he packed away the rest of the wine and bread and soon they were on their way again. Cassie maintained what she hoped was a dignified silence, but she was very much afraid Raoul Doulevant would think it more of a childish sulk. However, it could not be helped. She could not justify herself to him without explaining everything and that she would not do to a total stranger.

The sun was sinking when they met a farmer and his wife approaching them in a cumbersome wagon. Cassie listened while her escort conducted a brief conversation. The farmer confirmed that they were indeed on the road to Reims, but it was at least another full day's ride.

'You are welcome to come back with us,' offered the farmer's wife. 'It is an hour or so back the way you have come, but we can give you and your lady a meal and a bed for the night.'

Cassie froze. The idea of food was enticing, but these people clearly thought that she and this unkempt stranger were, were...

'Thank you, but, no, we had best press on.'

Raoul Doulevant answered for them both and exchanged a few more friendly words with the farmer before they parted. Cassie felt the hot flush of embarrassment on her cheek and it was all she could do to respond to their cheerful farewell with a nod of acknowledgement.

'It is fortunate I refused their hospitality,' he remarked, misinterpreting her silence. 'A farmer's hovel would not suit your ladyship.'

'You are mistaken,' she retorted. 'A bed and a good meal would be very welcome, since I suspect the alternative will be a night spent out of doors. But you were very right to refuse. I would like to get to Reims with all haste.'

'Certainly. We cannot get there too soon for my liking!'

'Good. Let us ride through the night, then,' Cassie suggested, rattled.

They rode and walked by turns until the last of the daylight faded away. Cassie was fighting to stay awake, but nothing would make her admit it. She was the daughter of a marquess, granddaughter of an Arrandale and it was beneath her to show weakness of any sort.

Thick clouds rolled in from the west, obscuring the sky and plunging the world into almost complete darkness. When the bay stumbled for the third time she heard Raoul Doulevant curse softly under his breath.

'This is sheer foolishness, *monsieur*,' she told him. 'We should stop until the cloud lifts.'

'That would delay our journey; I was hoping to make a few more miles yet.'

'If the horse breaks a leg that will delay us even more,' Cassie pointed out.

When he did not reply she admitted, albeit reluctantly, that she would like to rest. Immediately he drew the horse to a halt and helped Cassie to dismount. Without ceremony he took her arm and guided her and the horse from the near darkness of the road into the blackness of the trees.

'Stay here, *madame*, while I see to the horse.'

Cassie slumped down against the base of a tree. Stay here, he had said. Did he think she would run away? She had no idea where she was, or which way she should go. She recalled how she had complained that she could not sleep in the carriage. What luxury that seemed now, compared to her present predicament. Not only must she sleep out of doors, but in the company of a stranger. The fact that they had introduced themselves made no difference; she knew nothing of this man.

She listened to the rustle of leaves as Raoul Doulevant secured the horse before coming to sit down beside her. She felt his presence rather than saw him and his silence unnerved her. She tried to recall what he had told her of himself.

'So you are a sailor, *monsieur*?'

'I was ship's surgeon on the *Prométhée* for six years.'

'Really?'

She could not keep the surprise from her voice and he gave a short laugh.

'My clothes tell the different story, no? I was obliged to…er…acquire these to escape detection.'

'If you were being pursued, then clearly that did not work.'

'No. There is one, Valerin, who is very determined to catch me.'

'He holds a grudge against you, perhaps?'

'I stopped him from forcing himself upon my sister. I should have killed him, instead of leaving him alive to denounce me.'

Cassie shivered. The words were quietly spoken, but there was no mistaking the menace in them.

'Where is your sister now?'

'I sent her to Brussels. We still have friends there. She is safe.'

'No doubt she is anxious for you to join her.'

'Perhaps. Her last letter said she had met an old friend, a wealthy merchant who is now a widower. I think they will make a match of it. Who knows, they may already be married. She is a widow and does not need to wait for my blessing.'

It was the most he had said to her all day and his tone was perfectly polite so she pushed aside her animosity.

'All the same, *monsieur*, it is good of you to delay your journey for me.'

When he did not reply she wondered if he was regretting his decision.

'Try to sleep,' he said at last. 'I will wake you if the light improves enough to move on.'

'Will you not sleep, too?'

The black shape shifted, as if he had drawn up his knees and was hugging them.

'No.'

Cassie was too exhausted to wonder at his stamina or to fight off her low spirits. Eloping with Gerald Witney had been shocking enough, but she was very much afraid that her friends and family would be even more shocked if they could see her now, alone under the stars with a strange man. She sighed as she curled up on the ground. There was nothing to be done and she was quite desperate for sleep, so she made herself as comfortable as she could and closed her eyes.

Raoul sank his chin on his knees and gazed at the unremitting darkness. The track was well-nigh invisible now. They had been right to stop, he acknowledged, but he wished it had not been necessary. The sooner he was relieved of this woman's presence the better. He travelled best alone, he did not want the responsibility of a foreign female, especially an arrogant English-woman. She could find her own way from Reims. After all, Bonaparte had no quarrel with women, she could hire a carriage to take her to the coast. Raoul closed his mind to the fact that she had been duped once by an unscrupulous courier. He had problems enough of his own to think of. He glanced up, although the darkness was so complete it was impossible to see where the trees ended and the sky began. There was no sign that the cloud would lift any time soon, so eventually he laid himself down on the ground, knowing he would be wise to rest.

Dawn broke, but not a glimmer of sun disturbed the uniform grey of the sky. Raoul put his hand on Lady Cassandra's shoulder to rouse her. He could feel the bones, fine and delicate as a bird beneath his hand. But she was not that delicate. He remembered how she had brought her attacker down with the tree branch. He could not deny this aristo had spirit.

He shook her gently. 'We must be moving.'

She stirred, smiling as if in the grip of some

pleasant dream, and he thought suddenly that she really was very pretty, with her clear skin and a heart-shaped face framed by hair the colour of polished mahogany. Her straight little nose drew his eye to the soft curves of her lips and he was just wondering how it would feel to kiss her when she woke up and looked at him.

It was the first time he had looked into her eyes. They were a clear violet-blue, set beneath curving dark brows and fringed with thick, long lashes. He watched the violet darken to near black with fear and alarm when she saw him. He removed his hand from her shoulder, but the guarded look remained as she sat up. When she stretched he could not help but notice how the buttons of her jacket strained across her breast.

Raoul shifted his gaze, only to note that her skirts had ridden up a little to expose the dainty feet in their boots of half-jean. Something stirred within him, unbidden, unwelcome. He jumped up and strode off to fetch the horse. This was no time for lustful thoughts, especially for an English aristo.

Cassie scrambled to her feet and shook out her skirts before putting a hand to her hair, pushing the pins in as best she could without the aid of a mirror. She must look almost as dishevelled as her companion, but it could not be helped. He brought the horse alongside and held out his hand to her. As he pulled her up before him she marvelled again at his strength, at how secure she felt sitting up before him. She could not deny there was some comfort in being pressed close to that unwashed but decidedly male body. There was power in every line of him, in the muscular thighs beneath her and the strong arms that held her firmly in place. When she leaned against him, his chest was reassuringly solid at her back. Gerald had never made her feel this safe. Immediately she felt a wave of guilt for the thought and it was mixed with alarm. Raoul Doulevant was, after all, a stranger.

It was not cold, but the lack of wind allowed the mist to linger and the low cloud seemed to press on the treetops as they rode through the silent morning. Cassie's stomach rumbled, reminding her that she had not eaten since yesterday.

'There's a village ahead,' said Raoul presently. 'We should find a tavern there.' He drew the horse to a halt. 'It might be best if you give me a few coins before we get there. It would not do for you to be waving a fat purse before these people.'

'I do not have a fat purse,' she objected. Cautiously she reached into her skirts to the pocket and drew out a small stockinette purse. She counted out some coins and handed them to Raoul, who put them in his own pocket.

'Thank you. Now, when we get there, you had best let me take care of everything. You speak French charmingly, milady, but your accent would give you away.'

Cassie kept her lips firmly pressed together. He intended no compliment, she was sure of that. She contented herself with an angry look, but his smile and the glint of amusement in his eyes only made her more furious. If they had not been riding into the village at that moment she would have given him a sharp set-down for teasing her so.

The village boasted a sizable inn. When they had dismounted Raoul handed the reins to the waiting ostler and escorted Cassie into the dark interior. It took a few moments for Cassie's eyes to adjust to the gloom, then she saw that the room was set out with benches and tables, but was mer- cifully empty of customers. A pot-bellied tapster approached them, wiping his hands on a greasy apron. Raoul ordered wine and food and their host invited them to sit down.

'Been travelling long?' asked the tapster as he banged a jug of wine on the table before them. Raoul grunted.

'Takin' my sister home,' he said. 'She's been serving as maid to one of the English ladies in Verdun.'

'Ah.' The tapster sniffed. 'Damned English have taken over the town, I hear.'

Raoul poured a glass of wine and held it out for Cassie, his eyes warning her to keep silent.

'Aye,' he said cheerfully. 'But they are generous masters, only look at the smart habit my sister now possesses! And their English gold is filling French coffers, so who are we to complain?'

'You are right there, my friend.' The tapster cackled, revealing a mouth full of broken and blackened teeth. He slapped Raoul on the shoul- der and wandered off to fetch their food.

Cassie could hardly contain her indignation as she listened to this interchange.

'Sister?' she hissed in a furious undertone, as soon as they were alone. 'How can that man think we are related?'

His grin only increased her fury.

'Very easily,' he said. 'Have you looked at yourself recently, milady? Your gown is crumpled and your hair is a tangle. I am almost ashamed to own you.'

'At least I do not look like a bear!' she threw at him.

Cassandra regretted the unladylike outburst immediately. She chewed her lip, knowing she would have to apologise.

'I beg your pardon,' she said at last and through clenched teeth. 'I should be grateful for your escort.'

'You should indeed,' he growled. 'You need not fear, *madame*. As soon as we reach Reims I shall relieve you of my boorish presence.'

He broke off as the tapster appeared and put down two plates in front of them.

'There, *monsieur*. A hearty meal for you both. None of your roast beef here.'

Raoul gave a bark of laughter. 'No, we leave such barbarities to the enemy.'

Grinning, the tapster waddled away.

'Is that how you think of me?' muttered Cassie. 'As your enemy?'

'I have told you, I am not French.'

'But you served in their navy.'

He met her gaze, his eyes hard and unsmiling. 'I have no reason to think well of the English. Let us say no more of it.'

'But—'

'Eat your food, *madame*, before I put you across my knee and thrash you like a spoiled brat.'

Cassie looked away, unsettled and convinced he might well carry out his threat.

The food was grey and unappetising, some sort of stew that had probably been in the pot for days, but it was hot and tasted better than it looked. Cassie knew she must eat to keep up her strength, but she was not sorry when they were finished and could be on their way.

Raoul Doulevant's good humour returned once they were mounted. He tossed a coin to the ostler and set off out of the village at a steady walk.

'The tapster says Reims is about a day's ride from here,' he told Cassie. 'We might even make it before nightfall.'

'I am only sorry he did not know where we

could buy or hire another horse,' she remarked, still smarting from their earlier exchange.

'You do not like travelling in my arms, mi-lady?'

'No, I do not.'

'You could always walk.'

'If you were a gentleman *you* would walk.'

She felt his laugh rumble against her back.

'Clearly I am no gentleman, then.'

Incensed, she turned towards him, intending to say something cutting, but when she looked into those dark eyes her breath caught in her throat. He was teasing her again. Laughter gleamed in his eyes and her traitorous body was responding. She was tingling with excitement in a way she remembered from those early days following her come-out, when she had been carefree and had flirted outrageously with many a handsome gentleman. Now she wanted to laugh back at Raoul, to tease him in return. Even worse, she found herself wondering what it would be like if he kissed her. The thought frightened her. In her present situation she dare not risk becoming too friendly with this stranger. Quickly she turned away again.

* * *

Raoul closed his eyes and exhaled a long, slow breath, thankful that the lady was now staring fixedly ahead, her little nose in the air as she tried to ignore him. What was he about, teasing her in such a way? There was something about the lady that brought out the rake in him and made him want to flirt with her, even though he knew it would be much more sensible to keep his distance. He had no time for women, other than the most casual liaisons, and instinct told him that involvement with Lady Cassandra Witney would be anything but casual.

He glanced at the lady as she rode before him. His arms were on either side, holding her firm while his hands gripped the reins. The bay was a sturdy animal and did not object to the extra weight and Raoul had to admit it was not excessive. She was petite, slender as a reed. He was almost afraid to hold her too close in case he crushed her. She was trying hard not to touch him, but sometimes the movement of the horse sent her back against him and those dark curls would tangle with his beard and he would catch a faint, elusive scent of summer flowers. Confound it, he was enjoying himself! He could not deny that having her sitting up before him made the journey much more pleasurable.

It soon became clear that the tapster's estimate of the journey time was very optimistic. With only the long-tailed bay to ride progress was slow and in the hot September sun Raoul was reluctant to push the horse to more than a walking pace. He was glad when their road took them through dense woodland; that at least provided some welcome shade. The lady before him said very little. Perhaps she was still cross with him for teasing her, but he did not mind her reticence, for he was not fond of inconsequential chattering.

Raoul judged they had only an hour or so of daylight left and was beginning to consider where they would spend the night when the horse's ears pricked. Raoul heard it, too, the jingling sounds of harness and male voices from around the bend ahead of them. Lots of voices. Quickly he dragged on the reins and urged the horse into the shelter of the trees.

Their sudden departure from the road shook

his companion out of her reverie. She asked him what was happening and he answered her briefly.

'It may be nothing, but I think there may be soldiers ahead of us.'

Cassie's heart thudded with anxiety as they pushed deeper between the trees. It was bad enough that she had no papers to prove her identity, but she was also travelling with a fugitive. She could imagine all too well what would happen if they were caught. The ground had been rising since they left the road, but now it began to climb steeply and they stopped to dismount. In silence they moved deeper into the woods until they were out of sight of the road and the raucous voices had faded to a faint, occasional shout.

'Stay here,' muttered Raoul, tethering the horse. 'I will go back and see what they are about.'

'I shall come with you.'

'You will be safer here.'

'Oh, no.' She caught his sleeve. 'You are not leaving me alone.'

He frowned and looked as if he was about to argue, then he changed his mind.

'Very well. Come with me, but quietly.'

He took her hand and led her back through

the bushes, following the sound of the voices. At last he stopped, pulling Cassie closer and binding her to him as they peered through the thick foliage. She could see splashes of colour through the trees, mainly blue, but touches of red and the glint of sunlight on metal. The air was redolent with woodsmoke.

'They are making camp for the night,' breathed Raoul.

'What shall we do? Can we circle around them and back to the road?'

He shook his head. 'We have no idea how many of them there are. They may be the first of several units, or there may be stragglers. We must give them a very wide berth. We need to move deeper into the woods, too, in case they come foraging for firewood.'

It was at that inopportune moment, with French soldiers dangerously close, that Cassie discovered she did not wish to go anywhere. Raoul still had his arm about her waist and despite his rough and dirty clothes her body was happy to lean into him. She was disturbingly aware of that powerful figure, tense and ready to act. Growing up, she had always been impatient of convention and had craved excitement and danger. Instinct told her this man was both exciting and dangerous. A heady combination, she thought as he led her away. And one she would be wise to keep at bay.

They retrieved the horse and set off into the woods. Raoul was no longer holding her and Cassie had to fight down the temptation to grab his hand. She was perfectly capable of walking unaided and she told herself it was useful to have both hands free to draw her skirts away from encroaching twigs and branches. It was impossible to ride, the trees were too thick and their low branches were barely above the saddle. They walked for what seemed like hours. Cassie was bone-weary but stubborn pride kept her silent. As the sun went down it grew much colder and the thought of spending another night in the open was quite daunting.

It was almost dark when they saw before them a small house in a clearing. An old woman appeared at the door and Cassie stopped, knowing the deep shadows of the trees would hide them. She almost gasped with shock and surprise when Raoul put his arm about her waist and walked her forward into the clearing.

'Come along, *madame*, let us see if we can find a little charity here.' He raised his voice: 'Good evening to you, Mother. Could you spare a little supper for two weary travellers? We were taking a short cut and lost our way.'

The old woman looked at them with incurious eyes until he jingled the coins in his pocket. She jerked her head, as if inviting them in.

'I have salt herring I can fry for you and a little bread.'

'That would suit us very well, Mother, thank you.'

They followed her into the cottage. Raoul's arm was still about Cassie and he was smiling, but she knew he was alert, ready to fight if danger threatened. A single oil lamp burned inside and by its fragile light Cassie could see the house was very small, a single square room with an earth floor and a straw mattress in one corner. Cassie guessed the old woman lived here alone. A sluggish fire smoked in the hearth, but it was sufficient to warm the small space and Cassie sank down on to a rickety bench placed against one wall. The old woman gestured to Raoul to sit down with Cassie while she prepared their meal.

Cassie was exhausted. Raoul's shoulder was so temptingly close and she leaned her head against it, watching through half-closed eyes as the woman poked the fire into life and added more wood. Soon the pungent smell of the fish filled the room. Cassie's eyes began to smart and she closed them, but then it was too much trouble to open them again and she dozed until Raoul gave her a little nudge.

'Wake up now. You must eat something.'

Sleepily Cassie sat up to find a small table had been pushed in front of them and it was set now with plates and horn cups. They dined on salt herring and bread, but when the old woman offered them some of her white brandy Raoul refused, politely but firmly.

'Would it be so very bad?' Cassie murmured when their hostess went off to fetch them some water.

'Very likely,' he replied, 'but even if it is drinkable, to take it with the herring would give you a raging thirst.'

She accepted this without comment. She did not like the fish very much, but the bread was fresh and Cassie made a good meal. When it was finished the old woman cleared everything away. Raoul took a few coins out of his pocket and held them out.

'Thank you, Mother, for your hospitality. There

is double this if you will let us sleep on your floor tonight.'

The old crone's eyes gleamed. 'Double it again and I'll let ye have the paillasse.'

Cassie glanced from the woman to the bed in the corner and could barely suppress a shudder at the thought of what might be crawling amongst the straw. To her relief Raoul did not hesitate to decline her offer.

'We would not take your cot, Mother, nor your covers. We shall be comfortable enough before the fire.'

She shrugged and took the coins from his palm. 'As you please.'

The old woman banked up the fire and cleared a space before it, even going so far as to find a threadbare rug to put on the ground. Raoul went outside to attend to the horse and the old woman gave Cassie a toothless smile.

'You've got yourself a good man there, *madame*.'

'What? Oh—oh, yes.' Cassie nodded. She was too tired to try and explain that they were not married.

When Raoul returned the old woman blew out the lamp and retired to her bed with her flask of brandy, leaving her guests to fend for themselves before the fire. There was no privacy and they both lay down fully dressed on the old rug. Raoul stretched out on his back and linked his hands behind his head.

'Do not fret,' he murmured. 'I shall not touch you.'

Cassie did not deign to reply to his teasing tone. She curled up on her side with her back to Raoul. She was nearest the fire and glad of the heat from the dying embers, but she could not relax. She was far too on edge, aware of Raoul's body so close to her own. He was so big, and rough and...*male*. Gerald had been more of a gamester than a sportsman. He had been fastidious about his dress and she had never seen him with more than a slight shadow of stubble on his face. That is what she had loved about him; he had always looked like the perfect gentleman. She stirred, uncomfortable with the thought that he had not always acted like a gentleman.

Not that it mattered now, Gerald was dead and she would have to make her own way in the world. Sleepily she wondered why she had not told Raoul she was a widow. After all, it could make no difference to him, since as far as he was aware her husband was still in Verdun. But some deep, unfathomable instinct told her Raoul Doulevant was an honourable man. Now her hands came together and she fingered the plain wedding band. It was little enough protection, but it was all she had.

Cassie lay still, tense and alert until she heard Raoul snoring gently. The old woman had told them it was a full day's walk from here to Reims, so by tomorrow they would be in the city and she could be rid of her ragged companion. She closed her eyes. The sooner dawn came the better.

Cassie stirred. She was still lying on her side, facing the fire which had died down to a faint glow, and the room was in almost total darkness. She reached down to make sure the skirts of her riding habit were tucked around her feet, but she could feel the chill of the night air through the sleeves of her jacket. She tried rubbing her arms, but that did not help much. She sighed.

'What is the matter?' Raoul's voice was no more than a sleepy whisper in the darkness.

'I am cold.'

He shifted closer, curving his body around hers and putting his arm over her. The effect was startling. Heat spread quickly through her body and with it a sizzling excitement. It did not matter that Raoul was dressed in rough home-spun clothes, or that his ragged beard tickled her neck, her pulse leapt erratically as he curled himself about her.

'Is that better?'

Cassie swallowed. She could not reply, her throat had dried, her breasts strained against the confines of her jacket. She was wrapped in the arms of a man, a stranger. Even worse, she wanted him to kiss and caress her. Heavens she should move away, immediately! But somehow she could not make her body obey, and the idea of lying cold and alone for the remainder of the night was not at all appealing. It was confusing, to feel so secure, yet so vulnerable, all at the same time.

Raoul's arm tightened, pulling them closer together. So close she could feel his breath on her cheek, feel his body close against hers. She should protest, she should object strongly to being held in this way, but she was so warm now, so comfortable. The initial burning excitement had settled into a sense of wellbeing. She had never felt so safe before, or so warm. She felt a smile spreading out from her very core.

'Oh, yes,' she murmured sleepily. 'Oh, yes, that is much better.'

Raoul lay very still, listening to Cassie's gentle, regular breathing. It was taking all his willpower not to nuzzle closer and nibble the delightful shell-like ear, to keep his hands from seeking out the swell of her breasts. He uttered up a fervent prayer of thanks that the thick folds of her skirts prevented her knowing just how aroused he was to have her lying with him in this way.

He had been too long without a woman. How else could he explain the heat that shot through him whenever they touched? Even when she looked at him he was aware of a connection, as if they had known each other for ever. Fanciful rubbish, he told himself. She was a spoiled English aristo and he despised such women. By heaven, at eight-and-twenty he was too old to fall for a pair of violet-blue eyes, no matter how much they sparkled. And there was no doubt that Lady Cassandra's eyes sparkled quite exceptionally, so much so they haunted his dreams, as did the delightful curves of her body. Even now he wanted to explore those curves, to run his fingers over the dipping valley of her waist, the rounded swell of her hips and the equally enchanting breasts that he judged would fit perfectly into his hands.

He closed his eyes. This was nothing short of torture, to keep still while he was wrapped around this woman. He turned his mind to consider how he must look to her, with his dirty clothes and unkempt hair. She must think him a rogue, a vagabond. He was not fit to clean her boots.

And yet here she was, sleeping in his arms.

Chapter Three

They quit the cottage soon after dawn and followed the narrow track through the woods that the old woman told them would bring them to the highway a few miles to the west of Reims. They rode and walked by turns as the sun moved higher in the clear blue sky, but although Cassandra was cheerful enough her companion was taciturn, even surly, and after travelling a few miles in silence she taxed him with it. They were walking side by side at that point and Cassie decided it would be easier to ask the question now, rather than when they were on horseback. For some inexplicable reason when she was sitting within the circle of his arms it was difficult to think clearly.

She said now, 'You have scarce said a dozen

civil words to me since we set out, *monsieur*. Have I offended you in some way?'

'If you must know I did not sleep well.'

'Oh.' Something in his tone sent the blood rushing to her cheeks as Cassie realised that she might have been the cause. She had woken at dawn to find they were still curled up together but even more intimately, his cheek resting against her hair and one of those strong, capable hands cradling her breast. It was such a snug fit she thought they might have been made for one another. A preposterous idea, but at the time it had made her want to smile. Now it only made her blush. He had still been sleeping when she had slipped out of his unconscious embrace and she had said nothing about it, hoping he would not remember, but perhaps he had been more aware of how they had slept together than she had first thought.

Cassie closed her eyes as embarrassment and remorse swept over her like a wave. If eloping with Gerald had dented her reputation, what had happened to her since leaving Verdun was like to smash it completely.

Raoul Doulevant cleared his throat.

'How long have you been in France, milady?'

He was trying to give her thoughts a different turn and she responded gratefully.

'Just over a year. Gerald and I travelled to Paris last summer, shortly after we were married. The Treaty of Amiens had opened the borders and we joined the fashionable throng. Then, in May this year, the Peace ended.'

'Ah, yes.' He nodded. 'Bonaparte issued instructions that every Englishman between the ages of sixteen and sixty should be detained.'

'Yes.'

Cassie fell silent, unwilling to admit that she had already been regretting her hasty marriage. She had stayed and supported her husband, even though he had given her little thanks for it after the first anxious weeks of his detention.

'But now you return to England without him. I had heard the English in Verdun lived very comfortably.'

'Only if they have money. Our funds were running very low.'

'Ah. So now your husband's fortune has gone you have abandoned him.'

'No!' She bit her lip. She should correct him, tell him it was her money they had lived on, that she was now a widow, but the words stuck in her throat. Pride would not let her admit how wrong she had been, how foolish. Instead she said haughtily, 'You have no right to judge me.'

'Why, because I am not your equal, *my lady*?'

'You are impertinent, *monsieur*. I had expected better manners from a doctor.'

'But I have told you I am not a doctor. I am a surgeon.'

'But clearly not a gentleman!'

A heavy silence followed her words, but she would not take them back. An angry frown descended upon Raoul's countenance, but he did not speak. Cassie kept pace with him, head high, but his refusal to respond flayed her nerves. She tried telling herself that it was better if they did not talk, that it was safer to keep a distance, yet she found the silence unbearable and after a while she threw a question at him.

'If you are no deserter, why are you being pursued?'

'That need not concern you.'

Cassie knew his retort was no more than she deserved, after what she had said to him. Her temper had subsided as quickly as it was roused; she knew it was wise to keep a distance from this man, but that did not mean they had to be at odds.

She tried to make amends by saying contritely, 'I beg your pardon if my words offended you, *monsieur*, but you must admit, your appearance, your situation… We shall have a miserable journey if we do not discuss *something*.'

There, she had apologised, but when he said nothing she glanced at his angry countenance and thought ruefully that his pride was equal to hers. They were not suited as travelling companions. Cassie walked on beside him, resigned to the silence, but presently the strained atmosphere between them changed. The black cloud lifted from his brow and he began to speak.

'A year ago—about the time that you came to France—I quit the navy and went to Paris to live with my sister Margot. She and her husband had taken me in when I had gone there ten years before to study at the Hôtel-Dieu under the great French surgeon, Desault. Margot was widowed three years ago, so by moving into her house I thought I could support her. Unfortunately last winter she caught the eye of a minor official in Paris, one Valerin. Margo did not welcome his attentions and I told him so. He did not like it.'

'You were rather rough with him, perhaps,' she observed sagely.

'Yes. I came home one night and found him trying to force himself upon Margot. I threw him out of the house and broke his nose into the bargain. That was my mistake. Life became difficult, we were suspected of being enemies of the state, the house was raided several times. It became so bad that a couple of months ago I sent Margot to Brussels. I planned to follow her, once I had wound up my affairs in Paris, but Valerin was too quick for me. He accused me of being a deserter. When I looked for my papers they had gone, taken during one of the house raids, I suppose, and when I applied to the prefect to see the record of my discharge the files were missing.'

'And could no one vouch for you?'

He shrugged. 'My old captain, possibly, but he is at sea. A response from him could take months. I thought it best to leave Paris. And just in time. I was still making my preparations when Valerin came with papers for my arrest and I was forced to flee with nothing. He was so intent upon my capture that he sent word to the Paris gates, which is why you find me dressed *en paysan* and, as you put it, looking like a bear.'

Cassie bit her lip.

'I should not have said that of you. I am in no

position to preach to you now, *monsieur.*' She wrinkled her nose. 'I have never been so dirty. What I would give for clean linen!'

'I fear that will have to wait until we reach Reims, *madame.*'

They kept to the woodland paths and avoided the main highways. It made the journey longer, but Raoul was anxious to avoid meeting anyone who might ask for their papers. Their only food was some fruit, wine and bread they purchased from a woodsman's cottage and at noon they stopped on a ridge, sitting on a fallen tree to eat their frugal meal.

'Is that Reims ahead of us?' asked Cassie, pointing to the roofs and spires in the distance.

'It is. We shall be there before dark, milady.' He sensed her anxiety and added, 'I shall see you safe to a priest, or a nunnery, *madame*, before I leave you.'

'Thank you.' She sighed. 'Travelling alone is very perilous for a lady.'

She was trying to make light of it, but he was not deceived. She was frightened, as well she should be. It was no good to tell himself she was not his responsibility, Raoul's conscience told him otherwise. He made an attempt to stifle it, saying harshly, 'You should have thought of that before you left your husband.'

He glanced down at her and saw that she was close to tears. The urge to take her in his arms was so great that he clenched his fists and pressed them into his thighs. He searched for something to say.

'Why did you elope with him?'

One dainty hand fluttered.

'He was handsome and charming, and he swept me off my feet. Grandmama, who is my guardian, said I was too young, but I thought I knew better. When Gerald suggested we should elope I thought it would be a great adventure. I do not expect you to understand, but life in Bath was very…tame. Oh, there were parties and balls and lots of friends, but it was not enough. I wanted excitement. Gerald offered me that.'

'No doubt being in an enemy country and detained at Verdun has given you a surfeit of excitement.'

She frowned a little, considering.

'One would have thought so, but do you know, it was not so very different from Bath. There are so many English people there and they are determined to carry on very much as they always do. There are parties and assemblies, race meetings and gambling dens, everyone finding silly or frivolous entertainments to fill the time. In truth it is a very a foolish way to live. To be perfectly honest, I was *bored*.'

Raoul watched her. She had clearly forgotten to whom she was talking, there was no reserve as the words poured forth and when she turned her head and smiled up at him, completely natural and unaffected, it shook him to the core. He had the very disturbing sensation of his whole world tilting. The ground beneath him turned to quicksand and it threatened to consume him. It was not that she was trying to attract him, quite the opposite. Her look was trusting and friendly, and it cut through his defences like a sword through paper.

He dragged his eyes away. He needed to repair his defences, to put up the barriers again.

Cassie sucked in a ragged breath, unsure what had just happened to her. In telling Raoul about her elopement she had opened her soul to him in a way she had never done with anyone before. Even when she had thought herself hopelessly in love with Gerald she had never felt such a connection as she did with this dark stranger. It frightened her.

He rose, saying gruffly, 'We should go, we still have several hours travelling to reach Reims.'

Cassie nodded and followed him towards the horse. His voice was perfectly composed. He had not commented, displayed no emotion at what she had told him. No doubt he thought her an idle, frivolous woman, worthy only of contempt. When he sprang into the saddle and put his hand out to her she glanced up at his face, an anxious frown creasing her brow.

'No doubt you think me a silly creature. Contemptible.'

The black eyes gave nothing away.

'What I think of you is unimportant,' he said shortly. 'Come, let us press on.'

The afternoon grew warmer as they made their way towards Reims and the bay's walking pace slowed to an amble. The city was lost to sight as they descended into a wooded valley where the air was warm and filled with the trill of birdsong. It was enchanting, reminding Cassie of hot summer days in England, but much as she wanted to share her thoughts with her companion she held back, knowing she must keep a proper distance. She had already told him far too much and feared she had earned his disapproval. Her spirit flared in momentary rebellion. Well, let him disapprove, it did not matter to her in the least.

When at last they dismounted she was thankful that the rough path was wide enough to walk with the horse between them. There must be no accidental brushing of the hands and heaven forbid that he should be gentleman enough to offer her his arm, for she would have to refuse and that might give rise to offence. How difficult it was to maintain propriety in this wilderness! The heat in the valley was oppressive and the sun beat down upon her bare head. She sighed, regretting the loss of her bonnet.

'Are you tired, milady?'

'No, merely hot and a little uncomfortable.' She unfastened the neck button of her shirt. Even that was an indiscretion, she knew, but a very minor one, considering her situation.

'Would you like to rest in the shade for a while?'

'Thank you, but I would prefer to keep going and reach Reims. Perhaps there we can find some clean clothes.' She could not help adding, 'For both of us.'

His breath hissed out. 'Does my dirty raiment offend you, milady?'

'No more than my own,' she replied honestly. 'We are both in need of a good bath. I suppose it cannot be helped when one is travelling.'

He came to a halt.

'An answer may be at hand,' he said. 'Listen.'

'What is it? I cannot—'

But he was already pushing his way through the thick bushes. Cassie followed and soon heard the sound of rushing water. It grew louder, but they had gone some way from the path before they reached the source of the noise. Cassie gave a little gasp of pure pleasure.

They were on the edge of a natural pool. It was fed by a stream tumbling down the steep cliff on the far side and the midday sun glinted on the falling water, turning the spray into a glistening rainbow.

'Oh, how beautiful!'

'Not only beautiful, milady, but convenient. We can bathe here.'

'What? Oh, no, I mean—'

Cassie broke off, but her blushes only deepened when Raoul gave her a scornful look.

'You have warm air and clean water here, *madame*, I cannot conjure an army of servants for you, too. I am going to make the most of what nature has given us. I suggest you do, too.'

He tethered the horse and began to strip off his clothes, throwing his shirt into the pool to wash it. Cassie knelt on the bank and dipped her hands into the water. It was crystal clear and deliciously cool against her skin. From the corner of her eye she saw that Raoul had now discarded all his clothes. She looked away quickly, but not before she had noted the lean athletic body. How wrong she had been to describe him as a bear, she thought distractedly. There was only a shadowing of hair on his limbs with a thicker covering on his chest, like a shield that tapered down towards...

Oh, heavens! She must not even think of that.

She heard the splash as he dived into the pool and only then did she risk looking up again. Raoul was a strong swimmer, sending diamond droplets flying up as he surged through the water and away from her. For a moment she envied him his freedom before berating herself as a ninny.

He had said she should make use of what he had termed nature's gift and she would. The pool was large enough to keep out of each other's way. There were several large bushes at the edge of the water and she moved behind one of them to divest herself of her riding habit. She shook out the jacket and the full skirts and draped them over the bush where they could air in the sunshine, then she followed Raoul's example and tossed her shirt into the water. Once she had removed her corset she did the same with her shift, then she knelt at the side of the pool and washed the fine garments as best she could before wringing them out and hanging them over another convenient shrub. The sun was so high and strong she thought they would both be quite dry by the time she had bathed herself.

The pool was shallower in the secluded spot she had chosen and the cold on her hot skin made her gasp as she stepped in. Cautiously she walked away from the bank until the water was just over waist deep and she lowered herself until only her head was above the surface. Now her body was submerged she felt more comfortable. She moved into slightly deeper water and closed her eyes, feeling the heat of the sun on her face. Her body felt weightless, rocking with the gentle movement of the water, cleansing, relaxing.

'There, do you not feel better?'

Cassie gave a little scream. Raoul was only feet away from her, his wet hair plastered to his head and his eyes gleaming with laughter.

'G-go away, if you please,' Cassie ordered him, praying the sun glinting on the surface of the water would prevent him from seeing her naked body. 'Pray, go and wash your clothes, sir, and let me be private.'

'I came to tell you I have been standing beneath the waterfall,' he said, ignoring her request. 'It is refreshing, I think you will like it.'

'No, thank you.'

'Why not? I will stay here, if you wish to be alone.'

'I want to be alone *here*,' she said, trying to keep her voice calm. The amusement in his eyes deepened and she glared at him. 'Go away. I wish to dress. Now.'

'But your linen cannot be dry yet.'

'That is my concern, not yours.'

'It is not far to swim across to the waterfall. You would feel better for the exercise.'

'Most definitely I should not.'

His eyes narrowed. 'You cannot swim.' When she did not reply he reached out to her. 'Let me teach you.'

'No!' The word came out as a squeak. 'You c-cannot teach me.'

'It is very easy.'

She shook her head, backing away a little, towards the bank, but having to crouch down in the shallower water.

There was a splash as he pushed himself upright.

'Look, it is not so very deep, you could walk across, if you wished.'

Cassie was looking. Her eyes were fixed on those broad shoulders and that muscled chest glistening in the sunlight. Thankfully the rest of his body was still submerged.

'Come.' He held his hand out to her. 'I want you to stand beneath the waterfall and tell me if it is not the most invigorating sensation you have ever experienced.'

It was madness. She should dress immediately, but a glance at the bank showed her that her shirt and her shift were still too damp to wear. She could sit here in the shallows while the sun baked the skin on her face to the colour of a biscuit or she could go with Raoul into the shade beneath the waterfall.

No, it was not to be contemplated, but already her hand was going out to his and she was edging out of the shallows. As the water came up over her shoulders she felt its power rocking her off her feet. Raoul's grip tightened.

'Do not worry,' he said. 'I will hold you.'

It surprised Cassie just how safe she felt with her hand held so firmly in his warm grasp.

'Did you learn to swim in the navy?' she asked in an effort not to think about his naked body, just an arm's reach away from her own.

'No. My father taught me.'

'I would imagine it is a useful accomplishment for a ship's surgeon.'

'It is not difficult, you should try it. Even dogs can swim.'

'I am not a dog, *monsieur*!'

'No, I can see that.'

Cassie set her lips firmly together and suppressed an angry retort. If it wasn't for the fact that they had reached the middle of the pool and the water was so deep that she was forced to stand on tiptoe, she might have moved away, but she needed his support. She maintained a stern silence and kept him at arm's length as they moved forward. Cassie was also leaning away from her partner and she was reminded of seeing Grandmama performing a stately minuet. The thought made her want to giggle and she wondered what the marchioness would think if she could see her granddaughter now, naked as a babe and in the company of a strange man.

Raoul was guiding her to one side of the waterfall, where there was a gap between the sheer cliff and the falling water. Soon she began to feel the spray on her face, a fine mist that cooled her heated skin, but she did not have much chance to enjoy it, for an incautious step found nothing but water beneath her foot and she plunged beneath the surface. Panic engulfed Cassie before Raoul's strong arms caught her up.

'It's all right, you are safe now, I have you.'

She grabbed his shoulders, coughing, and as he pulled her close her legs came up and wrapped themselves about his waist.

'My apologies, milady,' he muttered, his voice unsteady. 'I had not noticed that the pool floor was so uneven here. I will carry you the rest of the way.'

She clung on, no longer concerned that they

were naked, all that mattered was that she was safe in his arms. Her face was hidden against his neck, the salty taste of his skin was on her mouth. Whenever she breathed in she was aware of the faint musky scent of him. The sound of rushing water was loud and constant, but she could also hear Raoul's ragged breathing and felt his heart hammering against her breast as he moved slowly, step by step, through the water. At last he stopped.

'You can stand down now, *madame*. It is not so deep. Trust me.'

Trust him? She had no choice. It had been sheer madness to come so far from the bank, to put herself at the mercy of a man she did not know. She swallowed. How could she claim not to know Raoul Doulevant, when their naked bodies had been entwined so intimately? Even now his hands were moving to her waist, supporting her, giving her confidence. Keeping her head buried against him, Cassie unwrapped her legs from his body. Gingerly she reached down to find firm, smooth rock beneath her feet. She stepped away from Raoul, but could not bring herself to release his hand as she gazed around. It was much darker here and she looked up to see that they were standing behind a curtain of water that cast a greenish hue over everything. Without the sun to warm her, Cassie realised that the parts of her body above the water were tensed against the cold. She glanced down, noting with relief that her hair was hanging down and concealing her breasts, then thought wryly that it was a little late for modesty, when moments ago she had been clinging like ivy to her companion. She glanced towards him and gave a little laugh of surprise.

'Your skin looks green!'

Raoul glanced at her.

'And you look like a mermaid.'

'Oh? You have seen one of those mythical creatures, I suppose.'

He grinned. 'Hundreds.'

She was laughing up at him. Raoul was inordinately pleased that she shared his delight in this place and it was the most natural thing in the world to lean a little closer and kiss her. He felt a tremor run through her, felt her body yield a little before she regained control and backed away from him, eyes wide and dark. She released his hand, clearly preferring to run the risk of drowning rather than touch him.

'We, we should go back now, *monsieur.*'

She would not meet his eyes and Raoul silently cursed himself. What was he about, consorting with this woman? He could not resist flirting with her, but she was not for him. Yet his body told him differently, it had known it from the first time he had pulled her into his arms and ridden away with her. Now it remembered every step he had taken with her in his arms, every moment of her warm flesh pressed against his, arousing him and sending the hot blood pounding through his veins and making him dizzy. Enough of such madness. He did not want her naked body in his arms again, she was too tempting. The instant and powerful arousal when she had flung her legs about him had almost toppled them both beneath the water. Yet she had felt as fragile as a bird when he held her close, her heart beating erratically against his chest, rousing in him a pro-tectiveness that he really did not wish to feel for any Englishwoman. He must get them both back to the far bank without further embarrassing the lady. He set his jaw. That would not be easy when her naked form was so temptingly close. The ap-prehension in her face told him that she, too, was wondering how they would get back.

He turned away from her.

'Put your hands on my shoulders and let your body float up behind you. If you relax you will find it easier.'

Obediently she placed her hands on his shoulders. Briefly he covered her fingers with his own.

'Hold tight now.'

Cassie was gripping as tightly as she could, feeling the knotted muscle moving beneath her hands as he used his arms to help pull them through the water. Her body was still vibrating from his kiss, her blood felt hot and she wondered what would have happened if they had not been standing up to their shoulders in the cold water. She thought it might then have been much more difficult to pull away from him, to remember the dangers of her situation. Even now she was not safe; she could not make it back across the pool without his help. She knew she must keep her body away from that broad back and not pull herself close and allow her breasts to rest against him, which was what some wild and wanton part of her wanted to do. She kept her body straight, pushing her legs up towards the surface of the water and keeping her eyes fixed on the tendrils of dark hair curling at the nape of Raoul's neck.

At first it took all her energy to concentrate, but gradually she managed to relax a little and discovered it required less effort. She was floating out behind him and where her back broke the surface she could feel the heat of the sun on her skin. Her grip on Raoul's strong shoulders eased, she tried a few tentative kicks with her legs and heard a chuckle.

'A few more trips across the pool and I think you might be swimming, milady.'

Quite unaccountably, his words pleased her, but she managed not to give herself away when she responded. 'No, I thank you.' They had almost reached the bank and her feet sank to the pool's floor. 'I can manage from here. If you will leave me I will dress myself.'

'Are you sure you would not like me to help you with your corset?'

She gritted her teeth. Really, he was quite infuriating.

'I will manage,' she told him. 'Pray, go and dress yourself, *monsieur.* Over there, out of my sight.'

Grinning, Raoul swam away. Milady was back, as haughty and commanding as ever, but when he had climbed out of the water and was pulling on his shirt he heard a faint but unmistakable sound coming from the other side of those concealing bushes. Lady Cassandra was singing.

When at last she emerged from the bushes she was fully dressed and she had removed the pins from her hair, letting the thick, dark tresses spread around her shoulders while they dried. She looked better, he thought. Less tired and her eyes were brighter. She looked beautiful. A sudden, exultant trill of birdsong filled the air, like a fanfare for the lady.

Scowling, Raoul turned away and busied himself checking the girth on the saddle. This was no time for such fanciful ideas. Resolutely he kept his eyes from her until he was mounted on the horse.

'Well, *madame*, shall we continue?'

He put out his hand. She sprang nimbly up, but from the way she held herself, tense and stiff before him, he knew that she, too, was trying to avoid touching him more than necessary.

Raoul pushed the bay to a canter and they covered the rest of the journey to Reims in good time. The sun was low in the sky when they reached the main highway and dismounted for a final time to rest the horse before they rode into the city. They had hardly spoken since leaving the pool, both caught up in their own thoughts, but as he waited for her to pin up her hair again he noted the frown creasing her brow.

'What is in your mind, *madame*?'

'How far is it from Reims to Le Havre?'

He shrugged. 'Three days, perhaps, to Rouen, then another two to Le Havre. Or you may be in luck and find a ship in Rouen that will take you to the coast. You might even find one to take you all the way to England.'

'But France is at war with England, will that not make it more difficult?'

Raoul shrugged. 'Difficult, but not impossible, if you have money.'

Le Havre could be bustling with troops. Dangerous enough for him, but a pretty young woman, travelling alone, would have to be very careful. He glanced at her. She had finished pinning up her hair, but even so she looked remarkably youthful. An unscrupulous man might take advantage of her. He might steal her money, thought Raoul. Or worse. He remembered when he had first seen her, about to be attacked by the courier and his accomplice. She had been prepared to fight, but without his help she might not escape so lightly next time.

'If you will help me to reach the coast and find a ship to take me home, I will pay you.'

The words came out in a rush and she fell silent after, keeping her eyes fixed on the distant horizon as if afraid to look at him.

Why not? Raoul asked himself. *Because she is English and an aristocrat. Everything you despise. Everything you have cause to hate.*

He glanced at the lady, noticed how tightly her hands were clasped together as she waited for his answer. She was also a woman and for all her bravado she was vulnerable and alone and it was not in his nature to turn his back on a defenceless creature.

He would prefer to travel to Brussels, but he had to admit that without money to pay his way any journey would be difficult. And once they reached a port he might well be able to find a ship to take him north along the coast.

'How much?'

She shook her head.

'I cannot say. I will pay for a carriage from Reims and our lodgings on the way and after that I need to find a ship to carry me home. I do not know how much all that will cost. However, if you will trust me, I will give you whatever I can spare, once I have booked my passage to England.'

Well, whichever way he went there was danger, but Raoul could not deny that the going would be easier if he had money.

'Very well,' he said. 'I will help you.'

She smiled, visibly relieved.

'Good.' She put out her hand. 'In England our tradesmen shake hands on a bargain. We will do the same, if you please.'

His brows went up, but after a brief hesitation he took her hand. Once they had shaken solemnly he did not let go, but carried her hand to his lips.

'Now I consider our bargain sealed, milady.'

He might have been holding a wild bird, the way her fingers fluttered within his grasp. Desire reared up again and he wanted to pull her into his arms. A shadow of alarm crossed her face. Had she read his mind? Perhaps she, too, was recalling that moment in the pool when she had wrapped herself about him, their warm bodies melding together in the cold water. Had she felt that tug of attraction?

'Yes, very well.' She pulled her hand free and

turned away from him, saying briskly, 'If we are going to travel together, then the first thing is to find you a decent set of clothes, and a razor. You are a disgrace. I cannot have my servant dressed in rags.'

His lip curled. There was his answer. That was what she thought of him.

'So, *madame*, I am to be your servant?'

The look she gave him would have frozen the sun.

'Of course. I am the daughter of a marquess and—'

He broke in angrily. 'I do not acknowledge that your *birth* gives you superiority over me.'

Cassie had been about to confess that it would not be easy for her to imitate the behaviour of a servant. She had intended it to be self-deprecating, but his retort sent all such thoughts flying and she responded with icy hauteur.

'I shall be *paying* you for your services, *monsieur*, since I have money and you do not.'

She was immediately ashamed of her response. It was ill bred, but his bitter interruption, the assumption that she was so full of conceit as to think herself superior, had angered her. Yet that in itself was wrong. What was it about this man that put her usual sunny nature to flight so easily? She was still pondering the problem when he jumped to his feet.

'Well, now we have settled our roles in this little charade we should be on our way.'

He held out his hand to her, his face unsmiling, his eyes black and cold. As he pulled her to her feet Cassie bit back the urge to say something conciliatory.

This is how it should be. You do not want to become too close to this man.

He would help her reach England, she would pay him. It was a business arrangement, nothing more.

When they reached the city gates the road was so crowded and bustling with traders and carriages they were able to slip through without being questioned. The savoury aroma of food emanating from a busy tavern tempted them to stop and dine.

'What do we do now?' asked Cassie, when they had finished their meal and were once more on the street, Raoul leading their tired horse. 'My preference is to find a respectable inn, like the one ahead of us, but...' she paused and, recalling their recent altercation, she chose her next words carefully '...I fear our appearance would cause comment.'

Raoul rubbed his chin. 'Yours may be explained by an accident to the carriage, but I agree my clothes are not suitable for a manservant. I have a plan, but I will need money, milady.'

Her eyes narrowed. 'What do you intend?'

'You will go ahead of me, tell them your servant follows. I will find new clothes and join you in an hour.'

Cassie dug a handful of coins from her purse and gave them to him, then she watched him walk away. There was a tiny *frisson* of anxiety at the thought that he might not return.

'Well if he does not come back there is nothing I can do about it,' she told herself as she turned her own steps towards the inn.

Despite her own dishevelled appearance Cassie's assured manner and generous advance payment secured rooms without difficulty. She requested a jug of hot water and set about repairing the ravages to her hair and her dress. She was only partly successful, but once she had washed her face and hands and re-dressed her hair she felt much more presentable. A servant came in to light the candles and Cassie realised with a start that darkness was falling outside now. Where was Raoul?

She sat down on a chair and folded her hands in her lap, willing herself to be calm. If he had taken the money and gone on his way she could hardly blame him, but she could not help feeling a little betrayed and also very slightly frightened at the thought of being alone.

Her ears caught the thud of quick steps on the stairs and she rose, looking expectantly towards the door, only to stare open-mouthed as a stranger entered the room.

Gone was the rough beard and shaggy, unkempt hair. Gone, too, were the ragged clothes. In fact, the only things about Raoul Doulevant that she recognised were his dark eyes, alight with laughter.

He was, she realised with a shock, devastatingly handsome. His black hair had been cut and brushed back from his brow. His cheeks, free of the heavy black beard, were lean and smooth above the firm jaw. His lips were so finely sculpted that Cassie felt a sensuous shiver run through her just looking at them. He stood tall and straight in a coat of dark-blue wool that stretched over powerful shoulders. The white linen at his throat and wrists accentuated the deep tan of his skin, while his long legs were encased in buckskins and top boots that showed his athletic limbs to advantage. To complete the ensemble he held a pair of tan gloves and a tall hat in hands. He flourished a deep bow and Cassie swallowed, unable to take her eyes off him. The laughter in his eyes deepened.

'Well, milady, do I have your approval?'

'Very much so.' Her voice was nothing more than a croak and she coughed, hoping to clear whatever was blocking her throat. 'Where did you find such elegant clothes in this little town?'

He grinned. 'There are ways.'

It was all he would say and she did not press him. On closer inspection it was seen that the coat and breeches were not new and although the boots were highly polished they bore signs of wear. However, Raoul Doulevant presented the picture of a very respectable gentleman and Cassie glanced ruefully at her own clothes.

'I fear the servant is now more grand than the mistress.'

'That *is* a concern,' agreed Raoul, coming further into the room. 'When I arrived the landlord took me for your husband.'

'Oh, heavens.' She put a hand to her cheek, distracted by memories of standing with him beneath the waterfall. Suddenly her mind was filled with wild thoughts of what it might be like to be married to such a man. She closed her eyes for a moment. It would be disastrous. She had rushed into a marriage once and had suffered the consequences. Falling out of love had been almost too painful to bear. She would not go through that again.

'Our host appears to be in some confusion over our name, too,' Raoul continued, unaware of her agitation. 'I told him we are Madame and Monsieur Duval.' Her eyes flew open as he continued. 'I believe, upon reflection, that it would be best if we travel as man and wife.' He put up his hand to silence her protest. 'I considered saying we were brother and sister, but although your French is enchanting, milady, you do not speak it like a native.'

'No, but—'

'And it would be impossible to pass you off as my servant, you are far too arrogant.'

'I am not arrogant!'

He continued as if she had not spoken.

'No, it must be as man and wife. It is settled.'

Cassie took a long and indignant breath, preparing to make a withering retort but he caught her eye and said with quiet deliberation, 'You asked for my help, milady.'

There was steel in his voice and she knew it would be dangerous to cross him. She doubted he had ever intended to travel as her servant. Well, she had a choice—she could dispense with his escort, and thus break the bargain they had struck, or she could go along with his plan. The infuriating thing was she could not think of a better one.

'Man and wife in name only,' she told him imperiously.

'Even after the…er…intimacies we shared in that shady pool?'

The laughter was back in his eyes, although his voice was perfectly serious. Cassie fought down her temper. He was teasing her, he *enjoyed* teasing her.

'We shared nothing but being in the same water,' was her crushing reply. 'It was a mistake and will not be repeated.'

'No, milady.'

'It should be easy enough to keep a safe distance between us. It is not as if we are in love, after all.'

'Indeed not.'

'And in my opinion,' she continued airily, 'love is an emotion that is best left to poets and artists. Its importance in real life is grossly exaggerated.'

'Truly? You believe that?'

He folded his arms and regarded her with amusement. Really, she thought angrily, he was much more at home in these new clothes. He was so assured. So arrogant!

Even as she fumed with indignation he said, grinning, 'Explain yourself, milady, if you please.'

Very well, she would tell him. Cassie had had plenty of time to ponder on this over the past year. She waved her hand.

'What passes for love is mere lust on the man's part. It makes him profess feelings he does not truly feel and engenders a false affection that can never last.' He was still grinning at her. Cassie said bluntly, 'Let us say that the man is led by what is in his breeches, not his heart. And for the woman, why, it is nothing more than a foolish infatuation that fades quickly once she becomes better acquainted with her swain. Marital bliss and heavenly unions are not to be had by mere mortals. I am right,' she insisted, when he had the audacity to laugh at her. 'I have been—am married, after all. I know what goes on between a man and a woman. It is not as special as the poets would have us believe.'

'If you think that, milady, it occurs to me that your husband is not an expert lover.'

Her brows rose. 'And you are, perhaps?'

'I have had no complaints.'

She met his dark, laughing eyes and for one panic-stricken moment she feared he meant to offer a demonstration of his prowess. She said hastily, 'This is a most improper discussion. Let us say no more about it.'

'Very well. But I fear my next news will not please you. Our host sends a thousand pardons to milady, but the servant's room is not available.' He patted his pocket. 'He has refunded your payment for it.'

Cassie's eyes narrowed and, as if reading her mind Raoul put up his hands.

'This is no plan of mine, I assure you. The prefect has bespoke the room for a visitor and the landlord dare not refuse him. We must think ourselves fortunate he did not throw us out on the streets.'

Cassie was in no mood to consider anything but the fact that she must now share a room with this insufferable man. She dragged two of the blankets from the bed and handed them to him.

'Then *you* will sleep on the floor!'

With that she threw a couple of pillows on to the chair, climbed up on the bed and pulled the curtains shut around her.

Cassie sat in the dark, straining her ears for every sound from the room. She was half-afraid Raoul might tear open the curtains and demand to share the bed. She remained fully dressed and tense, listening to him moving about the room, and it was not until she heard the steady sound of his breathing that she finally struggled out of her riding habit and slipped beneath the covers.

Raoul scowled at the blankets in his hand. By the saints, how would he make himself comfortable with these? But honesty compelled him to admit it was no more than he deserved. It was his teasing that had angered her, but for the life of him he could not help it. He had seen the flash in her eyes when he walked in. It had been a look of admiration, nay, attraction, and it had set his pulse racing. He had been determined to treat her as an employer, to convey the landlord's news dispassionately and then they might have discussed the sleeping arrangements like two sensible adults. Instead he had given in to the temptation to bring that sparkle back to her eyes. He grinned at the memory. Even now part of him could not regret it, she looked magnificent when she was roused, a mixture of arrogance and innocence that was irresistible. With a sigh be began to spread the blankets on the floor. And these was his deserts. Well, he would make the most of it. He had slept in worse places.

Cassie had no idea of the time when she woke, until she peeped out through the curtains to find the sun streaming into the bedchamber. Cautiously she pushed back the hangings. The room was empty, the blankets and pillows on the floor showing her where Raoul had slept, but there was no sign of the man himself. Cassie slipped off the bed and dressed quickly, but a strange emptiness filled her as she wondered if Raoul had left for good. Perhaps, when he had realised she would not succumb to his advances he had decided to go his own way. The thought was strangely depressing and she could not prevent hope leaping in her breast when she heard someone outside the door, nor could she stop her smile of relief when Raoul strode into the room, a couple of large packages beneath one arm and a rather battered bandbox dangling from his hand. His brows rose when he saw her.

'I hardly expected such a warm welcome, milady.'

'I thought you had gone,' she confessed.

'And break our bargain? I am not such a rogue.' He handed her the parcels. 'I had a little money left from yesterday, plus the reimbursement from the landlord, and I decided to see if I could find something suitable to augment your wardrobe. There is also a trunk following; to travel without baggage is to invite curiosity, is it not?'

She barely acknowledged his last words, for she was busy opening the first of the packages. It contained a selection of items for Cassie's comfort including a brush and comb and a new chemise. The second was a round gown of yellow muslin with a matching shawl.

'Oh,' she said, holding up the gown. 'Th-thank you.'

'I had to guess your size, but it is fastened by tapes and should fit you. And there is this.' He put the bandbox on the table and lifted out a straw bonnet. 'The fine weather looks set to continue and I thought this might be suitable.'

'Oh,' she said again. 'I—thank you. I am very grateful.'

'I cannot have my wife dressed in rags. My wife in name only,' he added quickly. 'Although after last night we must make sure we demand a truckle bed for the maid.'

'But we do not have a maid.'

'We shall say she is following on and then complain that she has not turned up. At least then I shall have a cot to sleep in.'

'You seem to have thought of everything, *monsieur.*'

'I spent a damned uncomfortable night considering the matter,' he retorted. 'Now, *madame*, shall we go downstairs and break our fast?'

Chapter Four

The lure of a fresh gown was too tempting to resist. Cassandra begged Raoul to wait for her downstairs and twenty minutes later she joined him in the dining room dressed in her new yellow muslin. She saw his eyes widen with appreciation and was woman enough to feel pleased about it. They were alone in the room at that moment and as Raoul held the chair for her Cassie murmured her thanks again.

'The gown fits very well, *monsieur*, and the maid has promised to have my riding habit brushed and packed by the time we are ready to leave.'

'Good.' He took his seat opposite and cast an appraising eye over her. 'The woman in the shop was correct, that colour is perfect for you.'

Cassie looked up, intrigued. 'How then did you describe me to her?'

'A petite brunette with the most unusual violet eyes.'

'Oh.' Cassie blushed. 'Th-thank you, *monsieur.*'

Raoul berated himself silently. She thought he was complimenting her, but it had not been his intention. It was true he thought her beautiful, but he did not wish her to know that. Confound it, he did not want to admit the fact to himself. He gave his attention to his breakfast. He had told the truth, nothing more.

While she was busy pouring herself a cup of coffee he took another quick glance. There was no denying it, she *was* beautiful. The lemon gown enhanced her creamy skin and set off the dusky curls that she had brushed until they shone. She had pinned up her hair, accentuating the slender column of her throat and her bare shoulders that rose from the low-cut corsage. His pulse leapt and he quickly returned his gaze to his plate. Strange how the sight should affect him. After all, he had seen her shoulders before, and more, when she had been bathing in the lake. But something was different. He looked up again. Yes, there was a thin gold chain around her neck from which was suspended an oval locket set with a single ruby. But it was not the jewel that held his attention, it was the fact that the ornament rested low on her neck, directing the eye to the shadowed valley of her breasts.

'You are staring at me, *monsieur*. Is something wrong?'

Raoul cleared his throat.

'I have not seen that trinket before.'

'The locket?' She put one hand up to her breast. 'Until today I have worn it beneath my riding shirt. It is the last of my jewellery. I sold the rest to pay for my journey.'

'It holds special memories for you, perhaps.'

Her hand closed over it.

'A portrait of my husband.'

'Ah. I understand.'

Cassie did not reply, but gave her attention to finishing her breakfast. It was better that he thought she loved her husband. She was now sure enough of his character to know he would not wish to seduce another man's wife.

They left Reims looking every inch a respectable couple. The trunk was packed and strapped on to the hired chaise, Cassie made herself comfortable inside, and Raoul rode as escort on the long-tailed bay. Their journey continued without incident. Cassie had given Raoul sufficient funds to pay for their board and lodgings, they were civil to one another when they stopped to dine on the road, and Raoul made no demur about sleeping in a dressing room at the wayside inn that provided their lodgings for the night. Their fear of discovery receded, too, for whereas the soldiers at the bridges and *gendarmes* at the town gates might question a pair of ragged travellers, a wealthy gentleman and his wife roused no suspicions and they were waved through without question. However, she agreed with Raoul that they should take a more circuitous route and avoid the main highway, which was constantly busy with soldiers. Their journey was going well. Raoul was very different from Merimon, her first, rascally escort, and she knew she was fortunate that he was such an honourable man.

Cassie wondered why, then, she should feel so discontented. Her eyes moved to the window and to the figure of Raoul, mounted upon the long tailed bay. She wanted him. She wanted him to hold her, to make love to her.

Shocking. Reprehensible. Frightening. She had already admitted to herself that eloping had been a mistake. How much more of a mistake to allow herself to develop a *tendre* for a man like Raoul Doulevant? A man whom she would not see again once she returned to England. Besides, it was nothing more than lust, she knew that. They were constantly at odds with one another and had he not told her himself he had no cause to like the English? Reluctantly she shifted her gaze away from him. No, much better to keep her distance, it would be madness to allow the undoubted attraction between them to take hold. If only she could forget what had happened in the lake, forget his kiss, the way it felt to have her naked body pressed close to his, the heat that had flowed between them despite the cool water.

She gave herself a little shake. The strong yearning she felt was because she was lonely. The last few months with Gerald had been very unhappy. She had no close friends in Verdun and loyalty had kept her from confiding her problems to anyone. Once she was back in England, living with Grandmama, taking up her old life again, she would be able to put from her mind her time in France. She smoothed out the skirts of her yel-

low muslin and tried to smother the quiet voice
that told her Raoul Doulevant would not be easy
to forget.

It was some time past noon and they were passing over a particularly uneven section of road
when there was a sudden splintering crash and
the carriage shuddered to a halt, lurching drunk-
enly into the ditch. Cassie was thrown from her
seat and was lying dazed against the side of the
carriage that now appeared to be the floor when
the door above her opened. She heard Raoul's
voice, sharp with concern.

'Are you hurt?'

Cassie moved cautiously.

'I do not think so.'

He reached down to her. She grasped his hand
and he lifted her out of the chaise and on to the
ground. She found she was shaking and clung
to Raoul for a moment until her legs would once
more support her.

'What happened?' she asked him.

'One of the wheels is broken,' said Raoul, adding bitterly, 'It is no surprise when you look at
the state of the road. We should be thankful the
windows did not shatter.'

'Ah, well, you see, now the aristos are gone there's no one to pay for the upkeep.'

They looked around to find a burly individual standing behind them. The man jerked a thumb over his shoulder.

'The great house back there. When the family was in residence they paid handsomely to maintain this road in good condition for all their fine friends. Since they've gone…' he shrugged '…no one around here cares to repair it for others to use.'

'Who are you?' Raoul asked him. 'Do you live at the chateau?'

'No, but I farm the land hereabouts and live in the grounds with my wife. Looking after the place, you might say.'

Cassie glanced through the trees towards the large house in the distance. The once-grand building looked decidedly sorry for itself, windows broken and shutters hanging off.

'Then you are not looking after it very well,' said Raoul, giving voice to Cassie's thoughts.

'Ah, good *monsieur*, I am but a humble farmer. The damage occurred when the family left.' He spat on the ground. 'They are either dead or fled abroad and I have neither the money nor authority to repair it. I merely keep an eye on it, so to speak.'

'Enough,' said Raoul. 'It is not our concern. We need to get this chaise repaired, and quickly.'

The man lifted his cap and scratched his head. 'The nearest wheelwright is back the way you came.'

'I was afraid of that,' Raoul muttered. 'Even if we were riding we would be hard pressed to get back there by nightfall. Is there an inn nearby and perhaps a chaise that we might hire?'

The man spread his hands and shrugged. '*Monsieur*, I am desolated, but I have only a tumbril. The nearest inn is back in the town.' He brightened. 'But all is not lost. I can provide you with shelter for the night.'

Cassie looked to Raoul, but he had gone to help the postilion free the horses from the overturned chaise. Only when they were securely tethered to a tree did he return. The postilion was beside him and it was clear they had been considering the situation.

'I think the best thing is for the post boy to take my horse and ride back to the town,' said Raoul. 'Tomorrow he can bring a new wheel and help to repair the chaise. In the meantime we need to stable the carriage horses.'

'Well, the stables were burned out some years ago, but you can put them in the barn,' replied the farmer genially. 'And in the morning I have a team of oxen that we might use to pull the carriage out of the ditch. For a price, of course.'

'Yes, well, we will come to that once the postilion has returned.'

Raoul issued a few brief instructions and the post boy scrambled up on to the bay. Cassie watched him trot away and turned back to where Raoul and the farmer were discussing the next problem.

'We require a room for the night. You say you can accommodate us, how much will you charge?'

'Ah, *monsieur*, my own house is small and my wife's aged mother is bedridden, so I have no bedchamber I can offer for you. But do not despair, you and your lady are welcome to sleep in the barn.'

'The barn!' exclaimed Cassie.

'But, yes, *madame*. It is a very good barn. The roof is sound and there is plenty of room for you and the horses. The animals keep it warm and there is plenty of clean straw.'

An indignant protest rose to Cassie's lips, but Raoul put a warning hand on her shoulder.

'Let us get the horses into shelter first,' he said. 'Then we will discuss our accommodation.'

Silently Cassie accompanied the two men as they led the horses off the road and through the gap in the hedge into the remains of the chateau's formal gardens. The wide gravelled paths were so overgrown with weeds they were difficult to discern from the flowerbeds, and what had once been parterres and manicured lawns were now grazed by cattle. As they approached the house itself she could see it was in a very sorry state, the stucco was peeling, tiles had shifted on the roof and weeds flourished on the surrounding terrace. Cassie could not help exclaiming at the sight.

'How sad to see such a fine house in ruins.'

'There are many such places in France now, *madame*.' The farmer grinned at her. 'But it is empty and you are free to sleep there, if it's more to your taste than my barn over there.'

The farmer indicated a collection of large buildings set back and to one side of the main house. Cassie guessed they had once been outhouses and servants' quarters. What looked like the stable block was no more than a burned-out shell, but the other buildings and a small house beside it were now the farmer's domain. He led the way to one of the large barns. The sweet smell of straw was overlaid with the stronger tang of cattle. Cassie quickly pulled out her handkerchief and held it over her nose. It did not surprise her that the carriage horses objected to being led inside, but with a little persuasion and encouragement from Raoul they were eventually stabled securely at one end of the great building, as far away as possible from the farmer's oxen.

'You see,' declared their host, looking about him proudly, 'there is plenty of room. So where would you like to sleep, here or in yonder palace?'

Cassie sent Raoul a beseeching look and prayed he would understand her.

Raoul grinned. 'We'll bed down in the chateau, my friend.' He winked and gave the farmer's arm a playful punch. 'My wife has always considered herself a fine lady.'

The man shrugged. 'It will cost you the same.'
He added, as Raoul counted out the money on
to his palm, 'You'll find it pretty bare, *monsieur*,
but 'tis weatherproof, mostly. I'll bring your dinner in an hour, as well as candles and clean straw
for your bed.'

Raoul added an extra coin. 'Can you have our
trunk brought in, too? I would not want it left at
the roadside overnight.'

'With pleasure, *monsieur*. My boy shall help
me with it as soon as I've told the wife to prepare dinner for you.'

The farmer went off, gazing with satisfaction
at the money in his hand.

'We might perhaps have argued for a lower
price,' observed Raoul, 'but I suspect the fellow
will serve us well in the hope of earning himself
a little extra before we leave here tomorrow.' He
turned to Cassie. 'Shall we go and inspect our
quarters?'

He held out his arm and she placed her fingers
on his sleeve.

'I am relieved that I do not have to sleep with
the animals,' she confessed.

'I could see that the idea did not appeal. However, I doubt the chateau will be much better. I expect everything of value has been removed.'

'We shall see.'

Her optimistic tone cheered him. He had expected an angry demand that they should go on to find an inn and was fully prepared to ask her just how she thought they were to get there with no saddle horse. There was also the trunk to be considered; having purchased it he did not think she would wish to leave it behind. But instead of being discontented the lady appeared sanguine, even eager to explore the chateau. They went up the steps to the terrace and carefully pulled open one of the long windows. The glass had shattered and it scrunched beneath their feet as they stepped into a large, high-ceilinged salon. A few pieces of broken furniture were strewn over the marble floor, the decorative plasterwork of the fireplace was smashed and there were signs in one corner that someone had tried to set light to the building. He heard Cassie sigh.

'Oh, this is so sad, to think of the family driven out of their home.'

'It was no more than they deserved, if they oppressed those dependent upon them.'

'But you do not know that they did,' she reasoned. 'In England we heard many tales of innocent families being forced to flee for their lives.'

'What else would you expect them to say? They would hardly admit that they lived in luxury while people were starving.'

'No doubt you believe it was right to send so many men and women to the guillotine, merely because of their birth.'

'Of course not. But I do *not* believe a man's birth gives him the right to rule others. Aristocrats like yourself are brought up to believe you belong to a superior race and the English are the very worst!'

Cassie smiled. 'You will not expect me to agree with you on *that, monsieur.*' She looked around her once again. 'But while I admit there are good and bad people in the world, I cannot believe that all France's great families were bad landlords. Some will have fled because there was no reasoning with a powerful mob.'

'But before that the king and his court were too powerful, and would not listen to reason,' Raoul argued.

'Perhaps.' She walked to the centre of the room and turned around slowly, looking about her. 'I grew up in rooms very like this. A large, cold mansion, far too big to be comfortable. I much prefer Grandmama's house in Royal Crescent. That is in Bath,' she explained.

'I have heard of it,' he said. 'It has the hot baths, does it not?'

'Yes. Many elderly and sick people go there to take the waters.' Her eyes twinkled. 'And many wealthy people who *think* they are sick enjoy living there, too, and pay high prices for dubious treatments. The doctors of Bath have grown fat giving out pills and placebos to the rich and privileged. It is not as fashionable as it once was, but it is still very pleasant with its concerts, and balls and the theatre, and all one's friends in such close proximity. I lived there very happily with Grandmama until...'

'Until you met your husband?'

'Yes. I have not seen Bath for nearly eighteen months.'

'You must have had the very great love to elope with this man,' he said. 'To give up your family and friends, everything you knew.'

He saw a shadow flicker across her eyes before she turned away from him.

'Yes.'

* * *

Cassie hurried across the room, giving Raoul no time to question her further. A very great love? It had been a very great foolishness. She had ignored Grandmama's warnings and thrown her cap over the windmill. She had been in love with Gerald then. Or at least, she had thought herself in love, but the last few months had brought her nothing but pain and disillusion. She had learned that love could not make one happy, it was merely a device used by men to delude poor, foolish females. She had witnessed it often enough in Verdun, especially amongst Gerald's friends. A gentleman would profess himself hopelessly in love, then as soon as he had seduced the object of his affection the passion would fade and he would move on to another lover. A salutary lesson and one she would never forget.

Pushing aside the unwelcome thoughts, Cassie grasped the handles of the double doors and threw them wide, drawing in a sharp breath at the sight of the once-magnificent ballroom before her. 'Oh, how wonderful it must have been to dance in a room such as this!'

She wandered into the cavernous space. The walls were pale primrose with huge blocks of darker yellow where large paintings had once hung. Between the windows were gilded mirror frames, the glass shattered and glittering on the floor. At each end of the room four Italian-marble pillars rose up and supported a ceiling that was decorated with a glorious scene of cherubs playing hide-and-seek amongst white clouds.

'Oh, how I loved to dance,' she murmured wistfully. 'Grandmama took me to so many assemblies in Bath and it is one of the things I have missed most since my marriage. Gerald never took me to balls.'

A wave of unhappiness washed over her, so suddenly that it took her by surprise. She pressed her clasped hands to her chest and was obliged to bite her lip to hold back a sob. It had been a shock to discover so recently that her husband had escorted plenty of other ladies to balls in Verdun. She was a fool to let it upset her now. Gerald could never resist a pretty woman. In the end that had been his downfall.

Raoul watched as sadness clouded her face and suddenly he was overwhelmed with the need to drive the unhappiness from her eyes. He stepped closer, saying recklessly,

'Then let us dance now.'

She frowned at him. 'I beg your pardon?'

'I say we should dance.'

She laughed as he plucked the shawl from her shoulders and tossed it aside.

'But we have no music, *monsieur.*'

'I will sing for us.' He took her hand. 'What shall it be, the Allemande?'

He started to hum a lively tune and bowed. Cassie looked a little bemused, but she followed his lead, singing along quietly as she twisted beneath his arm and stretched up to let him turn beneath hers. By the time they performed the rosette, holding both hands and twirling at the same time, she was giggling too much to sing. Raoul persevered, leading her through the dance steps again. He felt inordinately pleased that he had put that troubled look to flight and as they skipped and stepped and twirled about his imagination took flight.

They were no longer dancing in a derelict house, but in a glittering ballroom with the most accomplished musicians playing for them. The music soared in his head and he imagined them both dressed in their finery. He could almost feel the shirt of finest linen against his skin, the starched folds of the neckcloth with a single diamond nestling at his throat. And instead of that poor yellow muslin, Cassie was wearing a ball gown of silk with diamonds glittering against her skin, although nothing could outshine the glow of her eyes as she looked up at him. When they performed the final rosette and ended, hands locked, she was laughing up at Raoul in a way that made his heart leap into his throat, stopping his breath.

Time stopped, too, as their eyes met. Raoul had felt this same connection between them before, but this time it was stronger, like a thread drawing them together. He watched the laughter die from those violet-blue eyes, replaced by a softer, warmer look that melted his heart and set his pulse racing even faster. His heart was pounding so hard that he felt light-headed and quite unsteady. His grip on her hands tightened. Those cherry-red lips were only inches away, inviting his kiss.

Cassie's heart was beating so heavily that it was difficult to breathe. Raoul was standing before her, holding her hands, filling her senses. He was all she could see, his ragged breathing the only sound she heard. She was swathed in his powerful presence and it felt wonderful.

Kiss me.

She read it in his eyes. An order, a plea that went straight to her heart and filled her soul. She clung to his hands, trembling. She desperately wanted to close the gap between them and step into his arms, but above the excitement and exhilaration that filled her an alarm bell clamoured, faint but insistent. She knew there would be no going back if she gave in now. Raoul would take her, consume her, and she would be lost. It was a perilous situation; she was a widow, alone in an enemy country.

Strange, that this foolish, impromptu dance had so quickly driven all her troubles from her mind, but now that alarm bell could not be ignored. It was not just the physical perils that threatened her. She had thought Gerald had broken her heart, but now some instinct told her that if she gave herself to Raoul the parting would be much, much worse. That thought frightened her more than all the rest and made her fight for control.

She dragged up a laugh. 'Well, that has surprised me.'

Clearly not a gentleman!
Those scornful words echoed in Raoul's brain,

reminding him of the gulf between them. He dropped her hands and moved away, allowing his indignation to turn into anger. It was necessary, if he was to combat this attraction that could only end in disaster. He should be pleased she was in no danger of falling in love with him. He had no room for a woman in his life and he would not want her broken heart on his conscience.

'Yes, you considered me a savage, did you not?' he threw at her. 'Because I have not lived in your exalted circles. Whatever you might think of me, *madame*, my birth is respectable even if I was not born into the nobility. We moved amongst the first families of Brussels. My father was a doctor, a gentleman. It was *I* who let him down; I was determined to become a surgeon, despite the fact that many still regard them as mere tradesmen.' He turned his finger, stabbing angrily into the air. '*That* is where the future lies, in a man's skill and knowledge, not in his birth. But you and your kind do not recognise that yet. My father never recognised it, either. He was disappointed; he had such high hopes of me.'

Cassie saw the fire in his eyes and heard the bitterness behind his harsh words, but she knew

his anger was not directed at her. He had mis-
understood her, but in his present mood it would
be useless to try and explain so she made no attempt to correct him.

She said carefully, 'Parents are always ambi-
tious for their children. At least, I believe that is
the case. My own parents died when I was very
young, but Grandmama always wanted the best
for me. It must have grieved her most dreadfully
when I eloped.' She touched his arm, saying gently, 'There must still be a little time before the
farmer will bring our dinner. Shall we continue
to explore?'

Raoul shrugged.

'Why not?' he said lightly. He scooped her
shawl from the floor and laid it around her shoulders. She noted how carefully he avoided actually touching her. 'Lead on, *madame.*'

The magical moment was broken, shattered
like the ornate mirrors and tall windows. She
felt the chill of disappointment and tried hard to
be thankful that she had not weakened. A momentary lapse now would cost her dear.

The chateau had been stripped bare and they
did not linger on the upper floors. Cassie pulled

her shawl a little closer around her as the shadows lengthened and the chill of evening set in. She had been a child when the revolution in France had begun, only ten years old when King Louis had been murdered. It had been the talk of English drawing rooms and inevitably the news had reached the schoolroom, too. She had listened to the stories, but only now, standing in this sad shell of a house, did she have any conception of the hate and fear that must have been rife in France. She could only be thankful that such a bloody revolution had not occurred in England.

'It grows dark,' said Raoul. 'We should go down and look out for our host.'

Cassie readily agreed. The stairs were in semi-darkness and when Raoul reached for her hand she did not pull away. She told herself it was merely a precaution, lest she trip in the dim light, but there was no mistaking the comfort she gained from his warm grasp. They heard the farmer's deep voice bellowing from somewhere in the lower regions of the house and as they reached the hall he emerged from the basement stairs.

'So there you are,' he greeted them. 'We've put your dinner in the kitchen and my boy is lighting a fire there now. You'll find 'tis the most comfortable room, the windows are intact and there's a table, too.'

They followed him down to the servants' quarters and through a maze of dark corridors until they reached the kitchen. It was a large chamber, but a cheerful fire burned in the huge fireplace and numerous candles had been placed about the room to provide light. A plump woman with a spotless apron tied over her cambric gown was setting out their dinner on the scrubbed wooden table and the farmer introduced her as his wife. She looked up and fixed her sharp black eyes upon Raoul and Cassie. It was a blatantly curious stare and not a little scornful. Cassie's head lifted and haughty words rose to her lips, but she fought them down. She had no wish to antagonise the woman, so she smiled and tried to speak pleasantly.

'It is very good of you to let us stay here tonight.'

The woman relaxed slightly.

'*Eh bien*, your money's good and I suppose you will prefer this to sharing a bedchamber with the animals. The boy'll be over with a couple of sacks of straw later and he'll collect the dishes, too.' She pointed to a small door in the corner of the room. 'There's a water pump in the scullery. It still works, if you need it.'

'Thank you.'

The woman moved towards the door.

'We will leave you, then.' She gave a reluctant curtsy and followed her husband out into the dusk.

'We should eat.' Raoul indicated the bench.

They sat together and Cassie was relieved that there would be no awkward glances across the table. In fact, there was no need to look at him at all. They were facing the fireplace, where the fire crackled merrily and they could eat their meal in companionable silence. But it was *not* companionable, it pressed around her, pricking at her conscience and making her uneasy. At last she was unable to bear it any longer and had to speak, however inane her conversation.

'This is where they would have cooked the food,' she said at last, keeping her eyes on the dancing flames.

'Yes.' Raoul reached across to pick up the wine flask and poured more into their glasses. 'The turning-spit mechanism and all the cooking irons have been plundered. No doubt they have found a home elsewhere, or been melted down and turned into farm tools.'

Cassie picked up her wine glass and turned it this way and that, so that the crystal glinted and sparkled in the candlelight.

'These are very fine, perhaps the owners of this house used to drink from them.'

'And now they are being used by their tenants,' remarked Raoul coolly. 'It is merely a redistribution of wealth.'

Her chin went up a little and she turned to regard him. 'Something you heartily approve.'

Raoul met her eyes steadily. 'I have never approved of violence, Lady Cassandra. It is my calling to save lives, not take them.'

She turned her gaze back to the fireplace, knowing she did not wish to fight him tonight.

'So they cooked on an open fire. How old-fashioned,' she murmured, thinking of the closed range in Grandmama's house in Bath.

'There might well have been a dozen or more servants in here,' Raoul replied. 'Slaving to provide meals for their masters.'

'Not necessarily slaving,' Cassie demurred. 'In Bath my grandmother was at pains to provide the very best equipment for her cook. She said he is a positive tyrant.'

'Yet she has the power to dismiss him on a whim.'

Cassie shook her head, smiling a little. 'You are wrong, sir. The man is very aware of his own worth and paid well for his skills, I assure you. He also is the one with the power to hire or dismiss his staff as he wishes.' Her smile grew. 'And before you berate me again for the inequality of English society, I would tell you, *monsieur*, that the cook is a Frenchman.'

He grinned, acknowledging the hit.

'Very well, I will admit that it is in most men's nature to be a tyrant if they are not checked.' He turned slightly and raised his glass to her. 'A truce, Lady Cassandra?'

She returned his salute. 'A truce, Monsieur Doulevant.'

They returned their attention to the food, but the atmosphere had changed. Cassie no longer felt at odds with her companion and she was a great deal happier.

A basket of logs had been placed near the fireplace, but the size of the hearth was such that it was soon emptied and by the time the farmer's boy brought over their bedding and carried away the empty dishes the room was growing chilly.

'We should get some sleep,' said Raoul. 'We will have another busy day tomorrow.'

There were two sacks of straw. Raoul placed one on either side of the kitchen table and handed Cassie one of the two blankets that had been provided.

'Your bed awaits, my lady.'

She tried to make herself comfortable, but the sack was not well filled and the straw flattened quickly beneath her. She could not help a sigh that sounded very loud in the quiet, echoing kitchen.

'Is it not luxurious enough for you, my lady?'

Tiredness made her irritable and she snapped back.

'This is not what I expected when I left Verdun.'

'I am surprised your husband agreed to your travelling alone.'

'He did not agree. He's—'

She bit off the words.

'He what?' Raoul asked suspiciously. 'He does not know?'

'That is true.'

It was not exactly a lie. Cassie knew it would

sink her even further in his estimation, yet she was unwilling to admit she was a widow. She clung to the belief that there was some small protection in having a husband.

'But of course. You told me yourself that you grew bored at Verdun. *Tiens*, I feel even more sympathy for your spouse, *madame*. You have quite literally abandoned him, have you not?'

The darkness was filled with his disapproval. It cut her and she responded by saying sharply, 'That is not your concern.'

'No indeed. *Mon Dieu*, but you are a heartless woman!'

'You know nothing about me!'

Tell him, Cassie. Explain how you remained with your husband, endured the pain and humiliation of knowing he only wanted your fortune.

Pride kept her silent. Better Raoul should think her heartless than a fool. She turned on her side and pulled the thin blanket a little closer around her. 'Oh, how I pray there will be a ship in Rouen that will carry me all the way to England,' she muttered angrily. 'The sooner we can say goodbye to one another the better.'

He gave a bark of bitter laughter.

'Amen to that, my lady!'

Chapter Five

It took the best part of the morning to repair the chaise. Discussions with the farmer elicited the information that their meandering route, chosen to minimise the chances of encountering soldiers on the road or passing an army garrison, meant that they were a good half-day's drive away from Rouen and he doubted they would reach the city before nightfall, but Cassie was as anxious as Raoul to press on and echoed his refusal to remain another night.

She climbed into the chaise and watched Raoul scramble up on to the long-tailed bay. She was thankful he was not in the carriage with her, she did not enjoy travelling in the company of one who disapproved of her so blatantly. He saw her as a rich and spoiled lady who had run away from her marriage when the novelty had begun to pall. It would be useless to explain, because she knew that men saw these things differently. A wife was a mere chattel, was she not?

Cassie looked up as the chaise slowed. The road was winding its way between dilapidated cottages at the edge of a village. Through the window she watched Raoul exchange a few words with the postilion before bringing his horse alongside the carriage. Cassie let down the glass.

'This is Flagey, it is very small and the post boy tells me there is a much better inn about an hour from here where we may change horses and dine,' he informed her. 'If we do not tarry he thinks we may still make Rouen tonight.'

'Very well, let us push on. I—' Cassie broke off as a loud rumble, like thunder, filled the air. It shook the ground and the carriage jolted as the horses sidled nervously. 'What on earth was that?'

Raoul was already looking towards the cluster of buildings ahead of them. Above the roofs a cloud of dust was rising, grey as smoke. The bay threw up its head as the church bell began to toll.

'An accident of some sort,' he said, kicking his horse on. Cantering around the bend, he saw that a large building had collapsed on the far side of

the village square. People were already congre-
gating at the scene. Some of the women were
wailing, a few holding crying babies, but most
were helping the men to drag away the stones
and rubble.

Raoul threw the horse's reins to a woman with
a babe in her arms and immediately ran forward
to help, casting his jacket aside as he went.

'How many men are in there?' he demanded
as he joined the rescuers.

One of the men stopped to drag a grimy sleeve
across his brow.

'Eight, ten, perhaps more. 'Tis the tithe barn.
They were working to secure the roof before the
winter when the timbers collapsed.'

Raoul joined the group, scrabbling at the
wreckage. The dust was still rising from the de-
bris, making everyone cough. It was clear that the
roof had collapsed inwards, bringing down parts
of the old walls. Muffled shouts and screams
could be heard, so there were survivors, but
Raoul knew they must reach them and quickly.

The first man they pulled out had a broken arm,
but the next was badly crushed and groaning
pitifully. An old woman standing beside Raoul
crossed herself before trying to drag away an-

other rotted timber. There would be more crushed bodies, more broken limbs.

'You will need a doctor. Or better still, a surgeon.'

'Dr Bonnaire is ten miles away, *monsieur.*' The old woman took a moment to straighten up, pressing her hand to her back. She nodded to a group of young men working frantically to pull away more stones. 'Jean can go, he is the fastest runner.'

'Take the horse.'

Raoul heard Cassandra's voice and turned to see her leading the bay forward.

She said again, 'Take the horse. It will be much quicker to ride.'

'Then let me go,' said an older man, stepping up. 'I can handle a horse and Jean's strength would be better used getting those poor fellows out.'

'Good idea,' agreed Raoul.

He watched the man mount up and gallop away, calculating how long it would take the doctor to get there.

'What can I do?' asked Cassandra.

'Where is the carriage?'

'I have told the post boy to drive to the *auberge*

at the far end of the village. What may I do to help you?'

He regarded her as she stood before him. She was too petite to be of help moving the rubble; her hands were unused to any type of work at all. He was also afraid that they would be bringing bodies out soon and he did not want her to witness the carnage. He looked towards a group of women and children crying noisily as they watched the proceedings.

'Get them away,' he muttered. 'They are doing no good here.'

'Of course.'

She nodded and Raoul went back to the laborious process of dragging away the rubble stone by stone.

As word of the disaster spread more people turned up to help with the rescue. Raoul left them to finish digging out the survivors while he attended those they had already pulled out of the building. He had not wanted to reveal that he was a medical man, but there was no sign of the doctor and these people needed his help.

After sluicing himself down at the village pump he went to the nearest house, where the injured men had been taken. There were four so far: a quick glance showed him that the man who had been severely crushed would not survive. There was nothing he could do for the fellow so he left him to the care of the local priest while he set the broken arm and patched up the others as best he could. Thankfully they were not seriously hurt, but others were being carried in, each one bringing with him the damp, dusty smell of the collapsed building. He had no instruments and his equipment was limited to the bandages piled on a table, but there was hot water in a kettle hanging over the fire and a large flask of white brandy to ease the suffering of the injured men.

It was growing dark and Raoul was working alone in the little room when he heard the thud of horses and the sudden commotion outside the door. The doctor, at last. He looked up, his relief tempered by surprise when he saw a fresh-faced young man enter the room.

'You are Dr Bonnaire?'

'Yes. And you are?'

'Duval. My wife and I were passing through here when the accident happened.'

'It was good of you to stay and help.' Dr Bonnaire looked about him. 'Are all the men recovered, did everyone survive?'

'Everyone is accounted for now, nine men in all. Two are dead, four had only slight injuries. I patched them up and sent them home. These three are the most seriously injured.' He nodded to a man sitting by the fire. 'I have set his arm, but he has also had a blow to the head and is not yet able to stand.' He walked over to the two men lying on makeshift beds. 'These two are the worst. They were both trapped by their legs.'

As Bonnaire knelt beside the first of the men Raoul heard a soft voice behind him.

'I thought you would need more light.' Cassandra came in, followed by three of the village women, each one of them carrying lamps and candlesticks. 'We collected these from the other houses.'

The doctor shot to his feet. 'How thoughtful of you, Madame…?'

'Duval,' she said quietly.

'Ah…' he glanced towards Raoul '…your wife, sir. *Enchanté, madame.*'

Raoul saw the faint flush on Cassie's cheek and knew she was not happy with the subterfuge, but it was necessary.

'Aye, Madame Duval and her husband arrived most providentially,' put in one of the other women.

'Madame Deschamps owns the *auberge* at the far end of the village,' explained Cassie. Her eyes flickered over Raoul and away again. 'She and her husband have offered us a room for the night.'

'Well, 'tis too late for you to be travelling on now and 'tis the least we can do, for all your trouble.'

'You are very kind,' murmured Raoul.

'Nay, 'tis you and *madame* that have been kind, *monsieur*, helping us as you have done.'

Madame Deschamps appeared to be in no hurry to leave, but once the other women had gone Cassie touched her arm and murmured that they must not keep the good doctor from his work. She cast a last, shy glance at Raoul and ushered the landlady from the room. Bonnaire stood gazing at the door and Raoul prompted him gently.

'Well, Doctor, would you like to examine your patients?'

'What? Oh, yes. Yes.'

It did not take long. Raoul had already stripped the men of their clothing and cleaned their lacerated bodies. The doctor gently drew back the thin blanket from each of the men and gazed at their lower limbs.

'Legs crushed beyond repair,' he observed.

'Yes.' Raoul nodded. 'Both men will require amputation at the knee.'

The young doctor blenched. He placed his case upon the table, saying quietly, 'I thought that might be the situation and brought my tools.'

He lifted out a canvas roll and opened it out on the table to display an impressive array of instruments, very much like the ones Raoul had lost when he had fled from Paris, only these looked dull and blunt from lack of use.

Raoul frowned. 'Have you ever performed an amputation, Doctor?'

Bonnaire swallowed and shook his head.

'I saw one once, in Paris, but I could not afford to finish my training. These tools belonged to my uncle. He was an army surgeon.'

Raoul closed his eyes, his initial relief at finding a medical man on hand rapidly draining away. He sighed.

'Then you had best let me deal with this.'

'You? You are a surgeon, Monsieur Duval?'

'Yes. And I have performed dozens of these operations.'

The relief in the young man's face was only too apparent. A sudden draught made the candles flicker as the door opened and the priest came in.

'Ah, Dr Bonnaire, they said you had arrived. Thanks be! A sad business, this. Will the Lord take any more souls this night, think you?'

'I hope not, Monsieur le Curé,' was the doctor's fervent response.

'Good, good. I came to tell you that you are not to worry about your fee, Doctor. If these poor people have not the means there is silverware in the church that can be sold. You shall not go unrewarded for this night's work.'

The young doctor bowed.

'Thank you, but if anyone is to be paid, it should be this man.' He glanced at Raoul. 'He is the more experienced surgeon and is going to perform the operations necessary to save these two men.'

'Is that so indeed?' declared the priest, his brows rising in surprise.

'It is,' said Raoul, grimly inspecting the instruments spread out before him. 'But to do so I will require these to be sharpened.'

'But of course, *monsieur*! Give me the ones you need and I shall see it is done without delay.'

'And get someone to take this fellow home,' added Raoul, nodding at the man dozing in the chair by the fire.

'I will do so, sir, I will do so.' The priest gathered up the instruments and bustled away, leaving Bonnaire to fix Raoul with a solemn gaze.

'Thank you, *monsieur*, and I meant what I said about payment.'

'I do not want the church's silverware, but you should take it, Bonnaire, and when this night is done you should use it to go back to Paris and finish your training.'

They set to work, preparing the room and arranging all the lamps and candles to provide the best light around the sturdy table that would be used to carry out the operations. The situation was not ideal, but Raoul had worked in worse conditions during his time at sea. A woman crept in timidly and helped the injured man out of the room just as the priest returned with the sharpened instruments.

'Thank you.' Bonnaire took the honed tools and handed them to Raoul. 'Perhaps, *mon père*, you could send someone to attend to the lights and the fire while we work.'

'But of course. I will ask Madame Duval to step in.'

'No.' Raoul frowned. 'She is not used to such work.'

The priest stopped and looked at him in surprise.

'Really, *monsieur*? If you say so. Madame Deschamps, of course, is a woman most resourceful, but she is very busy at the *auberge*.'

'Well, there must be someone else who can come in,' said Raoul irritably.

The priest spread his hands.

'These are simple people, *monsieur*, uneducated. They are easily frightened and I fear they would be sorely distressed by the sight of their neighbours in such a situation as this.'

'But my wife...'

Raoul's words trailed off. What could he say, that his wife was a lady? That she was too cossetted and spoiled to be of any use here?

'Madame Duval has shown herself to be most resourceful in this tragedy,' the priest continued. 'The villagers turned to her in their grief and she did not fail them. While they could only weep and wail she arranged who should go to the fields to fetch the mothers and wives of those who were working in the barn. She helped to feed the children and put them to bed and it was *madame* who organised the women to prepare this house for you, to boil the water and tear up the clean sheets for bandages. Even now she is helping to cook supper at the *auberge* for those who are grieving too much to feed themselves or their families.'

'Practical as well as beautiful,' remarked Bonnaire. 'You are to be congratulated on having such a partner, Monsieur Duval.'

Raoul's jaw clenched hard as he tried to ignore the doctor's remark. He did not want to be congratulated, did not want to think how fortunate a man would be to have a wife like Lady Cassandra.

He shrugged and capitulated.

'Very well, let her come in.'

They had tarried long enough and he had work to do.

They lifted the first man on to the table. He and his fellow patient had been given enough brandy to make them drowsy and Raoul worked quickly. He was aware of Cassandra moving silently around the room, building up the fire to keep the water hot, trimming the wicks on the lights and even helping Bonnaire to hold down the patient when necessary. He glanced up at one critical point, fearing she might faint at the gruesome nature of the business, but although she was pale she appeared perfectly composed and obeyed his commands as steadily as the young doctor.

Midnight was long past before the operations were complete and the patients could be left to recover. Raoul felt utterly drained and when Bonnaire offered to sit with them through the night he did not argue. He shrugged on his coat and escorted Cassie to the *auberge*, where the landlady was waiting up to serve them supper.

Cassie was bone-weary and after all she had seen that evening she had no appetite, but she had eaten very little all day and she sat down opposite Raoul at the table while Madame Deschamps set two full plates before them.

The hot food warmed her and she began to feel better. She reached for her wine glass and looked up to see Raoul watching her.

'I am sorry we have had to delay our journey, milady.'

'I am not.' She continued, a note of wonder in

her voice, 'Truly, I do not regret being here. It has been a difficult day and a sad one, too, but I am pleased I could be of help.'

She took a sip of wine while she considered all that had happened. Raoul had thrown himself into assisting the villagers and she had done the same. The people had been shocked and frightened, unable to think for themselves. They had needed someone to take charge and it had felt like the most natural thing in the world for her to step in, deciding what needed to be done and setting villagers to work. They had not questioned her, instead as the day wore on they had looked to her even more for guidance. She glanced shyly at Raoul.

'For the first time in my life I think I have done something truly useful.'

Silently he raised his glass to her and, smiling, she gave her attention to her food. They finished their meal in silence and she sat back, watching as Raoul wiped a piece of bread around his plate. He was looking a little less grey and drawn than when they had come in, but she knew how tirelessly he had worked all day.

She said suddenly, 'You must be exhausted.'

He pushed away his empty plate.

'It has been a long day, certainly, and I cannot wait to get to my bed.' He drained his wine. 'Well, *madame*, shall we retire?'

Cassie had given little thought to the sleeping arrangements until the landlady showed them upstairs to what was clearly the best bedroom. A large canopied bed filled the centre of the room, its curtains pulled back to display the plump, inviting mattress. It was then that Cassie's tiredness fled, replaced by a strong sense of unease. She stopped just inside the door and did not move, even when the landlady left them.

'Ah. There is no truckle bed,' she muttered. 'I forgot to mention it.'

'Then we must share this one.' Raoul unbuttoned his coat and waistcoat and threw them over a chair.

'No!' Cassie was scandalised. To sleep in the open was one thing—even to curl up together on the floor before the fire had not felt this dangerous, after all the old woman had been sleeping in the same room and providing some sort of chaperonage. But to share a bed, to have that strong, lithe body only inches away— 'Out of the question,' she said firmly.

Raoul yawned. 'You need not fear for your virtue, milady, but if you think I will sleep on the floor tonight you are much mistaken.'

She eyed him suspiciously. If her own fatigue could vanish so quickly, she was sure his would, too. She remembered waking on the cottage floor to find his hand cradling her breast. The thought made her grow hot, but not with embarrassment. She began to recognise her own yearning for a man's touch. She watched in growing alarm as he sat down to pull off his boots.

She said quickly, 'I know how men use soft words and pretty gestures to seduce a woman, but I am not so easily caught, *monsieur.*'

'Confound it, woman, I am not using any soft words,' he snapped, but Cassie was so on edge she paid no heed.

'I know 'tis all a sham,' she continued, in an attempt to quell the flicker of desire that was uncurling inside her. 'A man must have his way and the result for the woman is always disappointing.'

'Disappointing, milady?'

With a growl he rose from the chair and came purposefully towards her. It took all Cassie's willpower not to back away from him. She tensed as he put out his hand and took her chin between his thumb and forefinger.

'Mayhap you have only had English lovers so far.'

She pulled her chin from his grasp. Her heart was hammering and panic was not far away, because she knew she was ready to fall into his arms at any moment. She started to gabble, trying to convince herself that such an action would be foolish in the extreme.

'Lovers? The word is too easily used, *monsieur*. Love rarely comes into it, in my experience. The coupling that ensues is for the man to enjoy and the woman to endure.'

His eyes narrowed and for one fearful moment she thought he might see that as a challenge, but after a brief hesitation he turned away.

'You might be the famous Pompadour herself and I could not make love to you tonight. I am too tired to argue the point with you now, *madame*. Sleep where you will, but I am going to bed.'

To Cassie's dismay he threw himself on to the covers. He could not sleep there! She must reason with him, persuade him to move.

'I am glad you will not try to woo me with soft

words,' she told him. 'It will not work with me. Let me remind you I have had a husband.'

'But not a very good one,' he muttered, putting his hands behind his head and closing his eyes.

'Gerald was a very accomplished lover,' she told him indignantly.

She turned away to place her folded shawl on the trunk. Would he notice she had used the past tense? Suddenly she did not want to lie any more and she exhaled, like a soft sigh.

'At least, he had any number of mistresses and he *told* me they were all satisfied with his performance. I confess I never found it very enjoyable, even when I thought I was wildly in love with him.' She clasped her hands together and stared down at the shawl, as if gaining courage from its cheerful, sunny colours. 'But perhaps it is wrong of me to say that, now he is no longer alive. You see, *monsieur*, I did not abandon my husband. I remained at Verdun, at his side, and would be there still, if he had not been killed. I made up my mind that I would not leave him, even though the provocation was very great indeed.'

There. She closed her eyes, feeling a sense of relief that she had at last confessed it. She was a widow and her husband had been unfaithful. Let him sneer at her if he wished.

A gentle snore was the only answer. Cassie turned to see that Raoul was fast asleep. Even a rough shake on the shoulder failed to rouse him. How dare he fall asleep while she was pouring out her heart! She looked at the sleeping figure. At least he was not taking up the whole bed. She blew out most of the candles and sat down on the edge of the bed, her indignation dying away as she regarded him. She reached out and gently brushed a stray lock of dark hair from his brow. He had worked tirelessly today, using all his strength and his skill to help the villagers. He deserved his rest.

Raoul surfaced from a deep sleep and lay still, eyes closed. He felt supremely comfortable, a soft mattress beneath him and a feather pillow under his head. He was still wearing his shirt and breeches but someone had put a blanket over him.

Someone.

Lady Cassandra.

He turned his head, expecting to see her dark curls spread over the pillow next to his, instead he found himself staring at a wall of white.

'What the—?' He sat up, frowning at the line of bolsters and pillows that stretched down the middle of the bed. On the far side of this downy barrier was Cassandra, wrapped snugly in a coverlet. He felt a momentary disappointment when he saw that her hair had been tamed into a thick plait.

She stirred, disturbed by his movements.

'It is called bundling,' she said sleepily.

'I beg your pardon?'

She yawned. 'The feather barricade between us. It is a device that I understand is often used in village courtships in England, so a man and woman could spend time together and find out if they truly liked each other without…committing themselves.'

'I do not think it would prove much of a deterrent, if the couple were willing.'

She was awake now and eyeing him warily.

'Well, in this case one of the couple was *not* willing,' she told him, throwing back her cover and slipping off the bed.

He saw she was still wearing her stays on top of a chemise that stopped some way above her very shapely ankles.

'I would consider that contraption of whalebone

and strong linen to be a more effective deterrent than a few bolsters, milady.'

'If you were a gentleman you would not be looking at me.' She added scornfully, 'But what else should I expect from a foreigner?'

Raoul picked up one of the bolsters and put it behind him, so he could lean back and watch Cassandra as she walked across to the washstand. He was well rested now and fully appreciative of the picture she presented.

'So it is only foreigners who look at pretty women? *Mon Dieu*, Englishmen are not only dull, they must have ice in their veins.'

She turned, clutching the towel before her.

'Of course they do not. They—' She stamped her foot. 'Ooh, you delight in teasing me!'

He grinned. 'I cannot resist, you bite so easily. By the way, how did you sleep in that corset? It must have been very uncomfortable.'

'I loosened the laces, naturally. And before you say anything more I do *not* need your help to tighten them again!'

He laughed and climbed out of bed.

'No, of course not, milady. I shall tease you no more. We must break our fast and move on.

What is the time?' He looked out of the window. '*Tiens*, it must be noon at least.'

'It was almost dawn before we went to bed,' said Cassie. 'I asked Madame Deschamps not to disturb us.'

She felt her cheeks burn as she remembered the landlady's knowing wink when she heard the request. When she had eloped she had been subjected to many such looks and rude jibes, too, but *then* she had thought herself too much in love to care about such things. How she was ever to explain these past few days she did not know. She could only hope that when she returned to England the details of this journey would remain a secret.

Raoul turned from the window.

'I had best go and see the patients. I hope Dr Bonnaire would have called me, if he needed my help in the night.' He grabbed his clothes and dressed quickly. 'We are still a good half-day's travel from Rouen. We will need to leave soon if we are to get there tonight.'

'Naturally we must stay here, *monsieur*, if you are needed.'

He looked a little surprised at her words and

nodded as he picked up his hat. 'I will go now to see how the men are doing.'

With that he was gone. Cassie finished dressing in silence, pushing aside the fleeting regret that Raoul had said he would stop teasing her.

Raoul spent an hour in the house that had become a makeshift hospital and when he returned to the *auberge* Cassandra was waiting for him at the door. His mood brightened when he saw her, pretty as a picture in her yellow gown, her dark curls brushed and pinned in a shining disorder about her head.

'Madame Deschamps insisted on cooking for us,' she greeted him. 'I have packed everything, and the carriage and your horse are ready to depart as soon we have broken our fast.'

At that moment the landlady herself came bustling out, insisting that they must not leave Flagey until they had eaten a good meal.

'I have bread and eggs and ham waiting for you, *monsieur*, and you will have the room to yourselves, you will not be disturbed.'

There was no point in arguing, so Raoul followed Cassie and their landlady into the little dining room.

'How did you find your patients?' asked Cassie as they settled down to their meal.

'The two men we operated on are awake and recovering. It will be slow, but I have hopes that with a little ingenuity they will be able to get around again. Most do and consider themselves fortunate they have only lost a leg and not their life. Bonnaire is happy to look after them now. And I called in on the fellow with the broken arm. His head has cleared, I think he will make a full recovery.'

'They must all be thankful you were here to help them.'

'They were. That is why it has taken me so long to get back. Everyone in Flagey wanted to speak to me.' He grinned. 'I cannot tell you the number of gifts I have had to decline, but I did not think you would wish to have a basket of eggs or a plucked chicken in the chaise with you, although I was tempted by the flitch of bacon.'

Cassie laughed.

'These poor people have little enough of their own. It is very generous of them to offer to share it with you. They are clearly very grateful for what you have done.'

'This is not just for me, milady, your efforts too were much appreciated.'

Cassie blushed. 'Truly?'

'Yes, truly.'

Raoul had received nothing but praise this morning for his 'good lady'. They had told him how she had supported everyone, organising them, comforting those in grief and cajoling the mothers into looking after their little ones. A saint, one man had called her. Raoul looked at her now, remembering how she had helped him during the operations, quietly and calmly doing as she was bid without question. He had expected that she would crumble at the sight of the crushed limbs, that she might cry, or swoon and need to be escorted away, but she had faced everything with a calm determination that surprised him.

And yet had he not seen signs of her resourcefulness even before they reached Flagey? There had been no tears, no tantrums during their time together. She had matched him step for step without complaint. His respect for her was growing.

Cassie was clearly pleased at his praise and he had to fight the urge to smile back at her. He dragged his eyes back to his plate. Heaven defend him from actually *liking* this woman! He scraped together the last of the ham and eggs.

But she would make a good wife.

Some demon on Raoul's shoulder whispered the words into his ear, but he closed his mind to them. He was not the marrying sort. He lived for his work. Surgery was his first love and a man could not have two mistresses.

'Our lack of a servant has not gone unnoticed, however.' He told her, sitting back in his chair. 'I have already set it about that you are so demanding no maid will stay with us.'

As he expected, she bristled at that. Her smile disappeared.

'Me, demanding?'

'Why, yes. They have experienced your managing ways for themselves. To their benefit in this instance, of course, and once I had explained that you were English they were not at all surprised when I told them you were extremely domineering.'

'Domineering?'

'I also said you were a scold.'

'You did not!'

'I did. A positive virago.'

She sat up very straight.

'You are insulting sir.'

'But truthful, milady. You have all the arrogance of your race. And your class.'

'Oh, you—you—' Her knife clattered on to her empty plate. She pushed back her chair and jumped up. 'I shall wait for you in the chaise!'

Raoul laughed as she stalked out. Best to keep her outraged. That way she was much less likely to end up in his arms.

Darkness had fallen by the time they reached Rouen. They found a small inn near the cathedral and Cassie stood silently beside Raoul while he enquired of the landlord if they had rooms. She waited anxiously, wondering if they would be questioned or asked for their papers but their host showed little curiosity about his guests, merely took their money and summoned a serving maid to show them upstairs.

Cassandra had been icily polite to Raoul on the few occasions they were obliged to speak during the journey and when they sat down to a late dinner in their private rooms she was determined to maintain her frosty manner. Her companion seemed unconcerned and applied himself to his food with gusto, while Cassie only picked at her own meal. Her lack of appetite drew an anxious look from the maid when she came to clear the table and Cassie was obliged to assure her that she found no fault with the inn's fare. Her smile faded once the servant had quit the room and she allowed her thoughts to return to the matter that had been worrying her all day. She could not forget what Raoul had said of her. It was very dispiriting and surely it could not be true.

'You are not hungry?'

Raoul's question cut through her reverie. She shook her head, feeling tears very close.

'Is something wrong, milady?'

'Did you mean it, when you said I was arrogant?'

'Aha, so that still rankles, does it?'

'Disdain for others is not a trait I admire,' she said quietly, keeping her eyes lowered. 'If the villagers thought me conceited yesterday, then I am sorry for it.'

She heard him sigh.

'No, no, they saw nothing but goodness in you. I said what I did this morning because...'

'Yes?' Cassie looked up hopefully.

Perhaps he had not meant it, perhaps he had been teasing and she had been too quick to take offence. He held her gaze for a moment and she was heartened by the sudden warmth in his eyes, but then it was gone. He looked away and she was left wondering if she had seen it at all.

'Because we needed a convincing reason for not having a servant with us,' he finished with a slight, contemptuous shrug. 'Your arrogance comes from your breeding, milady, it is hardly your fault.'

His words hit her like cold water. She had been selfish, yes, and thoughtless in eloping without any concern for the effect upon her grandmother, left alone to face the quizzes of Bath, but she had thought herself truly in love and Gerald had convinced her that they had no choice but to run away, or be parted for ever. Perhaps she had appeared arrogant towards Raoul, but only to keep him at a distance. She found him so dangerously attractive, but after what she had experienced with Gerald she had no intention of complicating her life by falling for the charms of another man. Ever.

Raoul watched Cassandra's countenance, saw the changing emotions writ clear upon her face. He had intended to make her angry, but his taunts had wounded her, she had not shrugged them off as he had expected. The hurt in her eyes tugged at his conscience, but it also affected him inside, like a giant hand squeezing his heart.

Bah. He was growing soft. The woman was an English aristo. She would take what she needed from him and then cast him aside without a second thought. She did not need his sympathy. He pushed back his chair and rose.

'It is late and we should sleep,' he said. 'As soon as it is light I will go to the docks and see if there is any ship there to take us to Le Havre. Who knows, I might even find a captain who is willing to take you all the way to England.'

'Yes, that would be the ideal solution and would suit us both,' she agreed.

Her tone was subdued and Raoul guessed she would be pleased to see the back of him.

Well, milady, the feeling is mutual!

'At least we have the benefit of two rooms here,' he remarked. 'If you will allow me to remove a pillow and blanket from the bed I will not bother you again tonight.'

She nodded her assent and he picked up one of the branched candles and went into the bedchamber. The large canopied bed looked very comfortable. Raoul found himself imagining Cassandra lying there between the sheets, her glossy hair spread over the pillows and those dark-violet eyes fixed upon him, inviting him to join her. It was a tempting picture and the devil on his shoulder whispered that a few soft words would bring the lady into his arms. There was no denying the attraction, he had seen it in her eyes, felt it in her response when he had kissed her. There was passion in her, he would swear to it, just waiting to be awoken.

Why not? In a few more days she will be safely back in England and you will be free of her. What have you got to lose?

'My honour,' muttered Raoul savagely. 'I will not demean myself to lie with my sworn enemy.'

Enemy? The word sounded false even as he uttered it. She might be a lady, and an Englishwoman at that, but over the past few days he had come to know her, to see the strength and resourcefulness in her character. The uncomfortable truth was that he was afraid. He could not give himself totally to any one woman and Lady Cassandra Witney was not the sort to settle for anything less. Brave and resourceful she might be, but she was born to command. To take, not give.

And what have you to give her, save perhaps a few nights' pleasure and that would demean you both.

Quickly he pulled the coverlet from the bed, grabbed a couple of pillows and returned to the sitting room.

'I have left the candles burning in there for you, milady,' he said, dropping the bedding on the floor. 'I will bid you goodnight.'

'Yes, thank you.'

When she did not move he turned. She was holding out her purse to him.

'You will need money tomorrow, if you find a suitable ship for us. For me. I do not know how much it will be, so it is best that you take this. I have kept back a few livres in case I need it, but you are attending to all the travel arrangements.' She looked up fleetingly. 'I am not so arrogant that I do not trust you, Monsieur Doulevant.'

Raoul took the purse, feeling its weight in his hand. She was giving him *all* her money? When he did not speak she gave a tiny curtsy and hurried away.

'Cassandra, wait—'

But it was too late; the door was already firmly closed between them.

Cassie undressed quickly and slipped into bed. She had done it. She had handed over her purse to Raoul, put herself wholly in his power. Perhaps that would show him she was not the proud, disdainful woman he thought her. It should not matter, but it did. She was a little frightened at how important it was that he did not think badly of her. She turned over, nestling her cheek against one hand. She had known Raoul Doulevant for little more than a week and yet she... Cassie shied away from admitting even to herself what she thought of the man. It had taken her months to fall in love with Gerald Witney and look how quickly she had recovered from that grand passion. Clearly her feelings were not to be trusted.

In the morning Cassandra's sunny spirits were restored. They had reached the Seine. From her window she could look over the roofs and see the masts of the ships on the quayside. With luck they would find a vessel to carry them to the coast. The inn was very quiet, so she guessed it was still early, but she scrambled out of bed and into her riding habit ready for the day ahead. She emerged from her bedroom to find Raoul already dressed. She responded to his cheerful greeting with a smile.

'Are you going out immediately, sir?'

'I have not yet broken my fast, so we may do so together, if you wish.' He picked up the bedding piled neatly on a chair. 'We had best put this out of sight before I ask the maid to bring up the tray.'

It was only a matter of minutes before they were sitting at the table with a plate of ham and fresh bread rolls before them. Cassie poured coffee and they fell into conversation like old friends. On this sunny morning it was easy to forget the harsh words of yesterday. And the fact that they were both fugitives, fleeing the country.

'How do you think you will go on today?' she asked when they had finished their meal.

'I have every hope of finding a ship, but it may take some time,' Raoul warned her. 'I shall have to be careful when I make my enquiries. Rouen is a busy port, there will be plenty of ships going to the coast, but not all of them will be prepared to take passengers without papers.'

He picked up his hat and she accompanied him to the door.

'Raoul, you will take care?' Impulsively Cassie put her hand on his arm. 'I would not have you put yourself at risk for me.'

He paused and gazed down at her, but she could not read the look in his dark eyes.

'I shall take care, milady.' He lifted her hand from his sleeve and pressed a kiss into the palm. 'Bolt the door and wait here for me. I shall be back as soon as I can.'

He went out, closing the door behind him and Cassie listened to his firm step as he went quickly down the stairs. She cradled the hand that he had kissed, rubbing her thumb over the palm for a moment before she turned and ran to the window. Their room overlooked the street and she saw him emerge from the inn. There was a pleasurable flutter of excitement in her chest as she watched his tall figure striding away. Excitement, but not fear; she had given Raoul nearly all her money, but she knew enough of the man now to know he would not cheat her. She trusted him. Smiling, Cassie turned from the window and looked about the room, wondering how best to amuse herself until Raoul returned.

* * *

The day dragged on and with no clock or pocket watch Cassandra had no idea of the time except from the length of the shadows in the street below. She reminded herself that it might take Raoul all day to find a suitable ship, but the shadows were lengthening before at last she heard a heavy footstep on the landing and she flew across the room to unbolt the door.

'Raoul, I was beginning to—'

Her smiling words ended abruptly. It was not Raoul at the door but a tall, pallid stranger in a black coat. At his shoulder was the weasel-faced Merimon, her rascally courier.

Merimon put up his hand and pointed an accusing finger at Cassie.

'That's her,' he declared. 'That's the woman who ran off with your deserter.'

Chapter Six

Cassandra stared at the men in horrified silence. Two uniformed *gendarmes* stood behind Merimon and the man in the black coat. Another look at the stranger showed her that his sallow face was badly marred by the crookedness of his nose. A memory stirred. Something Raoul had said, but for the moment it eluded her.

Gesturing to her to stand aside, they all marched into the room and the officers began to search it.

'What do you think you are doing?' she demanded angrily.

The black-coated stranger bowed. 'I am Auguste Valerin and I am here to arrest the deserter Raoul Doulevant.'

Cassie remembered now; Raoul had broken the man's nose. If that disfigurement was the result it was no wonder Valerin wanted revenge. She must go carefully.

'I have never heard of him,' she said with a dismissive shrug. 'I am staying here with my husband, Monsieur Duval.'

'But I heard you call him Raoul.'

'What of it?'

Cassie spoke calmly, but Valerin's sneering smile filled her with unease.

'A coincidence, perhaps, that your husband and the deserter should share the same name. It is also a coincidence that travellers coming into Rouen yesterday brought with them tales of a doctor helping to save the lives of peasants in a village not a day's ride from here. It is said he could set broken bones and even remove a crushed leg. Such skill is a rarity and news of it was bound to spread.'

The *gendarmes* emerged from the bedchamber.

'There is no one here, sir,' declared one of them.

'Stand guard on the landing,' ordered Valerin. 'Keep out of sight, ready to apprehend the deserter when he returns. I will question Madame Duval.'

'She is no more Madame Duval than I am,' put in Merimon.

'No,' Cassie admitted. 'You would know that, since you stole my papers.' She turned to Valerin. 'My name is Lady Cassandra Witney and I hired this man as a courier to escort me from Verdun to the coast. He and his accomplice stole my passport and would have murdered me if I had not escaped.'

Merimon threw an aggrieved glance at Valerin, his hands spread wide.

'What cause would I have to do that, *monsieur*? I am an honest man, why else would I have come to you with information about Doulevant?'

'For the reward,' Valerin snapped. 'Tell me your story again and we will see what Madame Witney has to say.'

Cassie drew herself up and said in her haughtiest tone, 'As the daughter of a marquess it is customary to address me as Lady Cassandra.'

She saw a slight wariness enter Valerin's eyes, but he replied coldly.

'We do not recognise such titles in France now, *madame*. And from what you have said, you do not have any papers to prove who you are, do you?'

'There are many people in Verdun who will vouch for me.'

'Possibly, but that is not my concern. Where is Doulevant?'

'I have no idea who you mean.'

'Do not lie to me, *madame*. The landlord described the man staying here with you, the man calling himself Duval. I am satisfied he and Doulevant are the same person. Now where is he?'

Cassie ignored the last question. She was thinking quickly and knew she must play a convincing part.

'La, so he is not Raoul Duval?' she said, opening her eyes wide at Valerin. 'That would explain a great deal.'

'Just tell me where he is, if you please.'

'But I do not know,' Cassie insisted. She decided it would be best to stick as close to the truth as possible. 'You are very right, I am not Madame Duval. The man calling himself by that name rescued me from this villain.' She pointed at Merimon. 'I was grateful and hired Duval to escort me to the coast. We were travelling as man and wife because there is no money to spare for servants and it seemed safer that way.' She clasped her hands together and assumed an anxious look. 'When we arrived here, he asked for my purse, that he might book me a passage on a ship for

England. I have not seen him since. I think perhaps he has abandoned me.'

'You seem to be singularly unfortunate in your choice of escorts, *madame*.'

She returned Valerin's glare with a steady look of her own.

'France seems singularly full of rogues, *monsieur*.'

He walked slowly to a chair and sat down, a deliberate insult while she was still standing. 'True, and I expect one of them to return here sooner or later.'

Cassie's blood ran cold. She could think of no way to warn Raoul and could only hope that he would see the *gendarmes* waiting on the stairs before they spotted him.

'You may wait if you wish,' she said with studied indifference. 'I told you, he has gone and taken my money with him. He will not be back.'

'We shall see,' purred Valerin. He looked round when the courier cursed impatiently. 'We need waste no more of your time, Monsieur Merimon. You may leave.'

'Not until I have had my reward.'

'The reward was for information leading to the

apprehension of one Raoul Doulevant. So far I have not seen him.'

'But I told you, she is his accomplice.'

Cassie replied to that bitterly. 'I was *forced* into his company when you attacked me!'

Merimon was inclined to argue the point, but Valerin put up his hand. 'Enough. We know where we can find you, citizen. Good day to you.'

'But I have received nothing for all my trouble,' Merimon whined. He turned his sharp little eyes to Cassie. 'She still owes me for my services.'

'I owe you nothing. I gave you half your fee when we set out from Verdun, the agreement was that you would get the other half when we reached Le Havre.'

'It was not I who ran off.' He turned to Valerin again. 'Believe me, sir, she is Doulevant's whore.'

'How dare you!' Cassie raged.

'You are in league with him.'

'He rescued me from your attack, that is all. And I have told you, I have no money.'

'None?' snapped Valerin. Cassie's slight hesitation was enough. He said coldly, 'Will you give me your purse, or shall I call in the *gendarmes* to search you?'

She did not doubt he would carry out his threat.

She pulled the remaining coins from her pocket and displayed them on her palm.

'You see, nine, ten livres, nothing more.'

Valerin scraped the coins from her hand. He held them out to Merimon.

'Take these, it will pay your passage back to Verdun.'

Merimon looked as if he would argue, but at last he took the coins and went grudgingly from the room.

'But that is all I have,' Cassie protested.

'If you are indeed in league with Doulevant you will find yourself in prison soon enough and will have no need of money.'

'And when you discover I am telling the truth, that I am innocent?'

Valerin's glance was sceptical.

'*If* you are innocent, *madame*, I shall personally escort you to the mayor and you may throw yourself upon his mercy.'

'Thank you,' she said coldly. 'I will ask him to write to my grandmother, the Marchioness of Hune. She will send funds for my passage home. Your First Consul himself has decreed that the wives of the English *détenus* are free to leave.'

'Providing they have not shown themselves

to be enemies of France,' said Valerin, adding sharply, 'Do not go near the window, *madame*. I would not have you warn your lover.'

'He is not my lover.'

'No?' Valerin got up and came closer. 'Then he is a fool.'

Before she could guess his intention he put his hand around her neck and dragged her close to kiss her. Cassie struggled against him and when he finally let her go she brought her hand up to his cheek with such force that it left her palm stinging. His eyes narrowed.

'A mistake, *madame*, to strike a government officer.' Holding her prisoner with one hand he drew a length of cord from his pocket and bound her wrists together. 'There,' he regarded her with an unpleasant smile. 'That should stop you scratching my eyes out while I show you—'

The door crashed open and one of the *gendarmes* burst in.

'Sir, we have him! The pot-boy says the deserter is in the taproom.'

Cassie's heart was hammering hard. Relief that she had been spared a loathsome groping was replaced by fear for Raoul. She saw the leap of triumph in Valerin's eyes.

'Very well,' he barked, 'arrest him. I will follow you.' He turned back to Cassie. 'What shall I do with you while I make my arrest?'

He glanced around the room, his eyes alighting on a stout peg sticking out high in the wall behind the door. He picked her up. Cassie kicked wildly but it was useless. He lifted her hands and hooked the cord over the peg. She was suspended, facing the wall, with the cord biting painfully into her wrists and her toes barely reaching the floor.

'Perfect. That should keep you safe until I return.' His hand squeezed her bottom through the thick folds of her skirts and Cassie shivered. She knew it was a promise of what he had in store for her.

Valerin went out, Cassie heard him clattering down the stairs, then there was silence. In addition to worries for her own safety Cassandra felt the chill of dread clutching at her insides. Had they caught Raoul? Had they hurt him? She tried to concentrate on her own predicament. Her toes just touched the ground, barely enough to relieve the pull on her wrists and stop the thin cord from biting deeper into the flesh. The wooden peg was angled upwards and strain as she might she could not reach high enough to lift her bound wrists free of it. The light was fading, soon it would be dark. In despair Cassie rested her forehead against the wall. Valerin would return for her and there was nothing she could do about it.

Her ears caught the faint sounds outside the door and she quickly blinked away her tears. This was no time for self-pity; she needed all her wits about her if she was to get through this. She heard the door open and close again. He was in the room. She turned her head, but the scathing remark on her lips died when she saw Raoul standing behind her.

Relief flooded through Cassie. She wanted to cry but would not give in to a weakness she despised and instead she took refuge in anger.

'Well, do not stand there like an idiot, get me down!'

Raoul had not known what to expect when he entered the room. His imagination had rioted and his blood had gone cold as he considered what Valerin might have done to Cassie. To find her apparently unhurt was a relief and it increased tenfold when she addressed him in her usual haughty manner. He could not stop himself from grinning, although the effect was like pouring oil on hot coals. Her eyes positively flamed with wrath.

'Get me down, this instant!'

He put his hands on her waist and lifted her so she could unhook herself from the peg. He lowered her gently to the ground and she turned, her arms still raised. Despite their perilous situation he could not resist the temptation to slide his hands up quickly from her tiny waist and pull her bound wrists over his head. He held her arms against his shoulders.

'Shall I steal a kiss, as my reward for rescuing you?'

His pulse raced even faster when he recognised the gleam of excitement that mixed with the anger in her eyes, a gleam that told him she was not averse to kissing him. It was gone in an instant, but he knew he had not been mistaken and it both thrilled and alarmed him; he could no more stop flirting with her than a moth could ignore a flame.

She shook her head at him. 'This is no time for funning, Raoul! We must go, quickly.'

Reluctantly Raoul released her.

'You are right,' he said, untying her wrists. 'I have bought us a little time, but not much.'

'How——?'

He put a finger to her lips.

'No time to explain now. Come.'

'Not so fast.'

At the words Raoul whipped about to find Valerin standing in the doorway. He pushed Cassie behind him, putting his body between her and the deadly pistol Valerin was holding. The sneering smile on that thin face made Raoul's blood boil, but he knew he must not lose his head.

'She said you had gone, but I knew you would not abandon your whore.'

'She is a lady, Valerin, as you would know if you had any intelligence.'

'Indeed? If that is so what is she doing here, with you?' His lip curled. 'Do you think any *lady* would look to you for protection? Why, you are not even a Frenchman.'

'And that is where I have the advantage of you,' Raoul drawled insolently.

The sallow face flushed with anger and hatred.

'You are nothing but a damned deserter. The

scum of the earth! I find you here, dressed like a gentleman—aping your betters, Doulevant! Men such as you should be whipped at the cart's tail.'

Raoul knew Valerin was goading him. He did not need Cassandra's warning hand on his arm to tell him Valerin was trying to make him attack, so that he would have an excuse to shoot. He must act and quickly. The hubbub of noise and confusion from below drifted in through the open door. At any moment Valerin's lackeys might return and then all would be lost.

He smiled and shifted his gaze to look over the man's shoulder.

'You would be wise to give me the pistol, Valerin. I have an accomplice behind you.'

'Do you think I am fool enough to believe that?'

Raoul's smile turned into a full grin.

'You are a fool if you do not. Any moment now you will feel my friend's pistol against your ribs.'

Raoul saw Valerin's certainty waver. There was a lull in the noise below that made the sudden creak of boards on the landing sound like a pistol shot. Valerin look around.

It was enough. Raoul launched himself at his opponent, one hand reaching for the pistol, the

other connecting with the man's jaw in a sick-
ening thud. Valerin fell back, catching his head
on the doorpost and collapsing, unconscious, in
the doorway.

Cassie had not realised she had stopped breathing, but now she dragged in air with a gasp and
felt her heart begin to thud heavily as relief
surged through her. On the landing stood the
pot-boy, grinning.

'Good work, master,' he told Raoul. 'I saw him
slip away and guessed he'd rumbled our plan.'

'Well, here's a little extra for your trouble.'
Raoul tucked Valerin's pistol into his belt and
tossed the boy a coin. 'Now we must be gone.
Milady?'

He reached for Cassie's hand, but she shook her
head. She pointed at Valerin.

'Pull him into the room first, then we can lock
the door. It will slow up his men when they come
looking for him, or for us.'

With the pot-boy's help it was done in a trice.
The lad pocketed the key and pointed to a door
further along the landing.

'That room's empty and the window will bring
you out on the back alley. I'll go down and see

if I can make 'em think you've gone out into the street.'

With that the lad dashed back down the stairs to the taproom, from where sounds of an altercation could still be heard. Raoul took Cassie's hand and they slipped into the empty bedchamber. He immediately went to the window and threw up the sash.

'Your skirts will make it more difficult,' he said to Cassie, who had followed him, 'but I think you will manage.'

The window looked out over a deserted yard and the sloping roof of an outhouse abutted the wall only feet beneath the sill. It was dark now, but there was the faint glimmer of a rising moon to light their way. Raoul jumped down into the yard and turned to help Cassie but she was already on the ground and shaking out her skirts, as if escaping from bedroom windows was an everyday occurrence for her. Together they crept out of the yard and into the alley.

Cassie glanced quickly right and left. The alley was deserted, but where it joined the street she could see people running towards the inn, eager to see what was going on. Raoul grabbed her hand and pulled her in the opposite direction,

where they soon found themselves in a labyrin-
thine mesh of alleys and narrow streets that led
down to the quay. He pulled her hand on to his
arm.

'We must go slowly, we do not want to attract
attention.'

Cassie nodded, forcing her body to a walk
while every instinct screamed at her to run. Her
eyes darted back and forth and her spine tingled
with fear. She had a strong conviction that they
were being watched and it was as much as she
could do not to look around. She took a deep
steadying breath, trying to match Raoul's apparent insouciance. He walked easily, head up, as if
he had not a care in the world and she must do
the same. They were an innocent couple, making their way to the quay.

She said quietly, 'You could have escaped easily, if you had not come back for me.'

Raoul heard the humble note in her voice, but
there was something else: wonder and a touch
of disbelief. He tried and failed not to feel aggrieved.

'Did you think I would leave you, *madame*?
We made a bargain.'

'We did indeed, but you risked your life to save me. I am very grateful.'

He was tempted to say he did not want her gratitude, that he was a gentleman and always kept his word. That he would have done the same for anyone, but he knew it was not true. He recalled the chilling fear that had gripped his heart when he realised Valerin would find Cassandra alone. A shudder ran through him as he thought again what might have happened to her. But she was safe and he must not waste time dwelling on what might have been. He forced himself to speak lightly.

'It was the greatest good fortune that I saw Valerin and his fools entering the inn as I was returning from the quay.'

'But they said you were in the taproom!'

'It was a man of similar build and dress. I met him in the street and persuaded him to go in and buy himself a drink. A few coins to the pot-boy did the rest. I am only thankful the lad had the wit to follow Valerin up the stairs.'

'That could have been very dangerous for him.'

'It *could*, although I'd seen Valerin cuff the lad even before he entered the inn, so I knew there'd be no love lost there. But enough of that, we have evaded capture and without much hurt, except to your wrists. And your dignity,' he ended with a laugh in his voice, remembering her outrage.

'Both of which will recover,' she told him, unmoved. 'That scoundrel Merimon was with him. He was hoping for a reward for your capture.'

'He will be disappointed, then. I suppose Valerin must have come upon him after we had made our escape from the forest.'

'That is what I think, too. But, Raoul, news has already reached here from Flagey, of how you helped the men caught under the collapsed barn. Valerin knew of it, that is why he was so certain you were here.'

'*Diable!* So soon? *Tiens*, if Bonnaire had known how to wield the knife I would not have needed to show my hand.'

Cassandra clutched his arm. 'You must not regret what you did for those poor people. I do not.'

'Truly?' He felt his heart lift a little. 'Even though it has put you in danger?'

She waved one tiny hand.

'Life is full of danger, Raoul. One must do what is right and helping the villagers was right.'

Raoul walked on, his head spinning at her words. She saw these things as he did. How had he ever thought her arrogant? Spirited, yes, head-strong and wilful, perhaps, but when he thought of the way she had worked with him to help the villagers and her bravery today, when Valerin had threatened her with heaven knows what, his heart was almost bursting with...

With what, respect? Admiration?

Her soft voice brought his wandering mind back to the present.

'Where do we go now? Did you find a ship to take us out of Rouen?'

They were approaching a tavern and he stopped, realising that hunger was affecting his ability to think logically.

'Let us go in here. I have not eaten anything since we broke our fast together this morning.'

'Nor I.'

'Then we shall dine in here and I can tell you of my success. Or lack of it.'

The tavern was gloomy, but that was to their advantage. He looked about and chose a small table in one shadowy corner where they could talk undisturbed. Raoul sat on the bench facing the entrance, keeping one eye on everyone who came in. He had deliberately chosen a table near the back door, where they could make their escape if necessary. A serving wench had brought them wine and bread and gone off to the kitchens to order their food.

'So you had no luck with finding a ship to take me home,' Cassie prompted him, once they were alone.

'I found one vessel that was going as far as Le Havre.' He stopped when a rough-looking fellow stumbled against their table. Raoul grabbed at his cup as the man muttered an apology and lurched off, falling on to a chair at the next table and impatiently calling for wine.

Raoul frowned. 'We should go.'

Cassie put a hand on his arm. 'No,' she whispered, keeping her eyes lowered. 'If we leave without eating that would cause comment.'

She was right. Raoul rested his elbows on the table and appeared to study his wine, but from the corner of his eye he watched as the landlord brought a bottle and cup to the fellow, who drank greedily. With a gusty sigh of satisfaction he dragged his grimy sleeve across his bearded mouth and looked about him. Catching sight of Cassandra, he grinned in a bleary fashion before settling back in his chair and closing his eyes. Within moments he was snoring.

Cassie held out her cup for Raoul to refill it.

'You see,' she murmured. 'The man is drunk, he will not trouble us.'

'And here is our dinner,' said Raoul loudly. 'And in good time, too, thank you, landlord.'

'So,' she said when they were alone again. 'You have booked our passage to Le Havre?'

He shook his head. 'I think it would be safer to go north by road to Dieppe. It would be easier for you to sail from there since it is closer to England and the crossing would be much quicker. I would wager an illicit trade still goes on between the two countries.'

'Do you mean smugglers?'

'Yes.'

She considered the matter. 'If they will take me to England, then I care not what they are. Very well, if you think that would be best, Raoul, we will go to Dieppe.'

If you think that would be best, Raoul...

The trustful look in her eyes unsettled him and he shifted uncomfortably in his seat. He had not suggested they go to Dieppe because it was best for Lady Cassandra. He would have to tell her the truth.

'There is another reason I want to go there.' He pushed his empty plate away. 'I learned today that the *Prométhée* is currently at Dieppe.'

He watched her tear off a little piece of bread and wipe it across her plate.

'That is the ship where you were surgeon?'

Raoul nodded, but his eyes were following that dainty morsel as she popped it into her mouth and licked her fingers. It was so neatly done, but the sight of her lips closing over one little finger tip was too fascinating for him to look away.

'The *Prométhée*, Raoul,' she prompted him gently. 'That was your ship?'

'What?' Raoul blinked, cursed himself for a fool and gathered his wits as best he could. 'Oh— yes, it was my ship. Captain Belfort will vouch for me, give me copies of my discharge papers and make everything *en règle*, I am sure.'

'Then of course we must go to Dieppe.'

She spoke with such cool certainty that Raoul's conscience pricked him still further.

'There is no need for you to undertake the journey. I could book your passage to Le Havre from here. The captain I spoke with today was a decent fellow. I would trust him to keep to his word and look after you.' He paused. 'I know we struck a bargain, we agreed that I would find you a ship to take you to England, but in truth, milady, the captain would be far better placed to do that, once you reach Le Havre. I will give you back what is left of your money and you can arrange matters directly with him.'

There, he had said it. He had told her the truth. If the lady had a particle of sense she would take her purse and quit his company as quickly as possible.

'And what of you, do you plan to go on to Dieppe alone?'

'Once I have discharged my duty to you, yes.' She sipped at her wine.

'From what you have told me of Valerin, he will have men on the quay here, looking out for us.'

'True, but that is a small problem. I could distract them while you slip aboard.'

'And put yourself in more danger?' She shook her head. 'I would prefer we took our chances together.'

'It will be dangerous to come with me to Dieppe. Valerin is no fool and he will have alerted the guards at the gates. You would be safer to embark upon a ship here in Rouen. You could be in England in a couple of days.'

A party of men pushed in through the door and made their way noisily to a table in the far corner. Raoul leaned forward as if to shield Cassie from view and once they had settled down he eased back, only to discover she had moved closer.

'I would rather stay with you. I have placed my trust in men before and been deceived.'

'Ah, you mean that scoundrel courier.'

'Not just Merimon.' Her eyes slid away from his. 'We have a saying in England, *monsieur*,' she said stiffly. 'We say 'tis better the devil you know. If I have a choice, I would rather take my chances with you than trust another stranger.'

'You think me a devil, milady?'

'All men are devils,' she retorted. 'But perhaps you are less of one than most.'

'*Merci, madame*, a concession indeed.'

She ignored that. 'Besides, Valerin will think it most likely that we will try to leave Rouen by ship, will he not?'

'That is my opinion.'

'Then we shall go by road and confound him. I am wearing my riding habit. Can you obtain a lady's mount for me?' She turned to him, a faint, shy smile lighting her eyes. 'I would rather not share a horse this time.'

'I think that can be arranged.'

He felt a smile tugging at his own lips. Her courage enchanted him. He wanted to pull her close and plant a kiss upon those cherry-red lips. To smell her, taste her...

He knew she had read his thoughts. Even in the dim light of the tavern he saw a flash of recognition in the violet depths of her eyes. She moved slightly away from him.

'Now, let us think how we are to get out of Rouen. Doubtless there will be sentries at the gate.'

Her cold tone sobered him, reminded him that they came from different worlds. A mutual attraction was not enough to bridge the differences between them.

'I met several fellows at the quay today who I am sure would help us,' he replied. 'Have you finished your meal? Then let us make a start.'

Chapter Seven

By dawn they were galloping north from Rouen. In the grey, misty half-light it seemed to Cassie that all the world was asleep, save her and Raoul. She was tired, for the night had been spent in preparation. She had accompanied Raoul as he held stealthy meetings with shadowy figures. She was at his side, silent and watchful while he made all the arrangements. She heard the soft chink of coins at times and guessed that their purse was now considerably lighter. It had been an anxious time, for Cassie could not shake off the feeling that they were being followed. She often glanced behind as they made their way through the darkened streets and peeped back as they slipped through doorways. She saw no one, yet her unease persisted.

Once away from Rouen they avoided the

main highways and rode along little-used tracks through the wooded countryside. Raoul had told her they would rest during the day and travel mainly at night to avoid detection and Cassie hoped she would not fall asleep and tumble out of the saddle as they pressed on northwards.

A blanket of cloud obscured the sun, but she guessed it was nearing noon when at last they made their first stop. The little-used road had led them deep within ancient woodland and Cassie followed Raoul as he turned off the track and pushed his horse through the thick undergrowth. The trees grew tall and close and the autumn gales had not yet arrived to strip the leaves from the canopy. As they moved away from the path they entered deeper into a murky half-light.

'We can rest here,' Raoul declared at last, dismounting and tethering his horse.

'Are we safe from pursuit?' She glanced back, peering anxiously between the trees. 'Are you sure we are not being followed?'

'I have seen no one and heard nothing,' he told her. 'We are far enough from the road now to escape detection, but we should not risk lighting a fire.'

'No, I would rather we did not. The cloaks you purchased will keep us warm.'

She considered jumping down before Raoul came over to help her, but her body was too weary for such independence. When he reached up for her Cassie slid down into his arms and when he held her for a moment she did not resist, but gave in to the temptation to rest her head against the broad wall of his chest.

'You are exhausted,' he said gently.

She summoned up a smile as she pushed away from him.

'I shall feel better for a little bread and wine.'

He handed her the saddlebag.

'Go and sit down. Rest and I will join you as soon as I have seen to the horses.'

Cassie unstrapped her cloak from the saddle and sought out a smooth piece of ground. The earth beneath the trees was soft and loamy. She wrapped herself in the voluminous folds of the cloak and sat down to wait for Raoul. When at last he settled beside her he began to take various packets of food from the bag. She took a small piece of bread and drank from the flask of wine that Raoul held out to her.

He said, when she handed back the flask, 'There is sausage, too. It is very good.'

'Thank you, I am too tired to eat more.'

'It will give you strength.' He cut off a slice with his knife and held it to her lips. 'Try it.'

The savoury smell was indeed enticing and she opened her mouth, gently taking the meat from him. Her lips touched his fingers, like a lover's kiss, and she felt the heat flowing up through her body. It set her cheeks on fire and her eyes flew to his face. What she read there made her heart pound. Quickly she looked away.

'Yes, you are right, it is very good. I am not usually fond of such meats, but perhaps the long ride has sharpened my appetite.' She was aware she was gabbling to cover her confusion.

He was cutting another slice for her and she put out her hand to take it from him. She could not risk another intimate touch. When Raoul offered her the flask again she shook her head. She watched him put back his head to drink, noting the powerful lines of his throat. There was a shadow of dark stubble on his lean cheeks and she thought by the evening it would be quite thick again, the beginnings of another bushy beard such as he had worn when they had first met.

How long ago that seemed. How far they had travelled since he had first taken her up before him and carried her away. Her ragged, bearded rescuer.

Cassie fell into a reverie, contemplating whether she preferred him clean shaven or hirsute. She had told him once he looked like a bear, but that was untrue. He had never looked anything other than a man. Strong, resolute, reliable.

Honourable.

'We should rest now, milady.'

Raoul was packing away the remains of their scant meal and she watched him in silence, wanting to thank him for all he had done for her, yet not knowing how to begin. Instead, without a word she pulled her cloak tighter around her and lay down. She fell asleep almost immediately, but following the deep repose of exhaustion came the memories. She was back in Verdun, trying to keep up appearances and eke out the little money they had left. She knew if she wrote to Grandmama the marchioness would find a way to send her more funds, but she did not tell Gerald that. She had realised soon after they had reached Paris that Gerald was an inveterate gambler. Even before they were detained and moved to Verdun their funds were running low, but Gerald would not economise, he was certain that the next evening the cards or the dice would prove lucky and they could repair their fortunes at a stroke.

She stirred restlessly, reliving the strained silences and heated arguments. When their disagreements became more bitter Gerald took to going out without her. He accused Cassie of not liking his friends and she could not deny it, she did not trust them. She was afraid to let him go out alone, but it was impossible to go with him. She rarely saw him sober, and as the weeks went on his taunts took an unpleasant turn, wheedling, cajoling, pleading, bullying, until she grew to dread his return to their lodgings...

'Cassandra. Cassie, wake up.'

The memories receded, angry voices were replaced by birdsong and the smells and sounds of the woods filled her waking senses. Her cheeks were wet with tears and she sat up quickly, alarmed. She never cried.

'I beg your pardon,' she muttered. 'Did I disturb you?'

'No, I was awake.' Raoul's hand had been warm on her shoulder, but now he drew it away and immediately she missed the comfort of his touch. He said, 'Your dreams were not happy, I think.'

She did not reply. She could not bring herself to describe them, shamed by the failure of her marriage.

Raoul was still sitting beside her, but his cloak was already folded neatly, ready to strap on to his saddle.

'Is it time to go?' she asked.

'Soon. You may rest more first if you wish.'

Cassie shuddered, her dreams still too vivid, too fresh.

'No.' She jumped up and shook out her skirts, saying resolutely, 'I would much rather we went on.'

Raoul threw Cassandra into the saddle and mounted his own horse. He would have liked to ask what her dream was about, but she was clearly not ready to share it. He had been awake when she had become restless, muttering incoherently, growing more distressed. More than once he had heard her crying out, 'Gerald, no!' Gerald was the name of her husband. Was he a cruel man, perhaps? A wife beater? Cassandra did not have the appearance of an abused wife, but just the thought of it angered him. Perhaps he had been too hasty in thinking she had abandoned her husband.

What did it matter? He asked himself the question as they made their way through the woods, weaving between the trees until they reached the road again. If it had been a bad marriage, then she was well out of it, but it could make no difference to him. He shifted uncomfortably in his saddle. That was not true; it would be easier for him to leave her if she was a selfish aristo, as he had first thought. Now he would remember her as a brave, noble creature and he would always regret what might have been, in another time, another place. He gave himself a little shake. No. Even if she had not been another man's wife there was no future for them. He had dedicated his life to medicine, there was no room for anything other than a casual liaison and he could not imagine Cassandra would ever agree to that. Raoul glanced across at her, noting the proud tilt to her head. She was a lady, so let her return to England, to her life of ease and comfort. It was what she knew, where she would be happy. And he would be happy for her. Another night and they would be at Dieppe. Then, with a little luck, she would be off his hands.

They made slow progress through the night as the clouds thickened to obscure the moon. Whenever they came to a river Raoul avoided the bridges with their sentries and searched for a ford where they could cross. It lengthened their journey, but the country was at war and especially near the coast the guards were on the alert. Without papers they could not afford to be stopped and questioned. By dawn a steady drizzle was falling, soaking into their cloaks and chilling the air. He saw a huddle of farm buildings ahead of them and struck off into the trees to wait and watch. Experience had taught him to be cautious; such buildings could be full of soldiers. The farm looked deserted save for a few hens pecking in the doorway of an old outhouse. He saw an old woman hobble outside to fetch water from the well. They had dismounted and Raoul glanced at Cassie, who was resting against a tree. Her face was grey and drawn in the dim light. She was shivering, too, and he made up his mind. He gathered the horses' reins, put one arm about Cassandra and walked purposefully towards the farmstead.

* * *

The farmhouse door was shut firm and only Raoul's repeated knocking brought any sign of life. A small casement window opened and the old woman looked out.

'Good day to you,' Raoul called cheerfully. 'My wife and I would be grateful if you would allow us to warm ourselves by your fire for a while.'

'No, no, I am too busy. Go away.'

Raoul pulled out a handful of coins and shook them.

'I can pay you.'

The old woman hesitated.

'You can shelter in the barn, yonder,' she said at last. 'You and your horses. I'll not have strangers in the house.'

'You are wise, *madame,* in these uncertain times. And could you spare us a little food? I would gladly catch one of those hens and wring its neck for you.'

Agreement was soon reached. Raoul took Cassie and the horses to the old wooden barn before going off to find a plump bird for the pot. When he returned he found the horses had been unsaddled and Cassandra was busy rubbing them down with sweet-smelling straw. He frowned.

'You should not be doing that.'

'Why not?' She turned, smiling. 'It was the least I could do, since you were catching our dinner. Besides, the exertion has warmed me and I feel better for that.'

He grabbed a handful of straw and began to help her.

'So, we dine on chicken today?' she asked him.

'Yes, but not until this evening. We are to fetch it from the window when we hear the bell ring.' He nodded to the sack he had brought in with him. 'She has sent over wine and some sort of cake to keep our hunger at bay for a few more hours.'

Cassie finished rubbing down her horse and threw down the straw, yawning. 'That is very good of her, but I think sleep is what I need first.'

She shook out their cloaks and threw them over a low wooden partition to dry off.

'And I.' Raoul scrambled up into the loft and pushed down a pile of hay for the horses to eat before collecting up some empty sacks and placing them over the straw piled in the far corner of the barn. 'I hope this will be soft enough for you, milady.'

She chuckled. 'I am growing used to such deprivation.'

'Hopefully it will not be for much longer.'

'No. I hope soon to be back in England.' She fell silent and he saw she was looking a little wistful. The pensive frown vanished when she realised he was watching her and she smiled.

'To be honest I am so tired I do not think I would notice if my bed was made of stone,' she admitted.

She made herself comfortable on the sacks and Raoul thought suddenly how much he would like to see her lying naked on the very finest feather bed. He turned away quickly. She had told him her husband was an accomplished lover, so he must have often seen her like that. Lucky man.

'Are you not going to sleep, too?'

Her question only flayed his raw desire. Sleep was the last thing on his mind. He dared not look at her.

'No, not yet. I will eat something first.'

He picked up the food bag and moved away, sitting down on the sacks of turnips piled against one wall. His appetite had quite disappeared and he only made a pretence of looking in the bag until Cassie's soft, steady breathing told him she was asleep. He found another empty sack and placed it on the straw, as far away from Cassie as possible. He was dog tired, but it was some time before his blood had cooled sufficiently for him to sleep.

Cassie opened her eyes. She had slept soundly, dreamlessly and was aware of a feeling of well-being. She stretched luxuriously. The straw beneath her was very comfortable and the patter of rain on the roof made her thankful they were not sleeping out of doors again. She reached out one hand, expecting to feel Raoul's solid body beside her and when it was not there she panicked, sitting up and looking about her wildly.

'Is anything wrong, milady?'

He was stretched out on the far side of the piled straw, lying on his back with his hands behind his head, watching her.

She answered him without thinking. 'I thought I had lost you.'

He sat up, saying shortly, 'I gave you my word I would see you safe aboard a ship for England.'

That had not been her concern, but it would be too difficult to explain so she did not try. Instead she rose and tried unsuccessfully to brush tiny wisps of straw from her skirts.

'I am thankful we found shelter here today,' she said. 'Even if it is only a barn.'

'The old woman thawed considerably once I handed over the bird for her to prepare,' said Raoul. 'She told me her son has been conscripted into the army and she has to manage here alone now, except for the occasional visits from her brother.'

'Poor thing, no wonder she is wary of us. But I do not mind staying in this barn. At least we are warm and we are protected from the rain.' She paused. 'What did you tell her, about us?'

'I did not need to say much at all. The old mother has a fertile imagination.'

'Oh?'

He grinned. 'I let her think we were man and wife, that is all. She guessed we had been on a pilgrimage to Rouen and I did not correct her.'

Cassie nodded. 'The French government may well have tried to abolish religion, but I am sure many people still cling to their beliefs, especially in remote areas such as this.'

'And marriage here still means a lifelong commitment, milady.'

The words were out before Raoul could stop them. Cassie looked up, her eyes flying to his face. He read the hurt there, but could not apologise. If she thought his words were aimed at her, then he could not deny it. He knew he should not blame her for the desire she roused in him, but he could and did blame her for abandoning her lawful husband. She looked away. He knew she was aware of his disapproval, but when she spoke her voice was calm enough, although he heard the note of reserve.

'Perhaps, *monsieur*, we should try a little of the food our hostess has supplied?'

The wine was rough, but palatable enough and it helped Cassandra to swallow the cake, which was dry and stale. She knew Raoul thought her contemptible for leaving her husband. She thought with a quick flash of annoyance that if he had not fallen asleep in Flagey he would know the truth. She had to admit she was reluctant to confess it all again. She did not want to tell Raoul she had lied to him in the first place. Understandable, perhaps, since he had been a stranger then and she had been wary of trusting him.

He was still a stranger, she reminded herself.

They had known each other such a short time, so why did she feel that she had known him all her life? It was strangely comfortable, sitting in the dim barn with horses snuffling in the far corner. She glanced up at Raoul under her lashes. She trusted him with her life, so surely she should trust him with her secrets.

'Raoul,' she began tentatively, 'what I told you, about my husband—'

She got no further. Raoul put up his hand to silence her. He was listening intently and Cassie heard it, too, the bright jingle of harnesses and beating tattoo of many of hoofs. Riders were approaching. Raoul ran to the wall of the barn. The planks had weathered and the gaps were large enough to look out.

'Soldiers.' He turned and came back to her. 'Quickly, up into the hayloft, out of sight.'

Cassie gathered her skirts in one hand and scrambled up the ladder. Raoul threw their cloaks and food bag into the hayloft and followed her, drawing the ladder up after him. Outside she could hear the soldiers' voices. Quietly, Cassie moved to the side of the barn and peered through a crack. The yard was filled with horses and the men were gathered about the well, filling their water canteens while the rain dripped from their hats. Two of the officers were standing at the farmhouse door, talking to the old woman. Cassie held her breath, expecting at any moment that they would turn towards the barn.

Raoul had crawled across beside her and he, too, was peering out through the gap. Cassie's heart almost stopped when one of the men moved away from the troop and headed for the barn. Instinctively she reached for Raoul's hand and gripped it as they watched the soldier approach. The man did not head for the door, but stopped to relieve himself against the wall just below them. Raoul put his arm around Cassie's shoulder and pulled her away from the wall. She looked at him, one hand across her mouth to stifle the giggle that was welling up. He frowned and shook his head, but his eyes were alight with laughter. Their amusement died, however, when they heard more footsteps approaching the barn. Cassie held her breath. Raoul was tense and alert beside her. She knew he had the pistol he had taken from Valerin, but what use would that be against a dozen or so soldiers?

A sudden crackle of musket fire from the woods

changed everything. Shouts went up, the soldiers were running back to their horses and moments later the whole troop had clattered away from the farm. A few more shots were heard, at a greater distance, and the thunder of hoofs died away, followed by almost complete silence. Cassie rolled on to her back, eyes closed and grinning with relief at their narrow escape. She heard Raoul's ragged laugh.

'You, milady, are a baggage. How could you give way to amusement at such a time?'

When she opened her eyes he was propped on one elbow, looking down at her.

'I did not give way,' she protested, still smiling broadly. 'I was as quiet as a mouse…'

Her words trailed away into silence as she held his gaze and recognised the hot glow in his dark eyes. She fancied that there were devils dancing there, but strangely the thought did not frighten her. Raoul cupped her face with his free hand, his thumb stroking the skin of her cheek. His touch left a burning trail in its wake and made the breath catch in her throat. She tilted her chin, running her tongue over her lips. She was inviting him to kiss her and he needed no second bidding.

* * *

Raoul captured her mouth, his heart jumping as he tasted her sweetness. It was every bit as delightful as he remembered. The bolt of desire that had shot through him as she lay laughing up at him drove itself deeper, sending the hot blood pumping through his veins and putting to flight all rational thought. His fingers slid from her cheek and down to the soft swell of her breast. She did not recoil, instead her body tensed and pushed against his hand. He deepened his kiss, allowing his tongue to tease and explore her mouth while he unbuttoned her jacket and the shirt beneath. Her arms wound around his neck, fingers driving through his hair as she gave him back kiss for kiss. She stilled, he heard the moan deep in her throat when his hand slipped beneath the stays and lifted one breast free, rubbing his thumb across the stiffened peak.

Cassie threw back her head, but pushed her body closer to Raoul, measuring her length against his as he trailed kisses down her neck, his fingers working their way beneath the hard linen of her stays to free her breasts. He cupped one in his hand, his thumb circling wickedly while his lips and his tongue played with the other. Her body ached with the sheer pleasure of his touch; he was wreaking havoc with her senses and turning her very bones to water. She cradled his head in her hands, aware of the silkiness of his hair between her fingers as he continued to caress her. When she felt his teeth tug oh so gently at one aching nub she could not suppress a soft, animal cry, a mixture of longing and delight.

She arched against him, excitement spiralling through her when she felt his body pressed against her. He was hard and aroused, she was aware of it, even through the folds of her skirts. She wanted to feel his skin against hers, to have him assuage the ache that was spreading through her body, taking control. When he raised his head she was bereft, but only for a moment, until his mouth found hers once more and she could return his kiss with a fervour that she had not known she possessed.

He slid one hand down over her hips, pulling aside the skirts and petticoats. His fingers smoothed over the fine silk of her stocking, moving up past the garter and on to the skin of her thigh. She trembled at his touch and her heart leapt and hammered with anticipation. All considerations of propriety, of caution, counted for nought. She wanted him inside her with a desperation that shocked her, but she had never felt so sure of anything in her life. Her hands scrabbled at his breeches until he pushed aside her fumbling fingers and unfastened the fall flap himself.

Cassie wrapped her arms around his neck again as he continued to kiss her. She slipped one leg around him, wanting him to satisfy the hunger that was consuming her. His fingers were stroking her thigh, moving closer to her heated core. She was almost crying out with her need, her head ringing.

Through the mist of her excitement Cassie realised that the ringing was not inside her head. It was coming from somewhere outside the barn. Raoul had stopped kissing her, his body was poised above her, but he had grown very still.

'Ah.'

Slowly, painfully Raoul fought for control as the insistent clamour of the hand bell forced itself into his consciousness. Could anything have been worse timed to prevent him sating his desires? Or better timed to stop him from taking another man's wife. As a boy he had seen how *Maman* had suffered at his father's neglect. How much more painful would it have been if he had actually committed adultery? Raoul had vowed then he would never succumb to the charms of a married woman and he had kept that vow. Until now.

He eased himself away from the warm, yielding body beneath him and sat up, turning his back on Cassandra. He dared not look at her lest his control should snap. He knew it was still as fragile as fine glass.

'A most judicious interruption, I think.' He spoke lightly, his tone completely at odds with the fire that was raging through him like a fever.

'Raoul.'

He heard the uncertainty as Cassie murmured his name and he closed his eyes, breathing deeply. He was fighting with everything he had not to turn back and finish what they had started. When she touched his arm he shook her off, saying harshly, 'I know you English think nothing of infidelity, milady, but in my world such betrayal is wrong. I could not forgive myself if I came between a man and his wife. I have seen the pain such an act can inflict.' He began to fasten his clothes, keeping his back to her lest he should look into her eyes. Even now he knew he might weaken. 'If I am not mistaken our hostess is calling us and not a moment too soon. Straighten your clothes, milady, while I go and fetch our dinner.'

Cassie watched as Raoul dropped the ladder back in place and quickly descended without sparing her another glance. Hot tears burned her eyelids and she blinked them away, determined that she would not cry. She crossed her arms over her stomach. She should be thankful for Raoul's restraint. A coupling here, with a man she would most likely never see again was sheer madness, but at this very moment, with her body still burning up with desire, it was hard not to regret the clamouring hand bell that had put an end to that madness.

She sat up and felt a slight tug on her neck as the locket she wore beneath her riding habit dropped back into place. She put up one hand to clasp the cool metal, her fingers tracing the outline of the large ruby fixed in the cover while she thought of the picture inside. Her husband. A handsome, smiling face that hid a weak and selfish nature. So different from Raoul. She felt dizzy, her body still thrumming from Raoul's touch, but she must forget how right it felt to be in his arms, how his kiss had thrilled her. How much it had hurt when he rejected her.

He still thinks you are a married woman, that you were about to commit adultery.

She must tell him the truth, then perhaps he would not hold her in such contempt. And then what would happen? She would give herself to him in the heat of passion, only to discover once again that she had mistaken her feelings. Or even worse, that his were transitory. She shivered. How could they be anything else, upon such a short acquaintance? Slowly she fastened the buttons of her shirt and jacket.

No, better to let him think ill of you, since you do not have the strength of will to withstand the attraction.

But as she carefully descended the ladder Cassie knew she would tell him the truth. Whatever the dangers, she could not bear to have him thinking badly of her.

Raoul returned a few moments later carrying a large tray laden with plates and dishes.

'Dinner is served, milady.'

He was smiling, his voice perfectly friendly, but his eyes were shuttered, and Cassie felt as if a barrier had come down between them. His demeanour was that of a stranger and she was too raw, too uncertain to confide in him now.

They consumed their meal sitting apart, like two strangers, and as soon as they had finished Raoul collected up the dishes and took them back to the farmhouse.

'We will set off again when it is dark,' he said when he returned. 'The rain has stopped and the sky is clearing, we should have the moon to light our way. I believe if we press on we will reach Dieppe by morning, but it will be a long ride, so we had best try to get some sleep.'

Without another word he threw himself down on his makeshift bed of straw and sacks and turned his back on her. Cassie swallowed a sigh and lay down on the sacks she had used earlier. They were lying at the far sides of the pile of straw so even if she threw out an arm she could not touch him, but the distance between them could not be measured now in feet and inches. It was imperative that she explain to him that she was not the selfish, adulterous wife he thought her, but not now. Now they both needed to rest before the long ride to Dieppe.

* * *

Their final journey started well enough. A light breeze blew small clouds across the sky, but rarely obscured the sliver of moon that hung above them. However as they rode north the air became heavier, the cloud thickened and thunder rumbled ominously in the distance. They followed a track through a narrow, wooded gorge with bare rock rising up like high black walls on either side. Cassie shivered and looked around nervously. As she did so a flash of lightning made the world as light as day and she screamed.

'Raoul, there is someone back there, in the trees!'

Immediately Raoul stopped and turned his horse, staring hard into the darkness. They both listened intently, but there was nothing, other than the keening wind that was rustling the leaves.

'Perhaps I imagined it,' she muttered.

'Perhaps, or it could have been an animal,' said Raoul. 'If there was anyone there they have gone now.' More thunder rumbled, accompanied by bright, searing flashes. 'Come along. I think we would do well to find shelter.'

The storm clouds were gathering rapidly, there was very little moonlight left and when Raoul spotted the black mouth of a cave just ahead he turned his horse from the path and made his way towards it.

They were just in time. Even as they approached the cave the first, fat drops of rain began to fall. They dismounted and led the horses towards the shadowy aperture. The cave turned out to be little more than a rocky overhang, but it was deep enough to provide shelter for them and the horses. They had barely reached it when the rain turned to a heavy, drenching downpour. The animals snorted nervously as a clap of thunder rent the air and rumbled around the skies. Apart from the occasional flicker of lightning it was very dark and everything was reduced to shades of black.

Cassie peered out into the gloom. 'Do you think there is anyone out there?'

'I doubt it. Valerin would not hesitate to move in if he had us in his sights.'

Cassie nodded. She tried to remember just what she had seen, but it had been so fleeting, a mere shadow moving quickly between the trees. It was nerves, she told herself. She was growing fanciful. She found a small ledge at the back of the shallow cave to rest upon while Raoul paced restlessly up and down, little more than a black shadow moving against the darkness.

'Will you not sit down?' she asked him. 'There is enough space here for two.'

'Thank you, no. I am glad to stretch my legs.'

'You would rather not be near me.' She stated it baldly, trying not to sound wistful.

'That is true.'

She clasped her hands tightly and screwed up her courage. It was time to speak.

'Raoul, I have to tell you, I...I lied to you. When we first met. I *was* married, yes, but I am a widow now. My husband died at Verdun and it was only then that I decided to return to England.'

He had stopped pacing, but she could not see his face. She fancied he had his back to her, looking out into the night. She would have to listen carefully to his reply and judge his reaction by his tone.

'Ah.'

There was nothing to be learned from that brief response. She felt rather than saw him turn.

'Why do you tell me this now?'

'Because I do not want you to think badly of

me. Or to blame yourself for…for what nearly happened in the barn.'

He said politely, 'I am grateful, milady.'

A flicker of lightning showed him standing before her, his face impassive. As the darkness returned he was moving again, muttering that he would just check the horses were securely tethered. Moments later he was back, a black presence, almost invisible in the darkness.

'These storms rarely last too long,' he said. 'We shall be able to resume our journey again soon.'

She frowned. Was that all? He had no other comment to make about her confession? She strained her eyes against the blackness.

'It is not just that you thought me a married woman, is it? There is something more. Is it my birth that makes you dislike me?'

'I do not…dislike you.'

'No.' She sighed. 'At times I have thought we might even be friends, but at others…'

'You are English. You are my enemy.'

'But you told me yourself you are from Brussels, that is not part of France.'

'True, but I wanted it to be, at one time. I was full of revolutionary zeal when I joined the French Navy to fight the English.'

'And you left it because you have no faith in the Consulate or in Bonaparte.'

'That does not mean I no longer hate the English.'

'Hate is a strong word, Raoul. What happened to make you so bitter?'

He cursed angrily.

'Damn your arrogance! You are paying me to escort you to Dieppe, nothing more. It does not give you the right to pry into my life.'

She reeled in dismay at his outburst and quickly begged pardon.

'I did not mean to pry, I...' She hesitated. What should she say; that she cared about him? She knew he did not want that. She murmured again, 'I beg your pardon.'

Silence. When Raoul did speak it was to say merely, 'The rain has stopped. We may continue our journey.'

The conversation was at an end and Cassie almost screamed with frustration. Raoul said he did not dislike her, yet he hated her race. She wanted to know why, but the moment was lost and he would not tell her now. She stood up and looked about her. She had been so intent on their conversation she had not noticed that the thunder

had moved away and the downpour had ceased.
The clouds were breaking up, too, and the crescent moon had once more made an appearance.

Raoul threw Cassandra up into the saddle before scrambling on to his own horse. He had
never been more thankful to be moving. He had
no wish to explain himself to this infuriating
woman. How dare she ask it of him? He owed her
nothing. She was no more than an arrogant, self-
seeking aristocrat. How did he know she was a
widow, how could he be sure she was not merely
saying that to placate him, now he had told her
he disapproved of adultery?

Even as the angry thoughts drove through his
brain he remembered the night they had met,
the black lace shawl fluttering in his face. He
had discarded it then without a second thought.
Perhaps it was true, she was a widow, but why
should she not admit it from the start? Did she
think a man would be deterred from seducing her
by the thought of an outraged husband seeking
vengeance? That might be so, but it did not alter
the fact that she was by birth a detested aristocrat, a proud, selfish creature.

No. Raoul could not pretend he truly believed

that. Cassie had made no complaint during their long journey although the hardships had been great for a gently bred lady. And he could not forget how she had wanted to help when they came upon the collapsed barn. She could have taken a room at the *auberge* and remained there safe and comfortable, instead she had worked tirelessly.

He glanced over his shoulder at the upright little figure riding behind him. When he had told her his reasons for going to Dieppe she had not hesitated. They could have parted at Rouen, she might well have been on her way to England by now, instead she chose to ride with him. Why should she do that? His mind shied away from the answer that presented itself.

A grey dawn was lightening the eastern sky when Raoul next looked back at Cassie. Through the gloom he could see unhappiness clouding her face. *He* had done that, he had turned on her, accused her of prurient curiosity when all she wanted was to understand.

He slowed his horse and waited for her to come alongside.

'I told you my father was a doctor,' he began, not wasting time with preliminaries. 'He was well respected in Brussels and amongst his patients were several grand English families. They had titles and money, even though most had fled from England to escape their creditors. They were also arrogant and demanding, none more so than a certain English countess. It was "Oh, Doctor, I have the headache…" and "Doctor, I am in pain…" This countess would think nothing of sending a servant to fetch my father in the middle of the night for the mildest of ailments. He was at her beck and call at all hours. He never complained, never delayed a visit or refused to go. She dazzled him, I think, even more so than the other English nobles. He was in awe of her title and her grand ways. So much so that he neglected his other patients and his family.' Raoul's jaw clenched as the memories flooded back. 'He did not even notice that his own wife was in failing health. In fact, I believe he deliberately avoided it, since to tend his wife would have given him less time to spend with the English milords. *Maman* sickened and died. I was just thirteen at the time, my sister was even younger. We did what we could to nurse her, but we could not save her. From what I have learned since I believe that if the growth had been diagnosed, if an operation had been carried out early enough, she might have lived, but my father would not even acknowledge that she was ill.

'Is it any wonder that I grew up with a burning resentment against the aristos with their money and selfish demands? And especially I hated the English. France was in the grip of its revolution then and I understood why the old regime had to go. I thought then that change was good, whatever the cost. I was young and idealistic, I thought Europe would be a better place under this new, fairer French government. I also believed that it would be a good thing to bring England under French rule, to destroy the aristocracy that bled its people dry. Older, wiser friends in Brussels tried to counsel caution, but I would not listen and my father showed no interest at all in my views. I did not understand then that he was crippled with guilt and regret. After *Maman's* death he threw himself even more into his work. His patients and his duty always came before any consideration for his family. We were left to fend for ourselves.'

'And yet you, too, wanted to study medicine?'

'Being a surgeon is not a choice for me, milady. It is what I am.'

'I know that,' she said quietly. 'I have seen you at work.'

Having started to explain, he could not stop now. 'Only when he was dying did my father admit that he had failed us, especially he had failed my mother. He blamed his calling, he had never wanted to be anything other than a doctor, it was his life, an all-consuming passion.'

She interrupted him. 'Forgive me, but your father believed his *calling* prevented him from seeing that your mother was ill? How can that be?'

'It was only a part of it. He confessed that being physician to the rich and privileged in Brussels had turned his head, especially the attentions of the English countess.' He added bitterly, 'He was so busy pandering to her imagined illnesses that he ignored the symptoms of illness that *Maman* displayed. He was always more interested in his patients than his family and that was his final piece of advice to me. He would have preferred me to be a doctor, but if I was determined to be a surgeon, then so be it, but he told me that medical men—physicians, doctors—should never marry. They live for their work, to the exclusion of all else. There can be no compromise.'

'What if they should fall in love?'

He had asked himself this question many times and the answer came easily.

'They must not. They may take lovers, yes, but there should never be any serious attachment.' He glanced towards her. 'You should appreciate such sentiments, milady, since you believe love to be overprized in your society.'

'I do,' she agreed, putting up her chin. 'There is much to be said for your view. I fell head over heels in love with Gerald and eloped with him, thinking the world well lost, but it did not last. Such a heady passion never could. Although *my* affection lasted considerably longer than my husband's,' she ended bitterly.

'How did he die?' asked Raoul.

'A duel.' She paused, her brows drawing together slightly as she frowned. 'A duel over another man's wife. I told you my husband would never take me to a ball. I would not play his games, you see. I did not wish to flirt with other men and I objected to his attentions to other women. So, I was left at home. He told me he was meeting friends, going to gambling hells, and I chose to believe that. In fact, he was escorting other ladies to balls and assemblies. Any number of them. One husband took exception and called him out.'

'I am very sorry.'

'Do not be. He had spent all our money on gambling and women. If he had lived he would have continued until we were deep in debt. His morals, too, were not what I first thought them. He was sinking into depravity and...' she swallowed '...and he was close to taking me with him.'

'Those dreams,' said Raoul. 'I heard you call out for him to stop. Did—was he—?'

He saw her shudder.

'A husband is entitled to his rights,' she said.

Raoul was silent. So he was wrong, she had not abandoned her husband. Or at least so she said. Could he believe her? The answer was already in his heart. He knew this woman now as if she was a part of him.

'Raoul.' Her voice broke into his thoughts. She was sitting straighter in the saddle, staring at the road ahead. 'There are some men on the road in front of us.'

Raoul heard the urgency in her voice, but he had already spotted the men and unease was prickling his skin. There were four of them approaching and at a point where the terrain would make it difficult to evade them.

'Stay behind me,' he muttered. 'If there is trouble you must turn and ride away, do you understand?'

It was light enough now for Raoul to see that the men were in ragged uniforms and two of them held short, heavy sticks in their hands. Deserters, perhaps, rogues certainly. They were in a line across the road, blocking the way.

'Good day to you,' he hailed them cheerfully. 'I hope you mean to move aside and allow two weary travellers to pass.'

One of the men, presumably the leader, stepped forward to answer him.

'With pleasure, my friend, once you have given us your purse and your horses.'

'I think not.'

The fellow slapped the club menacingly against his empty palm. 'Hand them over freely, *monsieur*, and you and your woman may walk on unharmed. Resist and I will smash your horse's knees and then we will kill you. And the woman, too, after we have taken our pleasure.'

Raoul pulled out the pistol. He would have to make good use of his one shot and pray he could give Cassie time to escape. He decided he would rather face them on foot, so he quickly slipped out of the saddle and took a few steps towards the leader, who bared his teeth in an ugly grin.

'One bullet against four men? The odds are not in your favour, *monsieur*.'

It was the truth and Raoul knew it, but he must give Cassie a chance to get clear. He was bracing himself for a tough fight when a voice spoke behind him.

'Then let us make the odds a little fairer, shall we?'

A tall black-bearded figure in riding dress emerged from the bushes at the roadside, a pistol in each hand and a serviceable-looking sword at his side.

'You see there are three pistols now,' the stranger continued. 'And I warn you that I am an excellent shot.'

He stepped up beside Raoul, but even as he did so the four ragged assailants were backing away and a moment later they were crashing away through the bushes.

Cassie had watched the whole from a distance, her chest constricted with fear, but now the immediate danger had passed she jumped down, collecting up the reins of the loose horse and walking towards Raoul and the tall stranger.

'We are very grateful for your assistance, *monsieur*,' she said, smiling up at the man and holding out her hand. 'Your arrival was most opportune.'

He bowed over her fingers. 'Do I have the pleasure of addressing Lady Cassandra Witney?'

Cassie stared up at him, surprised.

'Why, yes,' she said. 'How do you know my name?'

'I am your cousin, Wolfgang Arrandale.'

Chapter Eight

'Wolfgang!' Cassie exclaimed. 'But how—? What—?'

Raoul cut short her stammering questions with a wave of one hand.

'I suggest we move away from here. Those rogues might well return.'

'I agree,' said Wolfgang. 'My horse is hidden in the trees. I will collect him and we will ride on. There is an inn about half a mile ahead, we can talk there.'

He walked off, leaving Cassie to stare after him.

'Let me help you to mount.'

Raoul's words took a few moments to penetrate her bemused state, but at last she allowed him to throw her up into the saddle.

'So he claims to be your cousin,' said Raoul. 'Do you recognise him?'

'No, of course not. He fled England nearly ten years ago.'

'Fled?'

'Yes. He was accused of killing his wife and stealing her jewels.'

'And did he?'

A tiny crease furrowed Cassie's brow.

'I do not know,' she said slowly. 'Why would he run away, if he is innocent?'

Raoul was tempted to remind her that he was doing just that, but at that moment the man calling himself Wolfgang Arrandale trotted up on a glossy black hunter and instead Raoul turned to appraise horse and rider.

'I'd wager that beast is no hired hack.'

'No.' The man leaned forward to pat the glossy neck. 'Satan is my own. We have been through many adventures together.'

Cassie brought her mare alongside the black.

'Is that how you live, Cousin, as a soldier of fortune?'

Cousin. Raoul's brows rose a little. So she had decided to accept that he was who he claimed to be.

Arrandale gave a little shrug and said indifferently, 'Something like that. Shall we go?'

Raoul scrambled up into his saddle and trotted after the others. There was no doubt that Arrandale's intervention was timely, for the situation had been looking decidedly ugly, but Raoul could not help wishing it had been a chance stranger who had come to their aid. He might then have accepted their thanks and gone on his way. The fact that the fellow was Cassie's cousin could not be coincidence. If he *was* Wolfgang Arrandale. After all they only had his word for it.

He watched Cassie turn her head to look up at her companion and felt something twist in his gut. Something suspiciously like jealousy. He dragged his eyes away and glowered at his horse's ears.

'Do not be ridiculous,' he muttered savagely to the hapless animal. 'If the fellow is her cousin and he has come looking for her, then your job is done. He can take care of her'.

But as they clattered into the cobbled yard of the inn Raoul realised with a jolt that he did not wish to consign Lady Cassandra to anyone's care.

'So, Cousin, what are you doing here?'

Cassandra could hardly wait until the landlord

had left them at their table before she put the question.

'I have been following you.'

'So I was not imagining it.' She threw a triumphant glance at Raoul. 'I thought I saw something in the woods last night.'

'Yes, it was careless of me to get so close.'

'But why was it necessary for you to hide?' demanded Raoul. 'Why did you not declare yourself and ride with us?'

Wolfgang spread his hands. 'I could have been wrong. It wasn't until I looked my cousin in the eye just now that I was sure.'

Raoul nodded. Despite Arrandale's full beard it was possible to see a strong similarity between him and Lady Cassandra. Both had an abundance of curling dark hair and thick, dark lashes fringing those unusually coloured eyes. In Wolfgang's case his eyes were more blue than violet, but the likeness was sufficient to convince Raoul that they were related.

'Well I am very glad you decided to follow us,' said Cassie, smiling at her cousin in a way that made Raoul grit his teeth. 'You saved us from those horrid men.'

'I also saved your skin at the farm.'

'Ah,' said Raoul, remembering the musket shots that had sounded so opportunely. 'Was it you who drew off the soldiers?'

Those eyes, so like Cassie's, turned to look at him.

'It was the least I could do, for a fellow fugitive.'

'But how did you find us?' Cassie demanded. 'And why were you even looking for me?'

'Lady Hune.'

'Grandmama's letters reached you? I did not think they would. No one has had any word from you for years. To be truthful I thought you were dead.'

'My great-aunt—your grandmother—is very persistent. I believe she wrote many letters in the hope that at least one of them would reach me. She numbers amongst her acquaintances several members of the French aristocracy who survived the Terror and now live...er...outside the law. When I first came to France Lady Hune asked them to look out for me. Let us say I am returning the favour.'

Cassie frowned. 'But that does not explain how you found us, or what Grandmama expects you to do.'

'She wants me to spirit you back to England, of course.'

'*Could* you do that?' asked Raoul.

'Quite possibly. I went to Verdun with the intention of getting my cousin and her husband out of France, but I learned there that Witney was dead and his widow had left for England.' He looked at Cassie. 'I had only missed you by a matter of days and thought there might be a chance to catch up with you, so I went to Rouen. There was no trace of a Lady Cassandra Witney ever having arrived there. However, I did learn of an English milady and her husband staying in the town, so I thought I might take a look, in case you had got yourself into some sort of scrape.'

Cassie straightened in her chair and said indignantly, 'Why should you think I was in a scrape?'

'Because you are an Arrandale, Cousin. We have a talent for getting into trouble.'

Raoul laughed at that.

'Very true!' He saw the angry fire sparkling in Cassie's eyes and continued, before she could retort, 'But never mind that, now. You followed us from Rouen?'

'Yes. I arrived at the inn soon after the law officers. The tapster told me some government man from Paris was there to arrest a deserter and his English lover. The serving maid's description was enough to convince me the lady might well be my cousin. With so many *gendarmes* milling around the inn I thought it would be safer if I did not tarry so I retired to the street corner, keeping an eye on the place and trying to decide what to do. Then a commotion broke out. From my vantage point I think I was the only one to see a couple running away through the alley at the back of the inn. I followed you from there.'

Cassie remembered her unease as they had walked through the narrow streets.

'But I do not understand. Why did we not see you?'

'I had...*acquired* the clothes of a common seaman. It seemed more fitting, since we were so close to the quay.'

'The snoring sailor,' remarked Raoul, grinning.

'The very same.' Arrandale straightened in his chair and fixed Raoul with a piercing gaze. He said with a touch of hauteur that reminded Raoul strongly of Lady Cassandra, 'But I have not yet discovered why *you* are escorting my cousin, *monsieur.*'

'Oh, it is all quite simple,' Cassie rushed in to

explain. 'The courier I hired to take me to Rouen was a villain and Raoul rescued me.'

Her cousin did not look to be impressed. He kept his eyes upon Raoul.

'Word in Rouen was that you are one Raoul Doulevant, a deserter from the navy.'

'It is no such thing,' said Cassie indignantly. 'That horrid man Valerin destroyed Raoul's records and put out a false report about him.'

Wolf sat back in his chair. 'Really?'

'You do not believe me,' she exclaimed. 'It is true, Cousin, I assure you. Raoul is an honourable man.'

Without thinking she had put her hand over Raoul's, where it rested on the table, and he was obliged to quell the sudden soaring elation he felt at the gesture.

'Your cousin is rightly concerned for you,' he said, reluctantly withdrawing his hand. 'Rest assured, *monsieur*, we travel as man and wife in name only. Funds are low and milady has no maid to accompany her.'

'I can see that,' growled Arrandale. 'The question is, Doulevant, what is your plan?'

'To find a ship to carry milady to England from Dieppe.'

Arrandale nodded. 'The town is crawling with soldiers, but it should be possible. I have friends there who can help us.'

'You will come to England with me?' Cassie asked hopefully.

'Alas, I cannot return to England. You forget, Cousin, there is a price on my head. I am wanted for the murder of my wife.' He added bitterly, 'Even worse in the eyes of the English, I am accused of stealing a diamond necklace belonging to her family.'

'But if you are innocent—'

'Who would believe me? Even my own father thought I was guilty. He shipped me out of the country before I could be arrested. It is better that I remain in France. There is nothing for me in England now.'

'There is Arrandale,' said Cassie. 'And your daughter.'

He looked up at that. 'I have a daughter?'

'Yes, a little girl called Florence. Surely you knew that?'

He shook his head. 'I thought the child had died with her mother.' He was silent for a moment. 'I moved around a great deal when I first came to France and in truth I did not wish to keep in touch with my family. I was angry that they should believe the worst without giving me a chance to defend myself. I saw only the report in an English newspaper that there was a reward for my capture. Where is Florence now?'

'She lives with Lord Davenport's family.'

'Then she is better off without me.'

'But—'

'No, Cassandra. I cannot accompany you to England. It is impossible. You will have to make do with Doulevant's escort.'

'No, no, you misunderstand,' said Raoul quickly. 'It was never my intention to go to England. My service to milady ends once she is safely aboard ship.'

Cassie was still smarting from the way Raoul had pulled his hand away from hers and his last words stung her even more. She should not care, after all it would not be long now before they parted for ever, but she was surprised how much it hurt to discover that he would be very relieved once she was off his hands. Wolfgang was speaking and she tried to concentrate upon his words.

'You would send her alone? What do you think will happen once she reaches England?'

Cassie braced herself to hear Raoul say he neither knew nor cared. His reply was a tiny crumb of comfort.

'I have been thinking about that. Is there a way we can send ahead to this Lady Hune? Then she could send someone to meet Lady Cassandra.'

'That is possible, I suppose. It would mean delaying until we could get a message to the marchioness. Her letters to me were from London, but she may be back in Bath by now.'

'No, she is in Essex,' put in Cassandra. 'At Chantreys. The last letter I have from her says she will be staying at Lord Davenport's house there until December at least, to look after the earl's wards while he and his new wife are on honeymoon.'

Wolfgang looked up in surprise. 'James has married again?'

'Did you not know? James and his wife were drowned last winter. His brother Alex is now the earl.'

'Alex!' Wolfgang exclaimed. 'I did not think he was the marrying kind, he was always a wild one, but I suppose he must think about the succession.' He cast another searching look at Cassie. 'And Alex is now my daughter's guardian?'

'Yes, I believe so and also to James's daughter, Margaret. They are of a similar age.'

Her cousin frowned, as if digesting all he had heard, then he gave a shrug.

'Essex is closer than Bath, so in the event it works out better for us. I will send word to Lady Hune as soon as I have organised your passage and we know where on the coast you will be coming ashore, Cousin.'

'You seem to have forgotten the war,' put in Raoul. 'It may not be so easy to arrange all this.'

For the first time since they met Cassie saw her cousin smile.

'It is easy enough if you know the right people. I lived in this area for a few years when I first came to France and I still have friends along this coast. However, it may take a few days to arrange everything. In the meantime you would be best staying in Dieppe, I think. Strangers would attract less attention there than in any of the smaller ports along this coast.'

'That will suit me very well,' agreed Raoul. 'I have business in Dieppe.'

'Then it is settled.' Wolfgang drained his tankard and set it down on the table. 'We should press on, there will be much to do once we reach the town.' He leaned closer. 'One more thing, I am known here as Georges Lagrasse, a citizen of Toulouse. I think it will be best if I claim acquaintance with Doulevant rather than you, Cassandra. Your French is good, but you are clearly a foreigner.'

'Just what I told her, *monsieur,*' remarked Raoul, draining his own cup. 'We are in agreement on one thing, at least.'

Cassie, offended by this display of male solidarity, swept out of the tavern before them.

By the time they reached Dieppe it was past noon and beginning to rain again. Wolfgang gave them directions to an inn.

'It is clean and comfortable and I know the landlord, he is to be trusted. He is accustomed to travellers and is unlikely to ask you for your papers. If anyone *should* enquire, Cassandra, it would be best to say you are Irish. The recent bombardment of the town has made the people here less friendly towards the English.'

'Let us hope it is not necessary to say anything,' put in Cassie. 'I would rather we did not attract any more attention than necessary.'

'I agree,' said Wolfgang. 'Very well, get you to

the inn. I shall be in contact once I have secured for you a safe passage to England.'

'You are not coming with us?' she asked him.

'No. I have friends here who will give me a bed and help me find you a ship.'

Cassie was tempted to ask him about his friends, but decided it would be wiser not to know. From her conversations with her cousin during their journey she guessed that he lived a precarious existence in France, so now she merely wished him good luck and followed Raoul to the inn.

For Cassie it had become a familiar charade. She hung, exhausted, on Raoul's arm while he gave a false name and told the landlord they required accommodation with a separate bedchamber for their maid, who was following with the luggage. The recent storm accounted for their dishevelled appearance and they were shown upstairs to a comfortable suite overlooking the street. Their accommodation comprised a small anteroom which opened on to the main bedchamber and a truckle bed was prepared in the dressing room beyond. Cassie made no demur when Raoul ordered dinner to be served in their rooms. She was too tired to eat in public, knowing she would have to be on her guard against any slip of the tongue. Now all she had to resist was the growing attraction she felt for Raoul Doulevant.

'I am going out again,' he said as soon as they were alone. 'There is an hour or so before dinner and I must see if the *Prométhée* is in the harbour. I may be too late; she may already have sailed elsewhere.'

'Of course,' she replied. 'I wish you luck, Raoul.'

With a nod he went out and she moved restlessly about the apartment, making herself familiar with the rooms. She could not forget the last time Raoul had left her alone at an inn and she took time to look for possible routes of escape. But it was not fear of Valerin finding them that disturbed her most, it was Raoul's cool manner. It had become very marked since they had met her cousin and if Cassie didn't know better she would have thought he was jealous. But that was ridiculous, of course, and it was also quite ridiculous that she should *care*.

Cassie sighed and clasped her hands together. If only there was no war, no social divisions. If only they could meet and talk as equals. If only…

She found she was obliged to blink back a tear.

Angrily she stalked back into the anteroom. There was no point in wishing for the impossible. She could not deny her birth; she was the daughter of a marquess and her ancestors could be traced back to the Conqueror. She was going back to England, to the world she knew and understood. She thrust aside the shadow of loneliness that clouded her vision of the future. It was quite possible that Grandmama would find her a husband, a kind, generous man who would care for her and whom she would grow to love. It would be a safe, comfortable existence in a world she knew. It was where she belonged. Raoul could never be happy there, even if he had wanted to join her. And that was the point, wasn't it? He did not want her in his life. This new coolness was most likely a sign of relief that their time together was almost over.

'Which just goes to show that he is far more sensible than you,' she lectured herself. 'You have already made one *mésalliance*, but Gerald was at least English and a gentleman. To marry outside your sphere would be an even greater folly and not to be countenanced.'

Cassie made herself comfortable in a chair by the table and settled down to wait. She must concentrate now on the future. She would return to

Grandmama's care, Raoul would go to Brussels
and take up his life again as a surgeon. Perhaps,
one day when this wretched war was over they
might meet again, as friends. For the present she
could only hope that he would find his captain
and obtain the papers he needed to prove he was
no deserter.

Raoul returned just as the serving maid brought
in their dinner, and Cassie was obliged to hold
her questions until they were alone.

'The *Prométhée* was not there,' he informed
her at last. 'She was due here two weeks since,
but the English were attacking the town and she
narrowly escaped capture. She is expected to be
back in port here tomorrow. I am hopeful I shall
be able to see Captain Belfort then.'

'I am glad you have not missed him.' She
pushed a piece of chicken about her plate. 'Once
you have your papers you will be free to go where
you will, Raoul. I think you should do so, Dieppe
is not safe for you. You do not need to stay here
for my sake.'

'We are agreed, I shall not leave until you are
safe on board a ship for England.'

Safe? Cassie's spirit quailed, but she could not

let Raoul see how much she had come to rely upon his protection.

She said brightly. 'How long do you think it will take my cousin to secure a passage for me?'

'A day, two perhaps. *If* it is true that he is familiar with the town and the people, then he stands a better chance of striking a deal than I.'

'But you do not trust him?'

'I know nothing of the man, save that he is a fugitive, like myself.'

'I believe he is innocent,' said Cassie quietly. 'Like yourself.'

Raoul poured the rest of the wine into their glasses and sat back, staring moodily into the fire. There was no doubting Arrandale had proved himself useful, but he could not like the man. He wished Cassie disliked him, too, and immediately berated himself for such ignoble thoughts. By heaven, anyone would think he was jealous! A ridiculous idea. He shifted on his chair. Why, then, was it like a pinprick in his flesh every time she directed a smile towards her cousin, why the sudden burning anger whenever they conversed together?

His gaze moved to Cassandra. She was concentrating on cutting an apple into small pieces. The candlelight glinted on her dark curls and gave her skin a golden glow. He watched her take a piece of apple, holding it daintily between her fingers as she nibbled at it with her even, white teeth. She was a lady, from the tips of her toes to the top of those glossy curls. She was made for a life of ease and luxury, with servants at her beck and call. It was not her fault if she was bred to be no more than a selfish, arrogant ornament.

He had a sudden, vivid memory of her felling the postilion when he came to attack her. Another of her working beside him when he was operating on those unfortunate men in Flagey. He had known grown men to faint at the sights she had witnessed that night. Dr Bonnaire had been impressed. She had displayed no signs of arrogance then. True, she had taken charge of the village, organising the food, settling the children, comforting the grieving, but no one had complained. They had not called her arrogant. They had described her as a saint...

He pushed his chair back, saying roughly, 'I am going downstairs, I may be able to glean some news of how the war is going.'

'Oh, may I come with you?'

'No. I am going to the taproom. It is not a place for ladies.' He hesitated, then pulled the purse from his pocket. 'Perhaps it is time we divided up our remaining funds.'

'I need only enough to get me to England,' she said as he counted out the coins.

'We agreed we would share any surplus, did we not?' He held out the purse. 'There. It should be sufficient to pay for your passage to England, unless the captain is a rogue.'

'Thank you. And I still have my locket, I can sell that, if I am desperate.' She managed a smile. 'Let us hope Wolfgang can strike a good bargain.'

Raoul felt the now-familiar pain like a knife in his gut when she mentioned her cousin. He could only reply with a curt little nod before he left the room.

Cassie sat very still and watched the door close behind him. Only when she was alone did her shoulders slump. She could not ignore the fact now. They were no longer friends.

The serving maid came in to clear the table and Cassie moved away into the bedchamber, pretending to tidy her hair in the looking glass and avoiding the servant's scrutiny. It was very dispiriting to know that Raoul did not want her with him. They had gone together to make the arrangements to leave Rouen, she had remained cloaked and silent while he had negotiated with dubious characters in dimly lit taverns and shadowed alleys, but she had been there, at his side. Now, it seemed, he did not want her company and she must keep to her room. It went very much against her nature to remain idle, but she had little choice. For the moment she must allow Raoul and her cousin to make the necessary preparations for her repatriation.

When the maid had carried away all the empty dishes Cassie wandered back into the room. The long journey was beginning to take its toll, she felt very weary, but it was more than that. She pulled one of the dining chairs towards the fire and sat down, hoping the flames would dispel the chill of unhappiness that had crept into her soul. She should be happy. In another day or two she would be back in England, amongst her own people and she would be able to forget all about her disastrous marriage. She could forget about France. About Raoul.

* * *

The taproom was crowded and noisy, and most of the talk was on whether the English warships would return. The last bombardment had set fire to the town in three places and while the damage had been minimal the townsfolk were nervous that more attacks might follow. Raoul fell into conversation with a group of merchants who were in Dieppe to await the arrival of their ships, if they ever came. They bemoaned the English blockade of the ports, but none of them doubted for one moment that France would be victorious. After all, was not Bonaparte even now planning to invade England? Then the country would be annexed and brought under French rule, as had happened to the Southern Netherlands and so many other territories.

Raoul bit his tongue when they talked about his homeland. Growing up in the shadow of the revolution, he had been as keen as any that the people should be victorious, that the old tyranny should be ended and replaced with a just and fair system of government by the people, but that had not happened. He wondered what it would be like returning to Brussels, living under French rule. Not so bad, he told himself. As long as he was allowed to get on with his work he did not care. But to practise his trade he needed his papers and that meant finding Captain Belfort. He continued to talk to the merchants, asking them about the harbour and what ships were coming in, but they knew very little. He would have to make the trip to the quayside in the morning, not only to see if the *Prométhée* had docked, but also to try and ascertain if anyone would be willing to take Cassandra to England. She had pinned her faith on her cousin finding her a berth, but it would do no harm to have a second plan, should Arrandale fail.

Raoul spent a couple of hours in the taproom. Even after he had learned all he could he tarried there, fighting the urge to go back to Cassandra. Knowing they must soon part for ever, he wanted to spend every moment with her, to memorise her face, her smile, the sound of her laughter. He called for more wine. As if all those things were not already burned into his heart.

Eventually he made his way back upstairs. A good night's rest and an early start were needed now. With luck Cassie was already asleep with the curtains drawn tightly around the bed. He entered almost silently. Candles still burned on the mantelshelf and at first he thought she had left them to light his way. Then he saw her hunched on her chair, her hands over her face and her shoulders shaking as she cried quietly.

'*Tiens*, what is this!'

He crossed the room in a couple of strides, but Cassie had already jumped up and turned her back on him. She wiped her fingers across her cheeks.

'I did not hear you come in.'

He reached out, but his hand stopped just inches from her.

He said gently, 'What is it, *chérie*, why are you weeping?'

'I am *not* weeping. I abhor such weakness.'

She would have walked away, but he put his hands on her shoulders.

'Of course you do.' He turned her towards him and pulled her closer. 'You are far too sensible for such a thing.'

Her resistance was half-hearted. When he would not let go she leaned against him, burying her face in his coat.

'I am t-tired, that is all.'

Her voice caught on a sob and his arms slid

around, binding her to him. He rested his cheek on her hair and closed his eyes. They had been travelling for days and yet still there clung about her a faint summer fragrance. The subtle, elusive quality of it undermined his resolve to keep her at a distance. He raised his head and put two fingers beneath her chin.

'Cassandra, *chérie—*'

She called up every ounce of willpower to push herself out of his arms, reminding herself that the pain would be even worse if she allowed herself to succumb to this man's attraction, even for a moment.

'I do not want you to k-kiss me,' she lied, taking a few steps away from him and averting her face. 'I have told you I have no time for that, or your soft words. They bring nothing but pain.' Yes, that was better. She must remember that all men were deceivers. Had she not had proof enough of that in Verdun? She added, 'I know now that there is no joy to be found in any man's arms.'

'Ah, my dear, if we had time I would show you that is not true. But soon you will be back in England.'

'Yes.' She wrapped her arms around herself.

Scant comfort after being held in Raoul's embrace, but the greater the joy now, the greater the pain to follow, so it would have to suffice. Now and for ever. 'And you, I hope, will have your captain's testimonial and be free to return to your home.'

There was silence, as if they were both considering the future. It was as much as Raoul could do not to let out the howl of anguish that filled his soul. He watched Cassandra put her hands by her sides and straighten her shoulders, as though she was mustering all her strength. She picked up one of the branched candlesticks from the mantelpiece and held it out to him. 'You will need this to light you to bed. Goodnight, *monsieur.*'

Raoul did not move. She stood before him, head high, every inch a haughty aristo, but the hand holding the candles was not quite steady. Perhaps it was the wavering flames that made the air shimmer around them, but he could feel the tension, too, so great it was almost visible, yet even so he was aware that their whole future was balanced on a knife's edge. One false move, one unwise word and he would knock the candles aside and drag her into his arms.

He would kiss her until she succumbed to the

passion he knew she possessed. It was simmering just beneath the surface. The temptation was almost overpowering. He wanted to hold her again, to taste her, to have her body soft and yielding beneath his. Just once. But the consequences of that would be too great. *He* might walk away afterwards and immerse himself in his work, but what if he were to send Cassie back to England carrying his child?

Slowly and with infinite care he reached out and took the candlestick, making sure their fingers did not touch.

'Goodnight, milady.'

Just uttering those two words had been agony. Raoul turned and walked out of the room, every step an effort, his body stiff and burning with desire.

'Good morning, *monsieur.*'

Cassie greeted Raoul with cheerful politeness, determined that he should not guess the miserable night she had spent tossing and turning in her bed. Her dreams had been troubled by memories of her husband's infidelity. Even his death had been a betrayal, a duel fought over another woman, and Cassie awoke several times in the night, feeling wounded and defenceless, afraid to trust anyone. The dawn had brought resolution and she had fixed her mind on her return to England. Raoul Doulevant must be kept at a distance. He was a paid escort, nothing more, and must be treated as such.

While they breakfasted on hot, fresh bread washed down by scalding coffee they discussed their plans for the day. Raoul told her his first task was to ascertain if the *Prométhée* had docked.

'I think I shall do a little shopping,' she responded, keeping her tone light, as if she was discussing a trip to Bond Street. 'I would like to find a bonnet and veil.'

'You could ask the landlady to direct you,' Raoul suggested. 'I have already given them to understand that your maid and the rascally postilion have absconded with our baggage coach, so she would not be surprised at the question.'

Cassandra's errand was soon complete. She made her way to the shop recommended by the landlady, where the milliner commiserated with her upon the loss of her bags and was only too happy for her to make use of the mirror to fix the neat little bonnet over her dusky curls and arrange the veil. She also purchased a new reticule to complete the outfit. Thus attired, Cassie sallied forth and spent a pleasant hour or two browsing the shops and market stalls. Her purse was growing woefully thin. There was barely enough in it now to pay her way on the long journey home. However, when she came upon a stall selling a miscellany of goods she stopped. The stallholder hailed her with bluff good humour.

'Ah, *madame*, with what can I tempt you this bright morning? A pretty looking glass for your wall, or this fine bracket clock from the Netherlands? Or perhaps this sable-lined cloak, fit for a duchess. Everything was acquired honestly, *madame*,' he assured her, grinning. 'These days there are many who are only too glad to part with their possessions. After all, what good are such things if one cannot afford to eat?'

Cassie pointed to the large, leather-covered box that had caught her eye. 'That case—'

'This one? Why, 'tis is an old surgeon's set, *madame*. You see, it still contains the tools of his trade. It is a little worn, but it would make a fine addition to your baggage. As a dressing case, perhaps.' He added quickly, sensing a sale. 'I could remove the instruments—'

'No, no it is for a medical man.' She stared at the case. 'Where did you get it?'

'Where? It was amongst the goods sold by a bankrupt to pay his debts, *madame.*'

'And how much do you want for it?'

A sly look came into the man's eyes.

'Ah, now, here's the thing,' he said. 'I thought perhaps I might take it to the hospital in Rouen. There are many doctors and surgeons there who would pay me a good price for such a set...'

Cassie unfastened the chain about her neck.

'I will trade you the case and its contents for this chain and locket.' She held it out to him. 'It is solid gold and that is a real ruby embedded in the locket. It will fetch you a very good price.'

The man studied the locket, weighed it in his hand before shaking his head.

'Nay, *madame*, the surgeon's set is worth twice what this would fetch.'

Cassie was not accustomed to bargaining, but she had a stubborn streak and she was determined to put up a fight for the leather case. She held out her hand.

'I doubt that, but it is your choice,' she said indifferently. 'I will keep my trinket, then, if you would prefer a long and dusty ride to Rouen—'

As Cassie reached for the locket the stallholder closed his fingers over it.

'As you say, it is a long way to Rouen, whereas this pretty bauble I could sell much more easily.' He gave a gusty sigh. 'It is a great bargain for you, *madame*, and I shall most likely make a loss on this deal at the end of the day. But I will let you have the case in exchange for your locket and chain.'

It was done. Cassandra reached out to close the lid upon the gruesome-looking instruments and to lift the case off the stall while the stallholder was busy inspecting his new possession. He prised open the locket.

'A moment, *madame*. Who is this handsome gentleman portrayed inside?'

'My husband,' she said quietly. 'He is dead.'

'Ah, a thousand regrets! You are desolated to part with his likeness, no? But it need not be,' he said, holding the locket closer to his eyes. 'It is painted on ivory and it is a little loose...' She watched him take out a small knife and ease the miniature from its mount. 'There, *madame*, you may have your husband back again. It shows you that I have a great heart, have I not?'

'Thank you.' Cassie slipped the little painting

into her reticule. It was the last thing she had bought with her pin money before she and Gerald ran off together. It would remind her that she had thought herself in love with him and had been mistaken. Perhaps it would also help her avoid making the same mistake again.

In the privacy of the inn she inspected her purchase. The corners of the leather case were worn, but the instruments, although dull, looked to be in good condition and similar to the ones she had seen Raoul use at Flagey. Would he appreciate the gesture, or would he think her foolish? After all, what did she know of his profession? These instruments might be of poor quality. Not only would he think her foolish, he might be offended. The sound of his now-familiar step on the stair made her heart race. She would soon know.

Chapter Nine

When Raoul entered the room to find Cassie was waiting for him his spirits rose and the day seemed a little brighter. He noted immediately the new bonnet and the heavy veil which she had put back so that the black lace fell like a mantle over her shoulders. He thought how well she looked, a faint flush on her cheeks and a shy, tentative smile trembling on her lips.

'How was your morning?' she asked him, by way of greeting.

He stripped off his gloves and threw them on to a chair.

'There is news. The *Prométhée* was coming into the harbour even as I reached the quay. I did not wait. Captain Belfort will be busy for hours yet so I will go back later, after we have dined.' The delay was frustrating, but he had waited so long that he could be patient a little longer. He smiled at her. 'You have your hat and veil, I see. Very fetching.'

'I bought something else,' she said, waving towards the table. 'Something for you.'

For the first time Raoul saw the battered case upon the dining table.

'You bought this for me?'

He walked to the table while Cassie rushed to explain.

'I saw it in the market and thought you might be able to use it, since you left all your own instruments in Paris. I have no idea if these are the right tools for you, or if indeed they are any good, but I thought, I hoped they might suffice until you could find yourself a new set...'

Her words trailed off but Raoul barely noticed, he was too engrossed in assessing the familiar instruments. The contents were almost complete. No drugs or opiates, of course, that was too much to expect, but everything else was there: a few dressings and bandages, various types of knives and forceps, a bullet probe, even an amputation saw. The finish was dulled, but Raoul could see that they were all made from the finest cast steel.

'The stallholder assured me they were legally

acquired. He said they were from the sale of a bankrupt's effects.'

'Indeed?' Raoul murmured. 'One man's misfortune is another's gain, then.' He looked at her, frowning. 'But this must have cost you something. Have you spent your passage money?'

'No, of course not.'

'Then how did you pay for it?' When she did not reply immediately his imagination rioted as he considered what possible folly she might have committed. He said brusquely, 'The truth, milady, if you please.'

'I exchanged my locket for it.'

Raoul regarded her in silence as more wild thoughts chased around in his head. She had little enough money for her journey, so why had she sold her last item of jewellery to buy this for him?

'But it contained the picture of your husband.'

'The stallholder prised that out. I have it safe. Not that I really want it,' she said quickly. 'I thought I might send it to Gerald's family when I get back to England.' When he said nothing she gave a tiny shrug, 'I saw the case and thought you might be able to use it. However, if it is not what you require, I shall not be offended. Perhaps we could sell it back.'

He reached for her hand and carried it to his lips.

'No need for that, milady. I have never received a better gift. Thank you, a thousand times.'

Her fingers trembled and the blush deepened on her cheek.

'I thought perhaps it might help you to remember me,' she murmured.

I could never forget you.

Raoul heard the words in his head, but he dare not say them aloud. To do so would be to admit his weakness. He knew he should have left her at Rouen, insisted she take a ship from there, but somehow, he found it impossible to let her go. There was always some reason to keep her with him, just another day.

The long dark lashes had swept down so that he could not see her eyes, but she made no move to free herself from his grasp and he could not bring himself to release her. Silence settled around them and with each moment that passed the peace of it drained away. The air became charged with anticipation, as if an electrical storm was imminent. They were locked in a silent tableau, their bodies inching closer. Gently Raoul ran his free hand down her cheek.

'Cassie, look at me.'

He saw the nervous movement of her throat before she slowly raised her head and lifted her eyes to his. They were huge and dark with only a narrow ring of violet around the black centres and as Raoul stared into the liquid depths he thought that he was drowning. He saw himself mirrored in those luminous eyes and he had a sudden, wild idea that he had found his soulmate.

A knock at the door shattered the moment. They jumped apart as the door opened and a serving maid entered.

'A letter for *madame*,' said the maid. She handed over the letter then waited, wiping her nose on her sleeve. Cassie turned the note over and over in her hands. She was dazed and unable to concentrate. She felt like someone dragged suddenly from a deep sleep.

Raoul threw the girl a coin. 'You may go.'

At last Cassie broke the seal and read the note while the servant clumped noisily back down the stairs.

'It is from Wolfgang,' she said at last. 'He says the arrangements are in hand. He is going to join us here for dinner.'

'That is promising.' Raoul glanced towards the window. 'Judging by the sun's shadow there is still an hour or so until dinner, are you tired or would you like to stroll out with me? A little air might do us both good.'

'Yes, thank you, I would like that.'

Cassie carefully pulled the veil over her face and preceded him out of the room. She was still confused by the look she had seen in Raoul's eyes. What would he have said, if they had not been interrupted? Her heart skittered and she decided she would rather not know the answer. Therefore to walk out, where there would be much to see and discuss, would be infinitely preferable to sitting indoors together.

The town was bustling and it was easy for them to mingle amongst the crowds, enjoying the autumn sunshine. They talked very little, but they were comfortable together again and Cassie was glad of it.

'I am sorry the market stalls are empty now,' she said, when at last they turned to make their way back to the inn. 'I would have liked to show you where I purchased the case. I—'

Raoul put his hand over her fingers where they

rested on his sleeve and gave them a squeeze. She was silent immediately. A large group of uniformed riders was approaching.

'Keep walking,' Raoul told her quietly.

Obediently Cassie accompanied him along the street, but she peered out through her thick veil as the riders trotted past them towards the town centre. At their head was a figure she had seen only once before, but would never forget. Valerin.

'Has he come for you?' she murmured.

'It is most likely. He will know that the *Prométhée* is in port and has guessed that I would try to see the captain.'

They walked on unhurriedly, but the last few yards to the inn seemed to go on for ever and it was all Cassie could do not to glance back over her shoulder. When they reached the inn the landlord was looking out for them and told them somewhat severely that dinner was ready and their guest had already arrived.

'I have taken the liberty of setting a table for you in a private room,' their host informed them. 'Monsieur Lagrasse is waiting for you there.'

'Yes, very good,' said Raoul. 'Tell him we will be with him once we have washed the dust of the streets from our hands.' He followed Cassie up the stairs. 'I am very glad we chose to stay here under a different name, it will take Valerin a little longer to find us out. I hope, by the time he does, you will be safely on your way to England.'

It was an added worry, but Cassie tried not to let it show as she made her way into the private parlour. She waited impatiently for the servants to set out their dinner and leave the room and as the door closed behind them she asked Wolfgang for his news. He responded in a bluff, cheerful voice.

'I am very well, I thank you, and business is good.' He gave his head a little shake and said much more quietly, 'It is best not to take chances, even when we are alone. Someone may be listening on the other side of the panelling.' He beckoned to them to lean closer. 'We will meet at the church of St Valery at midnight tomorrow. It is barely five miles from here and there will be a boat standing off the coast, ready to sail for England. The captain is an old friend of mine. I did him a service some years ago and he is pleased now to be able to repay it.'

'I take it we should not ask what trade this ship is engaged in?' murmured Raoul.

Wolfgang shot him a quick grin. 'No, you should not.'

Cassie said eagerly, 'And he will take me to England?'

'Yes. He has agreed to put you ashore near Newhaven. I have already sent word ahead, informing Lady Hune and asking her to send a carriage to meet you there.'

Cassie was doubtful. Her fingers plucked nervously at the tablecloth.

'Do you really think she will do so?' she asked. 'After all the grief I have caused her?'

Wolfgang reached out and squeezed her hand.

'The marchioness was never one to turn her back on an Arrandale in trouble and you are her granddaughter. She loves you.'

'Yes, yes, of course.'

Cassie blinked back her tears and quickly drew her hand away as the door opened. When the servant came in with more dishes she forced herself to chatter about inconsequential things.

Raoul pushed his food about his plate, his appetite gone. It should not matter to him that Cassie and her cousin were getting on so well, but it did. He had to admit that Lady Cassandra had confounded his ideas about the English aristocracy. He had tried to tell himself she was spoiled and selfish, he had tried to hate her, but he could not. The only thing he could hold against her was her race and even that seemed less important now.

'And what of you, Doulevant, how goes your search for your sea captain?'

Arrandale's voice broke into Raoul's reverie and he realised they were alone again.

'I go to see him tonight,' he said shortly.

'No!' Cassie's knife clattered to her plate. 'You must not go near the *Prométhée* while Valerin is in Dieppe.' Without giving Raoul time to reply she turned to her cousin. 'The officer who accused Raoul of being a deserter rode into the town with a party of police officers this afternoon. He is bent on revenge and I am sure he will not allow Raoul to see Captain Belfort.'

'Revenge?' Raoul found himself subjected to an enquiring stare from Arrandale. 'What did you do to him, *monsieur*?'

'I stopped him forcing his unwanted attentions upon my sister.'

'Ah, I see. Well, Cassie is right. If he believes you are here he will surely prevent you meeting up with the captain.'

Raoul shrugged. 'He may try.'

'You must not go,' said Cassie firmly. 'His men will be looking out for you. At least leave it for a day or so. Valerin may begin to doubt you are here and relax his guard. Raoul, *please*, do not go.'

The pleading look in her eyes confirmed what he had seen there earlier, before the servant had interrupted them. She cared for him. He tried to be grateful for that interruption, to pretend the moment had no significance but he could not ignore what his heart was telling him. Yet there could be no future for them. Could there? The first tiny spark of hope flickered, but he quickly crushed it. Their lives were too different. He could never enter her world and he certainly could not allow her to sacrifice her life to stay with him. Even if he became the most successful surgeon in Brussels he could not ask her to give up everything she had known to become his wife. To risk being neglected, like *Maman*. No, his work was his life. There was no room for anything else. He shook his head.

'I cannot wait. The *Prométhée* is only in port to re-victual, then she will be off to sea again and I may not get another chance.'

'It is madness,' said Cassie. 'Valerin will have made sure every *douanier* and police officer in Dieppe has your description, they will stop you as soon as you go near the ship. You had as well walk into a lion's den.'

'She is right,' Arrandale agreed. 'If this Valerin is determined to destroy you he will not hesitate to shoot you on the least pretext.'

'That is a risk I must take. I need my papers if I am to practise my profession.'

'There is one way.' Arrandale was regarding him over the rim of his wineglass. 'Let me go for you.'

'Impossible,' said Raoul immediately. He did not want to be any more beholden to this man. 'I rely upon you to get Lady Cassandra safely out of the country.'

'I shall be back in time to take care of that.' Arrandale gave a careless shrug. 'And if not I will make sure you know all the arrangements before I leave here tonight.' He grinned. 'Trust me, Doulevant, I will see your captain and be back here before dawn with those papers for you.'

'But how?' asked Cassie. 'Is it not equally dangerous for you, Cousin?'

'Not at all. No one could mistake a longshanks

like me for Doulevant. And as you have seen, I can look far less respectable when I try! I shall become a common sailor. Believe me, I can do this. I have spent the past ten years passing myself off as someone I am not. Once more will be no problem.'

Raoul did not want to accept, but every one of his arguments was refuted and in the end he gave in. Arrandale drained his glass and sat back in his chair, grinning.

'Very well, then. You had best tell me all I need to know to convince this Captain Belfort to trust me.'

There was no possibility of sleep. Cassie sat with Raoul before the glowing embers of the fire while the night drifted slowly towards morning. After Wolfgang had left they had played at cards until midnight, but when Raoul suggested she should go to bed Cassie refused.

'*You* will not do so,' she told him. 'You cannot expect me to sleep while my cousin is risking his life.'

Raoul growled at that and looked angry, but Cassie was adamant. She would share his nighttime vigil and although she did not say so it was not only Wolfgang's plight that concerned her. She prayed that her cousin would secure the documents Raoul needed to prove his innocence.

It was some time shortly before dawn and Cassie was dozing in her chair when she was awoken by a faint scratching at the door. Raoul opened it carefully and the landlord slipped into the room.

'*Monsieur—madame*—your *friend* is below. He is waiting for you in the stables, I cannot allow him into the inn at this time of the night. If the servants should see him and talk, we would all be undone. Come, *monsieur*, I will take you down to him.'

Cassie tried to contain her anxiety. Wolfgang had said they could trust the landlord, but she was unsure. By the way Raoul hesitated she knew that he, too, was suspicious, but after a moment he nodded.

'Very well.'

As he moved towards the door she flew across the room to catch his arm. Her cousin might be in trouble, but she could not bear to think of Raoul walking into a trap.

'Raoul!' He looked down at her and all the

words she wanted to say caught in her throat. At last she managed just two. 'Be careful.'

He nodded silently, squeezed her hand and was gone. She closed the door and stood with her ear pressed against the wood, listening to the two men's stealthy footsteps fading into silence. An agonising wait ensued. She walked the floor, imagining the worst, and when Raoul returned to the room only minutes later she threw herself at him. His arms tightened around her for an instant before he gently held her away from him.

'What is this, milady? I thought you had no nerves.'

'I beg your pardon.' She moved away, trying to sound calm. 'I thought there might be trouble. You have seen Wolfgang?'

'Yes, and he has given me a packet of papers from Captain Belfort. The good captain was able to furnish him with a copy of my discharge as well as writing a testimonial for me. He is also sending copies to Paris, with a letter of explanation. Valerin cannot touch me now.'

'And Wolfgang is safe?' She saw immediately that something was wrong and pressed him for a reply.

'There was some shooting as he left the quay

and one bullet found its mark,' said Raoul, adding quickly, 'Arrandale told me it is only a scratch and he managed to get away quite easily. No one followed him here and he is gone now to prepare for tomorrow—no, tonight.'

Cassie closed her eyes for a moment, uttering up a silent prayer of thanks. 'And you have your papers.'

'Yes.' He patted the pocket of his coat. 'Your cousin told me Belfort was only too happy to oblige. It appears Valerin had already called and the captain did not take to him at all. He has sworn he will reveal nothing of my meeting with him.'

'That is good. And Wolfgang's injury, you are sure it is not serious?'

'He would not let me look at it, but assured me it was nothing.'

She nodded, relieved. He was standing temptingly close and she wanted nothing more than to walk back into the comfort of his arms, but it would not do. She turned away from him.

'So,' she said. 'You have your papers and by morning I will be on my way home. Our adventure is nearly over.'

'Yes.'

Her fingers were locked together, pressed against her stomach.

'I shall go back to England and you will join your sister in Brussels.'

'Yes, I will. And I have every hope that I shall be able to take up my profession again.'

Something was in her throat and she closed her eyes, praying the tears would not fall.

'I wish you success, *monsieur*. I am sure you will save many lives, even though I may never know of it. I doubt we shall ever meet again.'

Her words hung in the silence. Raoul wanted to go to her, to take her in his arms and kiss away the unhappiness he heard in her voice, but it must not be. The gap between himself and Lady Cassandra could not be measured in the arm's length that now separated them. She was a lady, daughter of a marquess, no mate for a common surgeon. Even if by some miracle he did not break her heart with his neglect she would be ostracised from the world she knew and over time she would grow to resent that and with resentment would come heartbreak. He must draw on every argument to keep from crossing that boundary and doing something he knew full well they would both regret.

'No,' he said quietly. 'It is unlikely we shall meet again. My country is part of France now, so we are at war. You are my enemy.' With that he picked up a bedroom candle and left her.

Cassie stared at the closed door, his final words echoing round and round in her head. Was this how they were to part, as enemies? She pressed her hands to her temples. It was barely two weeks since she had left Verdun, two weeks since Raoul had galloped away with her. Madness to think that in such a short time she could learn to know a man, but as she paced the floor she felt such a certainty that she knew Raoul Doulevant as well as she knew herself. He was no enemy.

With no servant to help her Cassie had become adept at undressing and she slipped into her nightgown, her thoughts revolving around the future. Raoul had his papers now. It was almost dawn. At midnight she would begin the final leg of her journey back to England and he would go north. All they would have of one another would be memories. She climbed into bed and blew out her candle. Memories. Her hands slid low across her body, trying to cover the aching, yearning void she felt there. She wanted one more memory to take with her.

The little dressing room was chilly. Raoul quickly threw off his clothes and slipped between the sheets. Even as he blew out the candle he knew sleep would not come easily. But he must rest. Once he had seen Cassie safely on her way to England, he would begin the long journey north, to Brussels. He was known there, he still had friends in the city and he doubted Valerin would follow him that far, and even if he did, he could now prove he was no deserter.

He could hear Cassie moving about in the main bedchamber. His blood heated at the very thought of her. He could not help but remember how it felt to hold her in his arms, to kiss her. He stirred restlessly. Just a few more hours to endure the torment of having her so near. He rolled on to his side, just in time to see the thin strip of light beneath the adjoining door disappear. Good. She would sleep now and so would he.

He closed his eyes, only for them to fly wide again a moment later at the sound of the door opening. Cassie was standing in the doorway, her white nightgown pale and wraithlike in the near darkness.

'I could not sleep,' she whispered.

Confound it, she was coming closer and his body was reacting violently.

'You have not tried hard enough,' he growled. 'Go back to your bed, milady.'

'I do not want us to be enemies, Raoul.'

In silence he watched her throw off her nightgown and slide down beside him on the low truckle bed. Her skin was cool as silk against his heated body and he could not resist taking her in his arms. She sighed and he felt her breath soft against his cheek.

'I want you to make love to me, Raoul,' she whispered. 'Show me you are not my enemy.'

He should send her away, but she was pressed against him and it was impossible to deny his arousal.

'Cassie, you should leave, while you can.'

'I do not want to leave you. This may be our last night together and already it is almost over. I want to remember it for ever.' She was nuzzling his neck and the last shreds of his resolve melted into the darkness.

'This is madness,' he muttered, even as he covered her face with kisses and breathed in the sweet, flowery perfume of her hair. 'You should not be here.'

'Love me, Raoul, just once, before we part for ever. I will ask nothing more from you, you have my word.'

She caught his face in her hands and kissed him with such passion that he was lost. A groan caught in his throat and he returned her kiss, deepening it until his senses were soaring. Gasping, he broke off the kiss and he heard her give a little cry as she threw back her head. The slender column of her throat was a pale blur in the darkness and he trailed a line of kisses along its length, flicking his tongue into the hollow at its base. Her sigh was pure pleasure and his mouth moved on to the soft swell of her breasts. While his tongue flickered and circled one hard nub his fingers caressed the other. Her body arched towards him and she cried out as her body trembled and shuddered with ecstasy. Her passion delighted him, but all the time he was holding back, refusing to acknowledge his own needs and desires until he was sure he had sated hers. He continued to caress one pert breast with his mouth, eager to bring her to that point of white-

hot heat again. Her fingers clutched at his hair
and she murmured restlessly, but he did not stop.
He caught her hands and pinned them against the
pillow above her head, holding them fast with one
hand while the other explored the soft curves of
her body and his mouth and tongue played over
her breast. Her hips tilted and he slid his fingers
into her hot, slick core, stroking and circling until
she was bucking and writhing against his hand.

With a cry Cassie arched her back and her body
clenched around the long, gentle fingers that were
causing such havoc inside her. Her hands were
still clamped above her head, but she was not
constrained, she was soaring, flying and falling
all at the same time. At last the pulsing spasms
ceased, every inch of her skin felt alive and sensitive to the lightest touch, but still the tongue
circling her breast and the fingers stroking her
core continued to move. They were feeding a fire
deep inside and she could feel the pressure building again, but this time she wanted more, she
wanted to feel Raoul's skin on hers, to join with
him. She wondered how to tell him. Would he
make her beg for the final union that she longed
for so much? She licked her lips and managed

to whisper his name. It was enough. While his fingers continued their inexorable rhythm he released her hands and stretched his hard, naked body against hers, at the same time seeking her lips with his mouth to join in a long, passionate kiss. He was so aroused she could not suppress a little mewl of delight deep in her throat. She clung to him, her body pliant, inviting, and when he rolled on to her she wrapped her legs around his waist and tilted her hips up to receive him. The invitation could not be resisted any longer. Their coupling was fast and furious, Cassie cried out, digging her nails into his shoulders even as his body tensed for the final push that carried her into oblivion.

They collapsed back against the pillows, gasping. Raoul kept his arms about Cassie, felt the tension leave her and he cradled her until she fell asleep. He rested his head against her hair and closed his eyes, reflecting ruefully that at the end his had not been the performance of an experienced lover. He had been as quick and hasty as a schoolboy, but he had wanted her too much, he had not been able to withstand the urgent demands of his own body. He smiled, planting a kiss on the dusky curls that tickled his chin. That did not matter. They would rest awhile and then he would take her again and show her just how skilled a lover he could be. But first he must sleep.

When Raoul awoke he was alone. Cassie was gone, but the memory of the night lingered, so fierce that he was sure he could smell her perfume. Daylight streamed in through the high little window and he lay very still, wondering if perhaps his longing had got the better of him and he had dreamed the whole thing. He quickly donned his clothes and went to the door. He knocked and hesitated briefly before entering the main bedchamber. It was empty. The door to the anteroom stood open and through it he could see Cassie, fully dressed and standing by the window. As he entered the little room she turned and one look at her face told him it had been no dream. Her cheeks were flushed and her lips had an added colour. She looked like a woman who had been loved.

Cassie had been dreading this moment. It was not that she regretted going to Raoul's bed. She had wanted a memory to take with her to England, but her longing for him had blinded her to the enormity of her actions. She had thrown herself at him, like a wanton. Was that the memory she wanted *him* to take away? She could not help the blood racing to her cheeks and hated the telltale blush. She eyed him warily: his bow was perfectly measured, his voice when he bade her good morning was coolly polite. He had hinted that he was an expert lover and most likely he was disappointed in her performance. She had wanted only to please him and had not intended to lose control so completely once she was in his arms. Just thinking about it made her body hot again. A searing disappointment swept through Cassie. She knew their lovemaking would not change the future, she and Raoul could never be together, but in her desperation to have him love her she had forfeited any respect he might have for her. She drew herself up. It was too late now to worry about that. Perhaps it was best if they ignored what had happened in the night.

She said, with a fair assumption of calm, 'I have sent down for breakfast. It should be here any moment.'

Raoul was regarding her solemnly.

'Milady, I think we should talk—'

Milady! Yesterday he had called her Cassie. If anything was needed to show how far they had moved apart that was it. She felt her panic rising and with relief heard the clatter of crockery outside the door.

'Ah, here is the servant now,' she cried gaily. 'I pray you sit down, sir, and break your fast with me.'

'As you wish.'

Raoul gave an inward shrug and closed his mind to his disappointment. She was an aristo, she had used him for her own amusement in the night, but with the day she had no wish to acknowledge what had happened. The hectic flush on her cheek and the way she avoided his eyes suggested she was ashamed of what she had done. Perhaps she was ashamed of him and he had to admit his performance had not been spectacular. Very well. It was forgotten.

But even as he watched Cassie pouring coffee for them both his body told a different tale. He could not forget those dainty hands clinging to him, the cherry-red lips fastened against his mouth, the slender body that was now clothed in demure linen pressed against his own, flesh upon flesh.

How he got through breakfast he could never afterwards remember. They talked of mundane matters like the weather, the possibility of rain, the excellence of their simple repast, but Raoul's head was bursting with words he dare not utter, lest he should see disdain or revulsion in her face.

As the breakfast dishes were being cleared away the landlord appeared and handed Raoul a note. 'This came for you, *monsieur.*' He dropped his voice. 'I brought it up myself, I would not entrust it to a servant in these uncertain times.'

Raoul pressed a coin into the landlord's hand and put the note in his pocket. He did not take it out again until the last of the servants had departed.

Across the table Cassie was impatient for information.

'What is it?' she asked. 'Is it from Wolfgang?'

'It is.' Raoul scanned the sheet, frowning. 'He says Valerin's men are patrolling the harbour and the guards have been doubled on all the roads out of Dieppe. Word is out that they are looking for a desperate criminal and they should not hesitate to shoot.'

A chill fear spread through Cassie.

'You think that means you?'

'Who else?'

She watched him tear the paper and throw it into the fire, where the pieces flared and burned.

'What will you do?' she asked him.

'Take you to the church of St Valery, as we agreed. Arrandale is sending someone to fetch us and show us a safe way out of the town.' He smiled. 'We will get you to your ship, never fear.'

'I am not worried for myself, Raoul.'

'You are all goodness, milady.' He picked up her hand and kissed it lightly. Cassie wanted to cling, to say something about what had happened in the night, but before she could find the words he had dropped her hand and was turning away, saying cheerfully, 'Now, we have the day to ourselves. Shall we sally forth and see how good Valerin's guards really are?'

'But if they are looking for you—'

'They will be looking for a skulking villain, not a gentleman enjoying the sunshine with his lady wife. Come, put on your bonnet and veil and let us go out.'

* * *

The town was even busier than the previous day. They strolled towards the quay and Cassie discovered that if anything was needed to make her forget the wonder of the night it was the effort of walking past the numerous *gendarmes* as if she had not a care in the world. True, she had her veil to hide her countenance, but she had to work hard not to grip tightly to Raoul's arm every time an officer glanced their way. She was constantly on the alert, looking out for Valerin. Raoul, by contrast, appeared totally at his ease. They made no attempt to approach the *Prométhée*, but even from a distance Cassie could see two men lounging at the foot of the gangplank and whenever anyone approached the ship they immediately stopped and questioned them.

'It would appear Valerin is taking no chances,' Raoul murmured. He gently guided Cassie away from the waterfront. 'I am indebted to your cousin for visiting Captain Belfort in my stead last night. Let us take a look at the other routes we might use to leave this town.'

They spent the day wandering through Dieppe, listening to the gossip in the market and noting the number of *gendarmes* at each of the gates leading out of the town.

By the time they returned to the inn for dinner Cassie was exhausted and it was a struggle to eat the delicious meal put before them.

'There are some hours before we will be leaving here,' remarked Raoul, noting her fatigue. 'We should try to sleep.'

His words immediately brought back memories of being in his bed and she felt herself blushing.

'You think I want a repeat of this morning?' His lip curled. 'I may not be a gentleman in your eyes, milady, but I have my own code of honour.'

'Forgive me, I did not mean—that is—' She stumbled over the words, distressed that he should misunderstand her, but he was already walking away to the dressing room, closing the door firmly between them.

Cassie lay down upon the covers. The comfort she had gained in his arms and the embraces they had shared seemed long ago. It had been a mistake, to throw herself at him in that way. She curled herself into a ball and nestled her cheek on her hand. What a fool she was to give in to a passion she knew only too well would fade and die. Well, she had her memory and perhaps in time it would not matter that she had sacrificed his respect to get it.

'Wake up, milady. We must leave.'

Raoul gently touched Cassie's shoulder. He watched her stretch and roll on to her back as her eyes fluttered open. She gazed up at him, looking so innocent, so vulnerable in the golden glow of the candles that it was as much as he could do not to place a kiss on her lips, parted now in the beginnings of a smile. She would not welcome it, so instead he stepped back and held out his hand to her,

'Madame?'

Perversely she did not approve his polite behaviour. Her face became a mask. She ignored his hand and slid off the bed, shaking out her skirts.

'Very well. Give me five minutes to collect my things.'

'One small bag only,' he reminded her. 'We cannot carry more.'

The landlord's son, Gaston, was waiting for them in the stables.

'You are our guide?' asked Raoul.

The lad grinned.

'Trust me, *monsieur*, it is not the first time I have helped people to leave the town. Let us collect your horses.'

They discovered their mounts ready and waiting for them and Gaston quickly fixed Cassie's small portmanteau to her saddle. When he took Raoul's saddlebags he swore roundly.

'By our lady, this is too heavy. Do you want to kill the horse?'

Raoul thought of the surgeon's box squeezed into the saddle bag.

'It is the tools of my trade,' he said. 'I must have them with me.'

Cassie's spirits lifted a little at his words. Raoul would not be taking the tools if he did not truly value them. It was a small comfort, but comfort nevertheless. As they led the horses out of the stables she noticed that each hoof was wrapped in cloth.

'We must walk them through the town,' explained Gaston. 'Quietly now.'

They followed the boy through a series of dark, deserted alleys, keeping away from the main streets. The dirt from the day's traffic was thick beneath their feet and Cassie was grateful for her serviceable boots. The night was very dark, the moon no more than a thin line in the sky, and Cassie found herself thinking that in a couple more days there would be no moon at all to light their way. A final, noisome alley ended at a large ramshackle building.

'My uncle's house,' Gaston informed them in a whisper. 'You will not see him tonight, but he has a very useful barn.'

He led them towards a wooden outhouse and opened one of the large doors for them to pass inside. When the door closed behind them the darkness was almost complete. Cassie knew a moment of chilling fear before she felt Raoul's hand close around hers, warm and comforting.

Gaston's voice came softly through the blackness.

'Wait here.'

They heard the lad moving around and suddenly a large panel in the back wall slid aside to reveal a small orchard.

'Walk your horses through the trees to the gate on the far side. The track there leads to open ground and a coast path to the church of St Valery.'

'Thank you,' Cassie began, 'We are most grateful—'

'There is more,' the boy interrupted her. 'The open ground is overlooked by the castle and there may be lookouts keeping watch.' He pointed. 'Head *away* from the coast once you are in the open. That will take you over the rise and out of sight of the lookouts in the quickest possible time. Keep going until you reach the crossroads, you cannot mistake it, there is a gibbet swinging there. Only then should you head back towards the coast. Ride like the wind,' he told them. 'There is always a chance that the soldiers will not see you.'

He beckoned to them to follow him into the orchard and helped them remove the cloth from the horses' hoofs before wishing them *bonne chance* and disappearing into the black shadows of the barn. The barn wall slid back in place and they were alone amongst the apple trees. As they began to walk away from the buildings Cassie felt her anxiety growing about their forthcoming ride. She was reluctant to ask Raoul if he was nervous, but he said, as if reading her mind, 'If anything happens and we are separated, you know the directions. Head for the church of St Valery and meet your cousin there.'

'You think there might be trouble?'

She saw his teeth gleam in the darkness.

'When we ride across that open ground under the castle walls we will be perfect targets.'

She tried to smile. 'Let us hope they are very poor shots.'

They continued in silence until they reached the gate, where Raoul turned to Cassie.

'Let me throw you up.'

'No, wait.' She caught his arm. 'Raoul, in case…in case anything should happen, I wanted to thank you. For last night.'

The shadow cast by his hat was too deep for her to see his face, but she had to continue, to let him know what it had meant to her. She forced herself to continue.

'I d-did not know being with a man could be so…satisfying. Thank you.'

She was aware of how woefully inadequate the words were to express her feelings, but at least she had tried. She sighed and was about to turn away when Raoul's hand came out and cupped her cheek. Gently he drew her into his arms, but when their lips met there was nothing gentle about his kiss. It was ruthless, demanding and it left her breathless. As he raised his head she remained within the circle of his arms, her head thrown back against his shoulder, gazing up into his shadowed face. His eyes gleamed with a fiery spark.

'If you thought last night was good, milady, you are woefully mistaken,' he told her. 'Only let us get through this alive and I will show you how good lovemaking can be.'

With something that was halfway between a sob and a laugh Cassie threw her arms about his neck and dragged his head down for another bruising kiss. There would be no more lovemaking, they both knew it, but she was grateful and comforted by his teasing words.

The soft breeze rustled the leaves, a whispered reminder that time was pressing. Reluctantly they broke apart and Raoul threw Cassie up into the saddle. He waited for her to arrange her skirts and checked the girth before he mounted upon his own horse. They trotted along the narrow lane, but drew rein when the track petered out into open ground. Cassie glanced back. Now they were away from the houses she could see the

massive black edifice of the castle looming behind them.

'Remember,' said Raoul, 'we go that way, up
the rise and on to the crossroads. Do not stop.
Whatever happens, you are to make your way
to the church, do you understand me? Now, are
you ready?'

Cassie gathered up the reins and dragged in a
long, steadying breath. They would be riding for
their lives.

'Ready.'

The horses sprang forward and they were away,
galloping across the springy turf. Cassie's cloak
billowed out behind her, the strings tugging at
her neck. Raoul's horse was bigger and stronger, but he remained at Cassie's shoulder and
she realised that Raoul was deliberately holding back, putting himself between her and any
marksman firing from the castle. The thought
made her feel quite sick with fear and she fought
against it, forcing herself to concentrate upon the
ride ahead of them. The ground rose steadily, but
to Cassie's overstretched nerves they seemed to
be getting no closer to the top. Her heart leapt
into her mouth when she heard the first crackle
of shots behind them. She put her head down

and urged the little mare to go faster, chillingly aware that Raoul presented the better target. Another brattle of musketry and she could not bear it, she had to take a quick glance behind. Raoul was still at her shoulder. His cloak, too, was flying out from his shoulders and she prayed any marksman taking aim would be distracted by its fluttering folds.

The shooting continued, but it was fading and she hoped they were out of range now. The mare was tiring, but they had at last crested the ridge and the land began to drop away. As soon as the town and the castle were hidden by the rise Cassie slackened her pace and turned to ask Raoul the question that was uppermost in her mind.

'Are you hurt?'

'Not a whit,' he said. The horses had slowed to a walk and he added, 'Would you care?'

A smile was growing inside Cassie, a mixture of relief that the immediate danger was past, elation from the gallop and the sheer joy of being with Raoul. Now as she turned to look at him that joy blazed forth and she did not care if he saw the raw emotion shining from her countenance.

'You know I would.'

She put out her hand and he took it, smiling at

her in a way that set her heart pounding and it leapt into her throat, sending her senses reeling when she read the message in his eyes. Even in the faint light of the setting moon it was unmistakable. Love.

The shock of revelation took Raoul's breath away. Here, on a lonely, windswept heath in the dead of night, he knew with certain, blinding clarity that he loved Lady Cassandra Witney. For the moment nothing else mattered, only that searing, soaring realisation. His heart was almost bursting with the joy of it and it was with some difficulty that he dragged his thoughts back to the present. The blazing look had died from Cassie's face, replaced by a sadness that sobered him. He was still holding her hand and now he squeezed her fingers.

'Cassie, I—'

She shook her head at him. 'Please, do not say anything Raoul. We must part and nothing has happened to change that.' She was smiling at him and at first he thought her eyes sparkled with starlight, but a second look told him it was tears. When she spoke there was a brittle, self-deprecating lightness to her voice that he had never heard before. 'You need not worry about me. Why, 'tis only two weeks since I buried my husband, so you may believe me when I tell you this type of grand passion never lasts. Let us say no more about it, if you please.' She pulled her hand free. 'Do you think we are safe yet?'

Raoul shook his head to clear his thoughts. She had retreated from him, but there was no time now to think of that or to consider her words. He must concentrate on their present situation. He looked about him.

'The danger is not over yet,' he said. 'They may have sent a party of riders after us, so we must push on. There is the crossroads ahead. We had best make haste to cover as much ground as we can before the moon sets.'

They turned their horses and cantered on towards the coast road. As they passed the crossroads Raoul glanced up at the gibbet with the caged remains of some poor soul swinging gently like a portent of doom.

Chapter Ten

Wolfgang had told them that the little church of St Valery was perched on the limestone cliff overlooking a sheltered cove with a pebble beach. Neither beach, cove nor the sea were visible when Cassie and Raoul reached the rendezvous shortly before midnight. The church was a black shape against the dark blue of the sky, but beyond it everything faded into blackness and only the fresh breeze and a muted roar told them that the sea was very close.

They had been riding hard, mostly in silence, and as they neared the coast Cassie was aware of the knot of unhappiness growing inside her. In a few more hours she would be leaving France, leaving Raoul. They must return to their own very different worlds, there was no other way. Occasionally she would glance across at Raoul and the set look on his face told her he, too, was not looking forward to their parting. He loved her, she had seen it in his face when they had slowed for a moment from their madcap ride, but following quickly on from the joyous realisation came the certainty that it could not last. Memories of the fierce passion she had shared with Gerald still haunted her. At first they could not bear to be parted for even a day, yet how soon their love had died, leaving only bitterness and pain. Just the thought of going through such agony again made Cassie shudder.

They tethered the horses in an old wooden shelter, as they had been instructed. Cassie was relieved to see Wolfgang's big black hunter was already there and she hurried after Raoul as he went softly into the church. Inside a single lantern burned near the altar, illuminating the scene. The lantern was held aloft by an elderly priest who was standing to one side while two men knelt over a prostrate figure. They were all so still that at first Cassandra thought she was looking at a religious sculpture, but at their entry the priest turned and the lantern's light fell more fully on the man lying on the ground. She ran forward with a cry.

'Cousin!' She fell on her knees beside Wolf-gang. 'What has happened here?' she demanded. 'What has occurred?'

The two men rose, touching their caps instinctively and introduced themselves as the captain and first mate of the *Antoinette*.

'He collapsed,' said the captain. 'We met as agreed, came in and then he staggered, complaining of an old wound.'

Raoul gently moved Cassie aside and began to examine the unconscious form.

'It would appear he received more than a scratch at the harbour,' he muttered. 'He has a bullet in his shoulder and he has lost a lot of blood. Why in heaven's name did he not tell me?'

Cassie touched his arm. 'Can you help him, Raoul?'

'Of course. He is strong, but the bullet will need to come out and quickly.'

'No, no, *monsieur*, you cannot tend him here,' cried the priest in alarm. 'If anyone should see the light, if you were to be discovered—'

'Is your house nearby?' said Cassie. 'We could take him there.'

The priest recoiled even more.

'No, no, *madame*. It is not possible. The *doua-*

niers patrol here regularly. They already suspect me of having links with the smugglers. I cannot risk having an injured man in my house.'

'Then it must be here,' she said. 'We cannot let him *die*.'

'There's the vaults,' suggested the captain. 'No one would see the light down there.'

'Very well, let us get him there now,' said Raoul taking charge. 'Monsieur le Curé, if you would be good enough to light the way. Captain, can you and your man help me carry him? Carefully now!' He glanced at Cassie, his voice softening. 'It appears I shall need your instruments sooner than expected.'

She nodded. 'I will fetch them.'

The vaults were cold but clean, as if regularly used. Raoul said nothing but he noticed the marks on the wall, as if something had been stacked against it. Barrels, perhaps. A flat-topped tomb to some ancient dignitary filled the centre of the biggest vault and Raoul helped the two sailors to lay the unconscious form gently on the top. It provided a perfect operating table. Lighted candles from the church were brought down to illuminate the space and the priest hurried away to fetch hot water and sheets to make bandages.

'What can I do to help?' asked Cassie.

The captain stepped up. 'Begging your pardon, *madame*, but 'tis time to leave. The tide will be turning and we need to get back to the ship.'

Raoul had shut his mind to this moment but he could do so no longer. It was as if a band of steel was tightening around his chest.

'He is right, milady. You must go.'

They were on either side of the tomb, facing each other across Arrandale's near-lifeless body.

'I cannot leave my cousin like this.'

Her voice shook and Raoul tried to reassure her.

'I will not let him die, Cassie.'

Her eyes sparkled with unshed tears. 'I cannot leave *you* like this.'

Her words were like a knife, twisting in his gut.

'My dear, there is no choice. The ship must leave with the tide.'

'Then I shall not go.'

The captain cleared his throat.

'Monsieur Lagrasse has been a friend for many years, *madame*. I told him I would see you safely to England. He would not forgive me for breaking my word.'

'Then I am sorry for it, Captain, but Monsieur Lagrasse is my cousin and *I* will not leave him until I know if he will live. I beg your pardon for your wasted journey.'

The captain rubbed his chin. 'We *could* stand off another day, perhaps, and come back tomorrow night.'

One more day. Raoul clutched at it, although he knew the parting would be no easier tomorrow. He looked at Cassie.

'You can help me tonight and nurse him tomorrow, until midnight. Then you must leave. Are we agreed?'

She nodded. 'Yes. Agreed.'

'Very well, then,' said the captain. 'I will return here for you at midnight tomorrow, *madame*. But you must be ready to leave; I put my men and my ship at risk coming back again.'

Cassie hesitated, wondering if Raoul would protest and beg her to stay. At that moment she knew she would willingly tell the captain not to return, she would remain in France and take her chances, but Raoul said nothing and she knew in her heart that it was for the best. She had said as much, had she not?

'Thank you, Captain,' she said at last. 'I will be ready.'

The sailors departed and she turned her thoughts to preparing Wolfgang for the operation. She had a few more precious hours here. She must try to remember everything.

Cassie worked with Raoul to remove Wolfgang's ruined coat and shirt, then she shifted the candles to provide the best light and prepared the instruments for him, making use of everything she had learned at Flagey. All the while the priest ran back and forth, bringing cloths and bandages from his house. He also brought a *réchaud*, or chafing dish, which not only kept the water hot but also provided a little warmth in the chill vault. She was relieved her cousin was oblivious when Raoul began to probe the wound, but by the time the bullet had been removed and the wound dressed, Wolfgang's continued unconsciousness was beginning to worry her.

'His heartbeat is strong,' Raoul reassured her, when she voiced her fears. 'If only he had let me look at his shoulder yesterday, instead of telling me it was nothing.'

She managed a little smile. 'We Arrandales do not like admitting our weaknesses.'

With the priest's help they moved Wolfgang to a bed of straw and blankets on the floor. Cassie wrapped herself in her cloak and sat down beside him, keeping watch. It was an anxious time, but there was little she could do save bathe his face and wait for him to come round.

She had dozed fitfully, waking once in a panic to find that she and Wolfgang were alone with a single lantern to light them. Her relief when Raoul reappeared must have shown on her face for he came over, directly.

'I have been to check on the horses and I helped the *curé* remove all evidence of his involvement. Now if we are discovered he can deny he knew anything about us being here.' He knelt beside the patient and laid a hand on his forehead. 'He is sleeping. There is no fever, that is a mercy, and his body will heal more quickly if he rests. Do not fret, Cassie, he will wake soon.'

He turned down the lamp and came around to sit beside her.

'Is it daylight now?' she asked.

'Yes, a fine day, too.'

She shivered. 'I do not like being here, I feel too...trapped. What if someone should come? What if Valerin should find us?'

'He cannot even be sure we were in Dieppe, unless Captain Belfort gives me away, which I do not believe he will do,' he told her. 'The most likely thing is that the *douaniers* might arrive, searching for contraband, but the *curé* has promised he will keep a look out for us and will send his boy to warn us if he sees anything suspicious. You should sleep while you can.'

'And you?' she asked him.

'I shall try to sleep, too.'

He had put his cloak on the ground beside her and stretched out on it. Cassie lay down, taking care that their bodies did not touch as she turned this way and that, trying to get comfortable. Eventually she heard Raoul give a loud sigh.

'What is the matter?'

'I beg your pardon, I did not want to disturb you, but the ground is so hard...'

He reached out one arm and drew her to him.

'There,' he said, nestling her against his shoulder. 'Is that better?'

'Oh, yes,' she whispered.

Tired as she was she knew she would not sleep, not even with the regular thud of Raoul's heart against her cheek, but she kept very still and silent, knowing he must be exhausted. However, it seemed that Raoul could not sleep, either.

'I cannot help but remember the last time I held you like this,' he murmured. 'Did you mean what you said, that you found our lovemaking…satisfactory?'

She sighed. 'It was more than satisfactory, Raoul. I never knew such happiness before.'

'Then your lovers were sadly lacking.'

'I have had no lovers,' she confessed. 'Only my husband.'

'And he did not give you pleasure?'

'At first perhaps, there was something like it, when I thought we were in love, but I wonder now if he ever truly loved me. I think perhaps he married me for the fortune I would inherit when I reached one-and-twenty.'

Raoul's arm tightened a little. 'He was a scoundrel, then.'

'Yes, but I was a fool. He had no money of his own, you see, but that did not matter to me. When we ran away I took all my jewels to sell.' She exhaled sadly. 'You would indeed think me spoiled if you had seen how many jewels and trinkets my family had lavished upon me. It should have been enough to live comfortably for years, but by the time we were sent to Verdun the money was running low and my husband needed more. Gambling had become an obsession. My grandmother warned me how it would be, she knew he was weak, although thankfully she had no idea just how low he would stoop and I will never tell her. But I should have heeded her.'

'But you need not have stayed,' Raoul pointed out. 'Once you knew what sort of man your husband was, why did you not go home to your family?'

She said simply, 'It would have been very disloyal to leave my husband at such a time. Although, I began to wish I had done so. He…he changed.'

He took her hand and said gently, 'Would you tell me?'

Could she? Cassie let her breath go in a long, low sigh. She knew she would never confess the whole to Grandmama, but lying here beside Raoul, her hand resting safely in his grasp, she thought perhaps it was time to give voice to it all.

'Gerald courted me so charmingly and it seemed such an adventure to elope, and the idea of going to France was so exciting! By the time we reached Paris I realised I did not love him. However, we were married by then and I knew I would have to make the best of it. Everything was well as long as there was money, but when it ran out—' Her hand trembled and Raoul's grasp tightened, giving her the strength to continue. 'Gerald wanted me to ask Grandmama to send more funds, but I refused. I would not ask her to pay for his gambling. He did not like that, it made him angry and we argued constantly. He said I was a burden, that I must pay my way.' She stopped, recalling the revulsion and fear of those last few months. 'He began to bring his friends to our rooms and to hint that I should…entertain them. He wanted to share me with his friends. To—to sell my favours.' She closed her eyes. 'I dreaded those parties and took to retiring to my room and locking the door, but I knew, sooner or later, Gerald would catch me out and make me do what he wanted. If he had not died when he did—' She broke off as the hot tears began to slide over her cheek. 'And now I feel so guilty,

because when they came to tell me I was a widow
I felt nothing but *relief*!'

Raoul had listened with growing anger to her
story, but now he could be silent no longer.

'Ah, my love.' The words were forced from him
and he turned, gathering her into his arms so she
might cry her heart out against his chest. When at
last the wrenching sobs died away he murmured
against her hair, 'You must not blame yourself.
The man was a brute to treat you in such a way.'

'B-but he was my husband, and he always
maintained he l-loved me.'

His arms tightened. 'That was not love, *chérie*.
You are well rid of such a monster.'

'He—he said I was cold,' she whispered. 'He
said I have no heart.'

'I can assure you that is not true.' He shifted
his position, cupping her face with one hand and
gazing into her eyes. 'Forget this man, *ma chère*.
He is not worth a moment's regret.' He dropped
a light kiss on her eyelids and another on her
mouth, where he tasted the salt of her tears.

'Raoul, I—'

'Hush now.' He settled her more comfortably
in his arms again. 'It is time to rest. Or are you
afraid of your dreams?'

She gave a sigh of contentment.

'Not now. Not when I am with you.'

Raoul closed his eyes, satisfied.

'Thank you,' she murmured, so softly he could barely hear her. 'Thank you for listening.'

He held her close, overwhelmed by the urge to protect the dainty, fragile creature beside him. Once she was in the care of her family it would be a different matter, but he hated the thought of her being alone and defenceless, even for a single day.

Arrandale's low groans woke Raoul. He gently disengaged himself from Cassie's sleeping form and went to tend his patient.

'Where the devil am I?'

'In the vaults of the church,' murmured Raoul, making a swift examination of the wound. 'I have removed the bullet from your shoulder. You fool, why did you not tell me about this the other night?'

'I was anxious to be on my way.' Arrandale drew in a sharp, hissing breath as Raoul touched a sore spot. 'I did not want to bring the officers to your door.' He raised his head to peer at his shoulder. 'How is it now?'

'The bleeding has stopped. It will heal, given time.'

'Good.' He sank back, closing his eyes again. 'Speaking of time, did Cassie get away?'

'No.'

'What!'

'She stayed to help you.'

Arrandale followed Raoul's glance towards Cassie's sleeping form and he muttered angrily under his breath.

'Your captain friend says he will return for her tonight,' said Raoul .

'Aye, he's a good man—' Arrandale broke off as Cassie stirred and sat up.

'Wolfgang. You are awake. How do you feel now?'

'I'll live. But what the devil do you mean by staying here?'

'I wanted to help,' she said simply.

'Confound it, Cousin, you have jeopardised your chances of getting to England. What if the weather is bad, tonight? What if—'

'Hush,' said Cassie, putting a hand on his good shoulder. 'Do not concern yourself, Cousin. Your captain has promised to return, I trust that he will.' She added shyly, 'Will you not change your mind and come back to England with me?'

'You know I cannot do that, Cassie. I am a wanted man.'

She shook her head.

'Grandmama has never believed it, I am sure she will help you.'

'Nay, Cousin, it will need more than that to save me from the gallows.'

Raoul listened in silence to their exchange. He was sure now that Cassie was not in love with her cousin, but he could not help a prickle of jealousy at her concern for Arrandale's welfare. He said curtly, 'You should go with your cousin, sir. She should not be travelling alone.'

'If that's the case, then you should go with her, Doulevant.'

'Impossible,' said Cassie immediately. 'Raoul is going back to Brussels to join his family and take up his work again.'

'He could work in England, now he has his papers,' Arrandale pointed out. 'If anything, my friend, you would be safer there than here, for if Valerin finds you before you reach Brussels he will not let you live long enough to prove your innocence.'

Raoul said nothing. Arrandale was right. The journey to Brussels was fraught with danger and he might even bring more trouble to Margot. But to go to England, to be so close to Cassandra, knowing he could never have her—

A sudden noise at the door had Raoul reaching for his pistol, but it was the *curé*'s servant carrying a heavy pot from which emanated a most appetising aroma.

'*Mon père* has sent you dinner, *madame*, *messieurs*. And he says to tell you it is growing dark now.'

'A thousand thanks to him for his goodness,' said Raoul, going forward to relieve the man of his burden.

By the time they had finished their simple meal of stew and bread Raoul noted that Arrandale was looking much better and was even talking about getting up.

'You should rest a little longer,' Cassie advised him. 'You are very weak.'

'Nonsense, I am as strong as an ox.' He struggled to his feet, wincing a little. 'Although an ox has four legs, which would help considerably.' He looked about him. 'Where is my shirt?'

'The priest took it away to burn it, along with your coat. They were both beyond repair.' For the first time that day Raoul grinned. 'He has left you some clothes from the poor box.'

'What? They are mere rags!' Arrandale looked with distaste at the old shirt and badly patched jerkin that Raoul was holding up. 'Well, help me into the shirt, if you please, it will at least keep off the damp chill of this place.'

It was soon done and despite Arrandale's protests Raoul fashioned him a sling from the remains of the sheet they had been tearing up for bandages.

'You will need to keep that arm still and rest the shoulder.' He took out his watch. 'It is nearly midnight. Your sailor friends should be here soon.'

'Aye. I will see my cousin safely away before I set off. Can I ask you to saddle the horses for me, Doulevant? I doubt I will be able to do that tonight and we shall have to take Cassie's mount away with us.'

'Of course,' said Raoul absently. 'I will slip out and see to it shortly.'

'Where will you go?' asked Cassie.

'It is best that you do not know that.' Arrandale

flicked her cheek with a careless finger. 'Trust me, I shall survive.'

'Perhaps Raoul will ride with you,' she suggested. 'At least for a few miles.'

'No.' Raoul had at last come to a decision.

You are a fool, man. You are only delaying the inevitable parting.

Perhaps he was a fool, but he could not bear to think of sending Cassie off alone into the night, with only strangers for company.

'If you will not go with your cousin to England, Arrandale, then I must go.'

'That is excellent news, my friend, and what I expected. You will find I have already paid for your passage, and sent instructions to the inn at Newhaven to expect you.'

Raoul's brow darkened and he scowled at Arrandale.

'You *knew* I would go?'

'I thought it very likely and made my plans accordingly.'

The tall Englishman was grinning broadly, but it was the soft shine in Cassie's eyes that alarmed Raoul. He should not be raising false hopes in her.

'It will be safer for me to quit France for a

while. I will not risk leading Valerin to my sister.'
He looked at Cassie and said meaningfully, 'This
changes nothing between us, milady. I will stay
with you only until you are safe in your grandmother's care.'

Cassie dropped her gaze.

'Of course,' she said quietly. 'I understand.'

She would have Raoul's company for another
few days and she could not help herself, she was
glad of it. She was not ready yet to say goodbye.

At a few minutes before midnight Cassie followed the men up the stairs, reaching the nave
of the church just as the *Antoinette*'s captain and
first mate entered. Wolfgang cut short their ex-
pressions of delight at seeing him on his feet
again.

'Never mind that, my friends. You have two
passengers tonight. Make haste to get them away.'

He broke off as the church door was flung
open. The priest's servant stood in the doorway.

'*Messieurs*, you must leave, now. This instant.
There are riders approaching!'

'Are they customs men?' demanded the captain.

The servant bent over his knees, gasping for
breath. 'No, no, they are not *douaniers*. They

are in uniform and look more like soldiers, or *gendarmes*. It is difficult to see in the dark. There are a dozen of them at least.'

'Valerin,' muttered Raoul, drawing his pistol. 'Captain, take milady and get her down to the beach. Arrandale and I will cover your escape—'

'No,' gasped Cassie.

Wolfgang caught Raoul's arm. 'Do not be foolish man, what do you expect us to do, fight them all?'

'Yes, or die in the attempt.'

Wolfgang put his hand on Raoul's shoulder, saying urgently, 'If we stay here we are all lost. Get Cassie away while you can, man. The path to the beach is perilous and she will need your help. I cannot manage it in my present condition, but I *can* ride. I am well acquainted with this coast, I'll take the horses and draw them off.'

'Quickly, quickly,' cried the servant, his voice rising with panic. 'They will be here any moment!'

Cassie held her breath. Time seemed to stand still as she waited in an agony of suspense for Raoul's answer.

'Very well,' he said at last. 'Take my pistol.'

'Aye, your hat and jacket as well,' said Wolfgang. 'If I hunch low in the saddle it should be enough to fool them that I am the man they want.'

Hastily Raoul exchanged his riding jacket for the worn leather jerkin. Wolfgang fixed the hat on his head.

'Goodbye, Doulevant. I rely on you to get my cousin safely to her grandmother.' He gripped Raoul's hand for a moment, then turned to Cassie.

She hugged him fiercely, being careful to avoid his injured shoulder.

'Goodbye, Cousin.' He held her close with his one good hand. 'Give my daughter a kiss from me.' He turned and grabbed the servant by the arm. 'Come along, my man, you can help me with the horses. Thank heaven Doulevant has already saddled them.'

He went off, dragging the protesting servant with him, while Cassie and Raoul followed the sailors out of a side door and through the grave-yard to the cove path.

At the cliff edge Raoul stopped, a stifled exclamation escaping him.

'My papers,' he muttered. 'Arrandale has them, they are still in my coat pocket.'

Cassie gave him a little push.

'Go after him, quickly,' she urged him. 'We will wait for you. Captain—'

The sounds of shouts and hoofbeats filled the night as Wolfgang rode out of the stable, leading the two spare horses.

'Too late,' said Raoul.

The captain gave a little grunt of satisfaction.

'It's so dark now the *gendarmes* might well think you are all riding away. Yes, look, there they go, after him.' He turned back to Raoul, saying urgently, '*Monsieur*, we must go.'

Raoul took Cassie's hand. 'Come on.'

They stepped on to the path. It dropped steeply away and the church was soon lost to sight. The descent was steep and they went slowly, picking their way in the darkness. Cassie held her cloak tightly about her with one hand, the other clinging to Raoul's fingers. They had not gone far when a shot sounded, quickly carried away by the breeze. They all stopped as several more followed, a distant sharp crackle of sound in the night.

'It looks like Lagrasse has got their attention,' muttered the captain.

Cassie said nothing, she felt sick with worry for her cousin, but there was nothing to be done now, except go on. By the time they reached the beach her whole body was aching from the strain of negotiating the steep path in near darkness. Every step was fraught with danger on the rocky, uneven path and without Raoul's firm clasp on her hand Cassie thought her legs might seize up altogether. On the beach they were sheltered a little from the stiff breeze, small waves lapped softly against the shore, and Cassie could just make out a small rowing boat pulled up out of the water, little more than a blacker shape against the darkness. As they scrunched across the pebbles several shadowy figures loomed up and pushed the boat back into the waves.

Without ceremony Raoul lifted Cassie into his arms and waded out to place her in the boat. Everyone else jumped aboard, she heard the scrape and splash of the oars, and they were moving swiftly away from the shore. A dark shape loomed up ahead of them and she guessed they had reached the *Antoinette*. She suffered in silence the indignity of being thrown over Raoul's shoulder as he climbed aboard and she sat with him in a sheltered spot on deck while the crew raced around them, weighing anchor and setting the sails.

'As long as we avoid the British warships we should make good time,' said the captain, coming up. 'We have a fair wind and the tides are in our favour. I expect to be putting you ashore near Newhaven early tomorrow evening.' He grinned. 'The gods are smiling on us; the weather is unusually good for this time of the year. You should enjoy an easy crossing.'

'Thank you, Captain.' Cassie put up her hand to smother a yawn.

'We have very few luxuries aboard this vessel,' he said, 'but there is one cabin below, if you would like to rest there?'

'Yes, indeed,' said Cassie. 'We are both in need of sleep.'

She reached for Raoul's hand, but he moved away from her.

'I will sleep on deck. Milady can have the cabin. Perhaps, Captain, you would show her the way?'

There it was again, that note of steel in Raoul's voice that told her he would not be moved. Silently she followed the captain down the ladder-like steps to the lower deck and resigned herself to a long, lonely night.

Chapter Eleven

England. Enemy territory. Raoul stood beside Cassie on the shingle beach as the rowing boat that had brought them to this shore slowly drew away. The moon was just rising and the *Antoinette* was no more than a shadow against the starry sky. A chill wind was blowing, cutting through the worn leather jerkin and making him shiver.

'We will be warmer if we walk,' said Cassie. 'And we must speak English now.'

'As you wish,' he replied in her own language. 'I do not speak it quite like a native, but enough to get by, I think.'

'You speak it very well, Raoul.'

They set off along the beach, heading for the distant lights that the captain had told them were from the port of Newhaven.

Raoul reached for her hand.

'You are tired, milady?'

'No.'

'Then what is it, why are you so quiet?'

'I am…sorry that this will soon be over.'

He laughed, deliberately misunderstanding. 'I am not. I cannot wait to get into clean clothes and a real bed!'

'Not that. Our time together.'

'Ah.' The lead weight that had settled in his gut that morning grew heavier. Perhaps it was better to speak the truth now and get it over with. He said gravely, 'After all that has occurred I should ask your *grandmère* for your hand in marriage, but she would not allow it. I have nothing to offer you, *ma chère*.'

'I do not expect you to marry me,' she replied quietly. 'I am a widow, not some innocent virgin that you have deflowered.' She fell silent. Then, 'What will happen to you, Raoul?'

'It is most likely that I shall be locked up.'

'But you are not French. You are not an enemy!'

'Who will believe that, when I have no papers to prove it? War, she is cruel, my love.' He tightened his grip on the leather-bound case in his hand. 'But look, I have my surgeon's tools now.

It is possible I shall be allowed to tend the other prisoners of war.'

'What if…?' She hesitated. 'What if I am with child?

He hesitated, torn between desperately wanting her to be carrying his baby and fear for a child he could not protect.

Misunderstanding his silence, she hurried on. 'You need not worry if that is the case. I am sure Grandmama will take care of matters.'

'I am sure she will,' he answered bitterly.

It took them an hour to reach Newhaven and they soon found the Bridge Inn, a busy hostelry where they discovered that they were expected. The landlord greeted them in person, bowing low.

'Good evening, my lady, sir. Your rooms are ready. I hope you will find everything is in order. Pray send word when you wish dinner to be sent up.'

They were escorted to an impressive suite of rooms on the first floor. Servants were waiting to show them to their separate bedchambers. Cassie followed the maid into a large chamber with a cheerful fire blazing in the hearth, hot water in a jug on the washstand and a clean set of clothes spread out on the bed. There was even a truckle bed made up in the corner for the maid, a tacit reminder to Cassie that the proprieties were to be observed now she was back in England.

When she emerged some time later she found Raoul waiting for her in the sitting room. He was attired in riding jacket, buckskins and top boots, the epitome of English country fashions, and with his sleek, dark hair, near black eyes and lean cheeks freshly shaved, he looked every inch a gentleman.

He turned to her and bowed.

'Your cousin, he surpasses himself with the arrangements,' he said, putting a hand to his snowy neckcloth. 'The coat, it is a little tight across the shoulder, but overall it looks very well, I think?'

He looked so handsome that Cassie felt almost sick with longing for him, but she hid it behind an even brighter smile.

'From the maid's chatter I believe he sent a full purse here with instructions for our every comfort. I have no idea where he came by so much money.'

'I think it is best not to enquire too closely into the affairs of your cousin,' said Raoul.

'Very true. I do hope he managed to get away.' Her smiled faltered, but after a brief pause she recovered, saying brightly, 'And this gown suits me very well, does it not?' She glanced down with satisfaction at her walking dress of pale-pink muslin over white cambric. 'In truth, it was too big at first, but with a little judicious pinning and tucking it now fits me perfectly. There are gloves, too, and a pelisse and bonnet for me to wear, when we go out.'

'Your cousin has truly thought of everything,' remarked Raoul. 'The landlord tells me the— what did he call it?—the *shot* here is paid until Lady Hune's coach arrives to fetch you, however long that may be.'

She looked up quickly. 'To fetch *me*? You will come with me to meet Grandmama, Raoul, will you not?'

The look he gave her tore at her heart.

'We must part sometime, milady.'

'Not yet,' she begged him. 'Please, Raoul, do not leave me until you have met the marchioness. She will be able to help you, I know she will.'

He inclined his head and said politely, 'As you wish. Shall I send down for dinner?'

Two days later Lady Hune's travelling chaise arrived to carry them to Chantreys.

'At least it is closer than Bath,' Cassie remarked as they set off. 'We should be no more than three nights on the road.'

Raoul said nothing, but kept his eyes fixed on the window as the houses dwindled and they rattled through the open countryside. How was he to survive another three nights, knowing Cassie was so close, but that he could not hold her? It must be done. They were both agreed there could be no future for them, but it cut him to the heart to see Cassie trying to be so brave. They were perfectly civil to one another, but occasionally he would look up to find her watching him, such sorrow in her eyes that he could hardly bear it.

Yet bear it he must. His mother had died as much of a broken heart as the growth in her body, pining for the man she loved. Raoul knew he was his father's son, he was committed to his work and he would not risk making the same mistake, of neglecting those he loved until it was too late. It was better that he left Cassie now, while she was young enough to find another man to love her, to cherish her. One who could give her the life she deserved, the life of a lady.

By the time they reached Chantreys, Raoul was exhausted. He and Cassie had maintained the pretence of being nothing more than acquaintances, retiring each night to their separate beds, but at one of the inns the walls were so thin that he had caught the sound of muffled sobs coming from her room. And in the morning she was looking so wan and hollow-eyed only his strong conviction that it was for the best kept him from taking her in his arms and kissing away her sadness.

As the chaise bowled up the drive he studied the house. It was a fine building, but it was not the grand palace he had been expecting. Cassandra had informed him that Chantreys was not the Earl of Davenport's principal seat, yet it was where he and his family had chosen to make their home. A house suitable for a gentleman, certainly, but with none of the magnificence Raoul thought essential for a peer of the realm. He wondered if he would ever understand the English.

When they alighted at the door they were met by the butler, Fingle, who informed them that the dowager marchioness was resting and would see them later. He then passed Lady Cassandra over to the care of the housekeeper and personally escorted Raoul upstairs to his bedchamber. The significance of this gesture was not lost on Raoul, who had half-expected to be treated as a hired courier and lodged in the servants' quarters. When a footman came in carrying a supply of fresh linen for him and asking if he would like hot water brought up for a bath, Raoul accepted readily. He was anxious to wash away the dirt of the road and refresh himself before his meeting with Lady Hune.

'There you are, my lady, this is your room.' The motherly housekeeper showed Cassie into a light, airy bedchamber overlooking the gardens. 'The fire has been burning all morning so 'tis nice and warm in here. Her ladyship's maid said she would come in when you are ready to dress, but perhaps you would like to rest, first?'

'Thank you, Mrs Wallace, I think I would like to lie down for a while. Tell Duffy I will send for her when I am ready.'

The housekeeper had been chattering non-stop and Cassie felt the beginning of a headache nagging at her temples. As soon as the woman left her she lay down on the bed and closed her eyes. Unhappiness weighed upon her like a heavy cloak. She felt so *tired*. Her body ached with longing for Raoul, with the effort of keeping that longing hidden from him. They had agreed that they must part and she was determined not to make it more difficult for him than necessary.

She heard a soft knock at the door and sat up. Had she slept without knowing it? Another knock followed and the door opened. A golden head appeared and a pretty, musical voice spoke.

'Ah, you are not asleep, Lady Cassandra. Good. May I come in?' Hardly waiting for Cassie's assent the young lady slipped into the room. 'I wanted to introduce myself to you, my lady. I am Ellen Tatham.'

'Ah yes. Of course.' Reluctantly Cassie slid off the bed. 'Will you not sit down, Miss Tatham?'

When they were sitting down on either side of the fireplace, Miss Tatham continued.

'Pray, do call me Ellen. Your grandmother has been kind enough to take me under her wing for my come-out. She has looked after me in London for most of the Season, but I wanted to assure you that I have not in any way usurped your place in her affections, Lady Cassandra. She has been so worried for you, but I hope I have helped her to bear it.'

'Thank you,' said Cassie politely. 'I am sure you have helped to divert her mind. But you must be sorry to have left London.'

'Not a bit of it,' Ellen reassured her. 'I had had quite enough of balls and parties. I was delighted to come here while Alex and Diana are away. And you must not think I allow Lady Hune to tire herself out running after the children. They spend most of their day with Nurse and myself.'

'Ah, yes, the children. I have not seen them for some years. How are they?'

'Quite delightful, and they are growing so fast, Florence especially. She celebrated her ninth birthday recently and is going to be very tall, I think.'

'Like her father,' murmured Cassie.

'I beg your pardon?'

'Oh, nothing. When do you expect Lord and Lady Davenport to return?'

'Lady Hune had a letter from them only today: they are even now on their way back to Chantreys and should be with us in two weeks. As soon as they return I shall rejoin my stepmama and the marchioness plans to take you to Bath with her.' Miss Tatham rearranged the folds of her white-muslin skirts. 'And the gentleman who escorted you to England—Monsieur Doulevant, is it not? Will he accompany you to Bath?'

'Oh, no, I would not think so.' Cassie hoped she sounded indifferent. 'Although I shall ask Grandmama to give him her patronage. He will require help, I think, if he is to avoid being taken as a prisoner of war. Not that he is French,' she hurried on. 'He is from the Southern Netherlands, which was under Austrian rule for a long time. Raoul deeply resents Bonaparte claiming his country as part of France.'

She felt the heat in her cheeks when she realised she had used Raoul's name, but her visitor feigned not to notice and she was grateful for that.

'And is he from a noble family?'

Cassie could not prevent a heartbeat's hesitation before she responded.

'No. He is a surgeon. A very skilled surgeon.'

'Ah. I see.'

Cassie doubted it, but she said nothing more.

'I had best go.' Miss Tatham rose gracefully. 'I am so pleased to have met you, Lady Cassandra.'

'Please, call me Cassie.'

'Very well, then, Cassie. We will meet again at dinner, when you shall introduce me to your very skilled surgeon.'

'Of course. Tell me, which room is Lady Hune occupying?'

'Her door is the last one on this passage and she may well be awake by now.' Ellen twinkled at her. 'You need not be afraid to go and see— her terrifying dresser will soon send you about your business if she is asleep!'

With that she whisked herself out of the room and Cassie was alone again, but she no longer wished to lie down. Quickly she washed her face and hands and went off to find her grandmother.

Duffy opened the door to her and Cassie was well enough acquainted with her grandmother's dresser to recognise the relief and affection behind the woman's brusque manner.

'Oh, so you've come back to us, have you, my lady? And about time, too, if you forgive my saying so.'

She was interrupted by an imperious voice.

'Who is it, Duffy? Is it Cassandra? Let her come in.'

The dresser stepped back and Cassie entered the room. Lady Hune was sitting in a wing chair by the window, regally attired in her customary black with white-lace ruffles at her neck and wrists.

'Yes, Grandmama, I am here.'

'Then come closer, where I can see you.'

Cassie took a few slow, hesitant steps forward, but then the marchioness put out her hands and with a sob Cassie threw herself on her knees before her chair and buried her face in her skirts. Her grandmother gently stroked her curls.

'Well, my love, what is the matter this time?'

Cassie gave a watery chuckle.

'You used to say that to me whenever I was in a scrape.'

'And is that not the case now?'

'No. *Yes!* Oh, Grandmama, I am so unhappy!'

Between gulping sobs and fresh tears Cassie told the marchioness what had happened since she had left Bath a year ago. The narrative was not quite complete; she spoke of Gerald's gambling, but not his weakness for women, nor did she describe those final few months in Verdun when money was short and Gerald's mood had changed. When it came to explaining her meeting with Raoul she said merely that he had been her escort. She did not mention the heavenly night she had spent in his arms, but Lady Hune was not deceived.

'This Monsieur Doulevant...' Lady Sophia handed Cassie a fresh handkerchief. 'You think you love him?'

'Yes.'

'You thought yourself in love with Witney.'

Cassie wiped her eyes.

'He is nothing like Gerald, Grandmama. Raoul is good and generous and so very kind. If you could have seen how he toiled to save those poor souls at Flagey! I love him so much.'

'And what is his family?'

'His father was a doctor in Brussels—'

'He is not French, then?'

'No, ma'am. His family are from the Netherlands.'

'Well, that's a mercy. I lost too many friends during the Terror to feel any warmth towards the French.'

Cassie gave a little huff of impatience.

'All this makes little difference, ma'am, since we are not to be married. We are both agreed on that.' Cassie tried to smile but it went sadly awry. 'We have known each other for such a short time, it is inconceivable that we can have formed a lasting attachment.'

If Cassie expected her grandmother to contradict her she was disappointed. Lady Hune gave a loud sigh of relief.

'Well, I am glad you both have the sense to see that.'

'That is what I have been trying to tell myself.' Cassie's head bowed and she said in a small voice, 'But he loves me, Grandmama.'

'Has he said as much?'

Cassie paused. There had been endearments, but no outright declaration.

'Not exactly.'

'Then I will give him credit for that, too.'

'He is a good man, an honourable man, Grandmama. He risked his life to help me, but he will not marry me, even though he has no money and he knows I shall come of age in a few months and will then have control of my own fortune. I will have enough money to keep us both.'

'I like him better and better!'

'Pray, ma'am, do not jest with me.'

'I have never been more serious, my love. Even if he were not from a country that is now annexed by France and therefore our enemy, to marry a man who is so far outside your sphere, a man with no money, no expectations—it would be a disaster. You would hate one another within the year.'

Cassie's head dropped even lower. She had tried to tell herself the very same thing. She wiped her eyes. She must try to forget her own unhappiness and think of Raoul.

'I want you to help him, Grandmama. I cannot bear the thought of his being locked away as a prisoner of war.'

'What do you expect me to do, child?'

'I do not think he will accept money, he is too proud for that. But perhaps you could use your influence to keep him from prison and perhaps to find him a position. Or help him to return to Brussels.' Cassie looked down at clasped hands. 'I quite see that we cannot marry, I am resigned to that, but I owe him a great debt, Grandmama.'

Lady Hune pursed her lips, considering. At last she nodded.

'I shall talk to Monsieur Doulevant at dinner and I will see what I can do for him.'

'Thank you, ma'am.'

Cassie leaned against the marchioness's skirts again and felt her grandmother's frail fingers smoothing her hair. It did not take away the ache that gnawed at her, but it was comforting.

'Let us move on to other matters,' said Lady Hune at last. 'You saw my great-nephew, Wolfgang Arrandale? I am glad my letters reached him.'

'So, too, am I,' said Cassie. 'We could not have escaped without his help, only I fear it might have cost him dear.' She raised her head and directed an anxious look at the marchioness. 'I have no idea if he is safe. We were pursued by French officers and he rode off to draw them away. We heard shots—'

'Worrying about him will do no good,' said Lady Hune prosaically. 'Wolfgang Arrandale has lived on his wits for the past nine years, we can only hope he has survived.'

'The thing is,' said Cassie, frowning, 'he did not know he had a daughter, for he has avoided all contact with his family until now. He told me to give her a kiss from him.' She looked up.

'Should we tell Florence, Grandmama? It would be heartbreaking to raise false hopes in such a little girl.'

'Then let us wait until we have word that he is safe,' said Lady Hune. 'Wolfgang was always a wild one, but I am grateful to him for helping to send you back to me.' She looked at Cassie, her eyes suspiciously bright, before saying in her usual sharp tone, 'But enough of this. It will soon be time for dinner and you must change, my dear. There was no time to send for your clothes from Bath—oh, yes, Cassandra, I have kept everything, just as it was when you eloped—but my protégée has looked out a couple of her dresses for you and Duffy will bring them to your room. Ellen is about your size, as you will see when you will meet her at dinner.'

'I have already done so, ma'am. She came to my room a little while ago. I thought her very charming.'

'She is a baggage,' said Lady Hune, not mincing her words. 'She reminds me very much of you, which must be why I like her so much.'

Cassie picked up one of the gnarled hands and kissed the beringed fingers. She said penitently.

'I am very sorry to have caused you so much trouble, Grandmama.'

'Yes, yes, well, be off with you now, or we shall both of us be late for dinner! And dry your eyes, Cassandra. An Arrandale does not show a woe-begone face to the world!'

Raoul received the summons to join the Dowager Marchioness of Hune and he made his way immediately to the drawing room. He passed a large mirror in the hall and it took a conscious effort not to stop before it and make a few final adjustments to his neckcloth. He was no lackey to fawn and cower before an English aristocrat. He entered the room to find the marchioness alone and sitting in a chair beside the fire. Her back was ramrod straight and her black dress was as severe as her countenance. She had an abundance of silver hair crowned by a cap of fine Mechlin lace and she held a black cane in one hand while the other rested on the arm of the chair, a king's ransom in jewels sparkling on her fingers. A matriarch, if ever he had seen one! She regarded him as he approached, her blue eyes sharp and assessing.

'I must thank you, Monsieur Doulevant, for escorting my granddaughter safely to England.'

He made his bow. 'It was a pleasure, Lady Hune.'

'My nephew Arrandale said in his message to me that you are a doctor.'

'No, ma'am. I am a surgeon.'

'Ah. That makes all the difference.'

'I am aware.' His pulled himself up a little straighter. 'In France, my lady, surgeons are beginning to receive the recognition they deserve.'

Those sharp eyes snapped at him.

'But we are in England, *monsieur*, and presently at war with France.'

Raoul held his tongue. It would do no good to antagonise the marchioness. He would be gone soon enough. He did not speak again until he was once more in control of his temper.

'Lady Hune, I do not know how much your granddaughter has told you of our journey together.'

'Enough.'

His neckcloth felt too tight, but he resisted the temptation to run a finger around it.

'I am aware, ma'am, in such circumstances, a gentleman should make an offer of marriage to Lady Cassandra, but as you say so truly, we are in England now and I am not regarded as a gentleman here. I believe you would think me presumptuous to aspire to the hand of your granddaughter.'

'You are correct, *monsieur*, I would. But it is not only the disparity in your birth that makes it an ineligible match. There is another, and to my mind an even more important, reason you should not offer for her.' Those sharp old eyes regarded him steadily. 'I do not believe you could make Cassandra happy. If she married you, society would turn its back on her. Would you really wish to remove her from the comfort of her family and friends, from the life she has known since birth?'

'No, ma'am, I would not.'

'We are agreed, then.'

He met her gaze.

'And if there should be…consequences of the time we spent together?'

'Let us speak plainly, Monsieur Doulevant. If my granddaughter should be carrying a child I shall deal with it. You need not fear that Cassandra will be cast penniless into the world, after all she is only recently widowed and might pass the child off as her late husband's.'

The idea filled Raoul with abhorrence and he said quickly, 'I do not believe she would do that.'

'Then she will be confined in the country until after the birth. There would be some talk, but it would pass.' She added with a hint of bitterness, 'The Arrandales are no strangers to scandal.'

'And the child?'

'Would be put with a good family.' The dowager marchioness regarded him for a moment and said in a softer tone, 'Do not worry, *monsieur*, whatever her decision I shall ensure that neither Cassandra nor her child shall want for anything. But all this is conjecture. There may be no baby—'

The old lady broke off as the door opened and Cassandra came in, looking very demure in a gown of pale-blue muslin, her dusky curls confined by a matching ribbon. She was looking down, her thick dark lashes accentuating her pale cheeks, and Raoul's heart contracted painfully. He wanted to take her in his arms, promise her that all would be well, but he could not. At this moment he could not promise her anything at all.

Cassandra looked quickly from the marchioness to Raoul, trying to read their faces, but both were inscrutable. She longed to ask Grandmama if she had agreed to help Raoul, but Lady Hune was already saying something innocuous about the weather. Raoul responded politely and Cassie joined in the conversation. She knew her grandmother too well to press her. She must bide her time and hope that over the course of the evening Raoul would make a good impression with the marchioness.

Miss Tatham's arrival lightened the mood slightly. She announced cheerfully that she and Cassie were now good friends and she greeted Raoul with unfeigned friendliness. She even cajoled Lady Hune into a smile within minutes of entering the room. Nevertheless dinner was a strained affair. Conversation was stilted. Raoul no longer supported the French, but his dislike of the aristocracy had not waned and Cassandra was careful to avoid any topics that were likely to put him at odds with her grandmother. The effort was quite exhausting and frustrating, too, for at the end of dinner Lady Hune announced that after such a long day the ladies would go directly to bed.

* * *

The following morning Cassie rose early. Her hope was to find Lady Hune alone and ask her what she thought of Monsieur Doulevant, but when she glanced out of the window and saw Raoul walking alone in the gardens, she quickly grabbed her shawl and ran downstairs to join him.

When he saw her on the path he stopped, suddenly feeling shy.

'May I walk with you, Raoul?'

He inclined his head and she fell into step beside him. He did not offer her his arm, and she kept both hands firmly holding her shawl about her shoulders.

'The sun is very pleasant,' she said, desperate for something to say, 'but it is has grown much colder these last few days.'

'Yes.'

His brief response was daunting.

'Would you rather be alone?'

He shook his head. 'I have been thinking that it would be best if I leave here.'

'No!' She stopped, turning to look up at him. 'I would like you to become acquainted with my grandmother.'

'To what end, milady, so that she might approve me as a husband for you?'

Cassie flushed and looked away. He was right, although she had hardly admitted it to herself.

'To stay would only bring us more pain, *ma chère,*' he said, smiling in a way that pierced her heart. 'You know there is no future for us. I cannot give you the things you deserve and I do not talk of just the things that money can buy,' he added quickly. 'You know my profession is my life.' He took her hand and pulled it on to the crook of his arm before starting to walk again.

'I have been thinking a great deal about this, Cassie, and I would not ask any woman to suffer as my mother did. To be sure my father was dazzled by the English lords and ladies in Brussels, but it was not for their titles and money that he attended them. He could not ignore those in need, any more than I could ignore those poor crushed men at Flagey.'

'You know I would not ask you to do so, Raoul.'

'I do know it, but I have told you, surgery is everything to me. I have dedicated my life to my profession and there is no room for a wife. I could not bear to think I would neglect you, as my father did *Maman.*'

Cassie drew a breath. 'I would take that chance, Raoul.'

'But I will not. That is why I must leave.'

'But not yet,' she begged him. 'Do not leave me just yet!'

With something between a sigh and a groan he stopped and pulled her round to face him.

'Ah, Cassie, do you think this is easy for me? I should have left you at Dieppe, but I was too weak. I told myself you needed me to see you safe to England, and when we reached Newhaven still I could not leave you. But now you are safe, there is no reason for me to stay longer.'

'But there is!' She clutched at his jacket. 'Grandmama will use her influence to help you find a position here in England, I know she will. At least stay here until we have secured you a place in a hospital. Please, Raoul.'

She was begging him, but she did not care. Perhaps if she kissed him he would give in. She reached up to cup his face, but he caught her hands, shaking his head at her.

'Do not do this, Cassie, in the end it will make no difference, I must go.'

'At least stay until the end of the week,' she said desperately. 'That will give Grandmama time to write letters of introduction for you. It is the least you deserve after all you have done for me.' She placed her hands on her stomach. 'And if I *am* with child, I would rather its father was not locked up like a common felon.'

She was being cruel and the shadow of pain in his eyes tore at her heart, but it was her last argument.

He exhaled, a long, sighing breath. 'Very well. I will remain here until the end of the week, but not a moment longer.'

'Thank you.'

She closed her eyes. Four more days. It was not long, but it was something. All she could do now was pray for some miracle.

Cassandra made her way back indoors alone. She could not help thinking that there was something she had missed, that somehow there was a way for them to be happy together. She did not see Raoul again until late in the afternoon, when her grandmother asked her to accompany her for a stroll on the west lawn. She was aware of a stab of jealousy as she watched Raoul joining in a lively game of cricket with Ellen and her two young charges.

'Miss Tatham is certainly at ease with little Meggie and Florence,' she observed, trying hard to sound unconcerned.

'I am much indebted to her,' replied Lady Hune. 'I was at first against the idea of our looking after the little girls while my nephew and his new bride went away, but it has indeed been more restful than escorting Ellen to an endless round of parties in town. And now she is initiating Monsieur Doulevant into the mysteries of cricket.'

Cassandra saw her chance.

'What do you think of him, Grandmama?'

'Is it right to judge a man on such short acquaintance, Cassandra? I am naturally disposed to like him because he has brought you home to me and I think at heart he is a good man.'

'He *is*, Grandmama,' said Cassie. 'He is the bravest man I have ever met and also very kind, and honourable—'

'My love, he may be all those things, but he is still not the husband for you.' Lady Hune took her hand. 'We may be able to keep him out of prison, but he still has nothing to live on.'

'I know it,' said Cassandra unhappily. 'He has told me he will only remain at Chantreys until the end of the week.'

'I respect him all the more for curtailing his visit here. Forgive me if I speak frankly, Cassandra, but I believe he knows in his heart that you would make a disastrous wife for him. He needs someone of his own rank, someone who understands his world and can support him in his work.'

Cassie nodded and glanced down at her hands, encased in chicken-skin gloves to protect them while the blisters and cuts of the past few weeks healed.

'What a useless creature I am, Grandmama.'

'Nonsense. You have all the accomplishments of a lady and in time I do not despair of you finding another husband, this time one who will make you happy.'

Cassie did not attempt to argue, but at that moment she doubted she would ever be happy again. She must not think of that.

'But you will help Monsieur Doulevant, Grandmama, will you not?'

'Certainly, my dear, if I can. Now, this wind is too chill to remain out of doors for long, even with the sunshine. We shall go in. That is, unless you wish to remain here and join in their game?'

Cassie glanced at the laughing group running

happily about the lawn and resolutely looked away again.

'No, Grandmama, I shall come indoors with you.'

Raoul watched Cassandra walk off with the marchioness and the unhappy droop of her shoulders tore at his heart. Having delivered her safely into Lady Hune's care he should have left Chantreys immediately. Now he had promised Cassie he would remain, when every day was torture for them both. He decided he must break that promise, since remaining here was merely prolonging the agony. He fixed his smile in place and tried to concentrate upon this foolish English game. He still had a little money left from the purse Cassie had shared with him, he would use that to hire a chaise and leave at first light in the morning. Where he did not know and did not care.

As soon as he had changed for dinner Raoul went off in search of Fingle. He ran lightly down the stairs to the hall, turning the last corner just as the butler appeared.

'Ah, Monsieur Doulevant. Her ladyship would like you to join her in the drawing room.'

'But certainly,' replied Raoul, descending the last few steps. As he accompanied Fingle across the marble floor he quickly explained his requirements for a carriage the following morning.

'I wish to be leaving at dawn,' he reiterated as they reached the drawing room door. 'Is that understood?'

Fingle bowed. 'Perfectly, *monsieur*. Allow me to announce you to her ladyship.'

Lady Hune was sitting in her customary chair, but Raoul's eyes were drawn immediately to Cassie, who was standing by the window and outlined by the late afternoon sun that was pouring in through the glass. She was wearing the pale-blue gown again, the muslin so fine that the sun shone through it and he could see the slender body beneath. Quickly he averted his gaze and turned away from her to greet his hostess.

'Ah, Monsieur Doulevant.' Lady Hune held out her hand to him and he bowed briefly over her fingers. She continued without preamble. 'I am under an obligation to you and I need to repay it. I have been making enquiries and I understand a medical degree may be obtained quite easily from some universities, especially those of Aberdeen or St Andrews. I am willing to purchase such a degree for you and to give you my support to set up a practice in Bath—'

He stepped back, frowning.

'I have heard what it is to be a doctor in Bath, madam. To quote your granddaughter, they have grown fat giving out pills and placebos to the rich and privileged. No, I thank you!' He pressed his lips together to prevent any further outburst and took a few slow, steadying breaths so that he could say politely, 'I am obliged to you, my lady, but I will make my own arrangements.'

'Oh? And just how will you to that, *monsieur*? Do you have papers, proof that you are not a Frenchman?'

'Grandmama!'

He heard Cassie's anguished whisper and curbed his temper.

'You know I do not, Lady Hune. I served with distinction in the French Navy for six years—'

'That is hardly going to recommend you to the English government! You are most likely to be taken up and imprisoned the moment you leave Chantreys.'

'So be it. I will ask them to contact my captain. He would vouch that I was conscripted into the navy and that I was honourably discharged.'

'My grandmother will help, will you not, ma'am?' He looked down to see Cassie standing beside him. 'She managed to get word to my cousin so I am sure she could find Captain Belfort. She will not let the war prevent her from doing so, will you, dearest Grandmama?'

'We can try,' admitted Lady Hune. 'But that may take months if the man is at sea.' She stared pointedly at Cassandra, who refused to move from Raoul's side. 'In the meantime,' she continued, 'what is to become of Monsieur Doulevant?'

Raoul said quickly, 'I will not live as your pensioner, ma'am!'

'No, I did not think that would be acceptable to you.'

With Cassie beside him he was emboldened to give voice to a plan that had been forming.

'I know that there is now a Royal College of Surgeons in London, Lady Hune. If I could gain membership *there*—members have to pass an examination, I believe, but I have no fear of failing. I studied at the Hôtel Dieu before I entered the navy, and went back there upon my return to Paris. In time I could prove myself, I could even make a reasonable living.'

'Then you could come to Bath and call at Royal Crescent to keep us informed of your progress,' put in Cassie.

Lady Hune put up her hand.

'You do not understand, Cassandra. A doctor might be considered acceptable as a visitor, but a surgeon's presence would never be countenanced in our circles.'

'No, Grandmama, forgive me, but *you* do not understand,' cried Cassie. 'Raoul is very skilled at his profession, I have seen him at work, he has saved many lives—'

Lady Hune's ebony cane banged on the floor.

'That is not the point, Cassandra. One might invite a doctor to dine with us, to visit. But a surgeon—it is an admirable trade, I am sure, but it is a trade nevertheless. Let me speak plainly, my child, as a surgeon's wife you would never be acknowledged in society. You would do as well to marry a shopkeeper!'

Raoul looked into the haughty face of his hostess.

'If we are speaking plainly, ma'am, permit me to ask: are you saying that if I were to become a doctor you would allow me to marry Lady Cassandra?'

The marchioness compressed her lips and after a long silence she pronounced judgement.

'Once your practice was established and if the attachment between you proves lasting, then, yes. You have charm, *monsieur*, I can see that. It will not take you long to make a success in Bath and with success comes money. And in the meantime I would sponsor you and introduce you to my acquaintance.'

Raoul said nothing. It was a compromise, but would it be so very bad? He would be at the beck and call of just the sort of persons he most despised, but he would be able to practise a little medicine. At least he would have Cassandra and he would not feel the same obligation towards his pampered patients so there was little chance of his neglecting her. She would be his whole world.

She would have to be.

'Lady Hune, there is something you should know.' He glanced towards Cassie. 'When I left the French Navy and joined my sister in Paris, she had just received word from our father's lawyer in Brussels. It concerned an English countess.'

'The one who ruined your lives?' put in Cassie.

He nodded. 'The very same. It appears that

when she died she remembered me in her will. She has left me a house in England. Perhaps at the end her conscience pricked her.'

'Perhaps she had fond memories of your father,' said Cassie. 'It may have been that she was lonely in Brussels.'

'Perhaps. I was so young then. The situation may not have been quite as I perceived it.'

'But what of this property?' demanded Lady Hune. 'Where is it, what is it?'

'That I do not know, the lawyers mentioned a small bequest, probably not enough to provide an income. At that time I wanted nothing to do with the lady or her money and I never made enquiry. Now, however...' He turned to the marchioness. 'I know I have no papers, ma'am, but with your help perhaps, I might go to London and approach the lawyers.'

'That is possible,' replied Lady Hune. 'Certainly a doctor with property would be a more acceptable suitor for my granddaughter.'

He bowed. 'That is what I thought, ma'am.'

Cassie caught her breath. Could Raoul truly love her so much that he would consider giving up his work, his vocation, to marry her? That was a sacrifice indeed. She closed her eyes. Gerald had wanted everything from her, no compromise, no sacrifice on his part at all. She had happily given up everything, her family, friends and her fortune, to be with him. It had been an unequal partnership and inevitably it had ended in disaster.

Suddenly she knew what must be done. She forced her unwilling limbs to move across the room until she was standing beside her grandmother.

'No, Raoul,' she said quietly. 'I will not let you sacrifice yourself in this way. It would destroy you to give up the work you love.' She met his eyes steadily, drawing on all her Arrandale blood and breeding to get her through the next few minutes. 'You told me yourself you had no choice, that being a surgeon is what you are. You *must* be allowed to practise. I have seen the good work you can do. I cannot allow you to give that up for me. You said yourself there could be no happiness for us. You would resent me and I could not blame you.' She took a deep breath. 'Before you came into the room, my grandmother was telling me that she has an acquaintance who is patron of a hospital on the coast, near Portsmouth. I am sure Grandmama would be willing to write to him and together they could help you become a member of the Royal College of Surgeons and find you a post at the hospital. With the Dowager Marchioness of Hune as your sponsor they are unlikely to turn you away.'

Raoul's dark brows snapped together.

'Cassie, I—'

She put up her hand. 'We are at war again and it is unlikely to be over quickly. Your services will be in great demand, I am sure, and your skills would save many lives.'

There, it was done. Raoul was looking stunned, Grandmama was silent but approving. Cassie felt her spirit disintegrating. She must go if she was not to disgrace herself. She forced a smile to her lips.

'Now, I pray you will both excuse me if I do not join you for dinner tonight. I shall lie down for a little while and ask Fingle to send me up a supper tray. So I will say goodbye to you now, Monsieur Doulevant, but believe me when I say I wish you every happiness.'

With that Cassie gave a little curtsy and, keeping her head high, she walked quickly from the room.

* * *

Raoul stared at the closed door, trying to bring his chaotic thoughts into some sort of order. He was hardly aware of the marchioness's deep sigh.

'My granddaughter must love you very much to put your happiness before her own.'

There was a rustle of silks as the old lady hunted for her handkerchief.

She gave a little *tsk* of impatience, 'Oh, go after her, sir. Ask her to be your wife. Tell her if she wishes to marry a mere surgeon I will not stand in her way.'

Slowly Raoul shook his head.

'Lady Cassandra deserves better than to take second place to my work.'

'I doubt she would agree with you,' replied Lady Hune.

'She will, in time. Whatever I choose to do I will hurt her, but if I may use the analogy, I know that sometimes one must lose the limb to save the life.' He was still staring at the door, but slowly his thoughts settled and he turned to face the marchioness. 'Very well, then, ma'am, if you can help me to find a post as a surgeon I will accept your help and I will thank you for it.'

Her hand clenched upon the black cane and

she said sharply, 'Let us understand one another, *monsieur*. I will fund you while you obtain the necessary membership of the College of Surgeons and I will do what I can to find you a position. You will be paid adequately, I have no doubt, but there can be no advancement in society, no opportunity to make a fortune.'

'I do not want a fortune.'

'But without the means to support her you cannot hope to marry my granddaughter.'

'I understand that, ma'am. I have no hopes in that quarter.'

'And you will not try to contact Cassandra again?'

'You have my word.' Raoul met the faded old eyes steadily. 'It is over.'

He left Chantreys the following morning, driving away into a grey dawn with the first chill of winter frosting the grass.

Chapter Twelve

Gosport, Hampshire—February 1804

'I have shut up the house, sir, and made up the fire in your bedchamber. If that is all, sir, I will bid you goodnight.'

'Yes, thank you, Slinden. Goodnight.'

As the servant closed the door Raoul leaned back in his chair and stretched his feet towards the crackling blaze in the hearth. Perhaps he would have just one more glass of wine before he went to bed. Only one, though, because he would have to rise betimes and return to the hospital. He had received word only this evening that another ship had docked and the wounded would be transported to Gosport overnight.

Even in the few months he had been at the small hospital the number of injured men returning from the ongoing war with France had risen.

It was already being suggested that he should be promoted to chief surgeon, the trustees recognising his superior knowledge and ability, but the daily round was gruelling. He and his fellow medical staff—surgeons, physicians and medical assistants—worked through all the daylight hours and often Raoul would continue far into the night. Even when he had finished at the hospital local people would turn up at his door with a variety of injuries and ailments, for word had soon spread that kind-hearted 'Mr Doolevant', as they called him, would help them if he could. And without charge, too, if they had no money. He rarely had a moment to himself.

One would have thought that such a busy life would leave him little time to think of Cassandra, but it was not the case. He missed her so much it was a physical pain. She was like a ghost at his shoulder; whenever he was operating he remembered how she worked with him at Flagey, if he saw a pretty brunette in the street he would think of Cassie and when he lay down each night she haunted his dreams. Cassie as he had first seen her, fighting off her attackers; Cassie laughing and teasing him; Cassie naked in his arms...

It was five months since he had driven away

from Chantreys and the heartache was as strong as ever. Impatiently he pushed himself out of his chair and poured a glass of wine from the decanter on the table. It was contemptible to feel so sorry for himself when the hospital was full of men who were injured or dying. He heard the faint thud of the knocker and closed his eyes. Another poor soul requiring his help. In the past months he had become adept at setting bones and stitching broken heads, not to mention advising his neighbours on all sorts of bodily ailments from chilblains to childbirth. He had never wanted to become a doctor yet here he was administering to the sick, albeit those who were too poor to pay for medical help. At first Raoul had thought his services might offend the local physician, but Dr Radcliffe was sanguine.

'There's more than enough sickness and ailments to go round, young man,' he had said, when Raoul had voiced his concerns. 'These unfortunates cannot afford to pay, so you are not robbing me of my livelihood.'

They had discussed the possibility of setting up a charitable trust to help the townsfolk. Nothing had come of it yet, but it was something Raoul was determined to pursue, when he was not so overworked. The knock sounded again and he closed his eyes. Let them go away. He was too tired to deal with anything more tonight.

He was refilling his glass when Slinden came in.

'Mr Doulevant, sir, there is a lady wishing to see you.'

Raoul turned, intending to rebuke his servant for disturbing him, but when his eyes fell upon the figure standing beside Slinden the words died away.

Cassandra pushed back her hood and looked nervously at Raoul.

'I beg your pardon for calling so late.'

Perhaps she should have waited until the morning. He was frowning so direfully that she was about to withdraw when he came towards her, hands held out.

'No, no, it is not yet ten. Come, sit here by the fire, let me get you a glass of wine. Have you eaten? Slinden shall bring you bread and cheese, or there is a little chicken broth—'

'No, no, I dined on the road,' she told him, relief at his reception making her laugh a little.

She sank on to a chair and accepted a glass of wine.

'Please sit down, Raoul. You look so tired, are you working very hard?'

'Yes, but it is very rewarding.'

'I am glad.' She fell silent, sipping her wine while the servant withdrew and closed the door upon them. Raoul was devouring her with his eyes like a starving man might survey a banquet.

'Why have you come here?' he demanded.

She saw his glance drop to her stomach.

'Not to tell you I am carrying your child.'

She watched him carefully and was heartened when he looked a little disappointed at her words. He frowned at her.

'Have you come from Bath, alone?'

'No, no, I have my maid with me.' She added, when he raised his brows, 'I left her at the Globe.'

'You should not be here.'

'We made very good time and spent only one night on the road,' she said, ignoring his comment and untying the strings of her cloak. 'Grandmama's chaise is prodigious comfortable and very swift.'

'And does Lady Hune know you are here?'

He was still staring, as if memorising every detail, and her heart fluttered. His eyes were every bit as dark and intense as she remembered, but then it was hard to forget him when he filled her thoughts by day and haunted her dreams every night.

She said now, 'I came of age last month, Raoul, I do not need Grandmama's consent, but, yes—' she smiled at him '—she knows I am here and I have her blessing.'

She waited expectantly, hoping he might drag her out of her chair and kiss her. Instead he looked down into his wine, scowling.

'I thought she had more sense than that. Finish your wine, milady, and I will escort you back to the Globe. I take it you have bespoke rooms there?'

Cassie was disappointed, but not downhearted. She had been thinking about this meeting for the whole of her long journey and his reaction could have been so much worse. She took another sip of her wine.

'Very well. But first I must give you this.' She reached into her reticule and pulled out a bundle of folded papers which she handed to him.

He opened them and studied the contents in silence.

'This is my testimonial from Captain Belfort. And the copy of my discharge papers...'

'Yes. Grandmama received them two days ago.'
He looked up. 'But how?'

'They arrived with a note from my cousin.' Her smile grew. 'Wolfgang is alive. He successfully escaped from Valerin's men, but a bullet grazed his temple and eventually he collapsed. He was taken in and nursed by some kind villagers, but when he came round he had no knowledge of who he was. They found these papers on him and assumed he was you. As did Wolfgang.' She chuckled. 'He says in his letter he knew something was wrong when he was confronted with his first patient and had not the smallest idea of what to do! Thankfully, a few weeks ago, his memory returned and as soon as he was able he sent the papers to my grandmother.'

She waited, but when he said nothing she continued. 'It means that you can claim the house that was left to you by the English countess.' She saw his mouth twist in distaste, observed the slight shake of his head and said quietly, 'Or you could go home, now you have proof against Valerin's lies.'

'Home?' He shook his head. 'Brussels is no longer home, it is under French rule and Bonaparte is greedy for more power. He has already established his own system of law and made his brother-in-law Governor of Paris. It would not surprise me if Bonaparte declared himself king. It seems no one can stop him, but at least the English are trying to do so. I shall remain here, where thanks to Lady Hune I can continue my work. And there is much to do. The trustees here are forward-thinking men and I hope eventually we may establish a medical school.'

Cassie noted how the tiredness left him and his face lit up with enthusiasm as he spoke of his plans.

'For that you will need money,' she said. 'And perhaps someone to help you.' She sat forward, saying in a rush, 'My fortune is mine to control, or my husband's—'

'No! I have told you, Cassie, we cannot marry. It is impossible.'

'Why is it impossible, unless you do not love me?' She held her breath waiting for his answer.

He exhaled, something between a sigh and a groan as he said, 'Oh, my dear, I love you more than I can say, but I cannot give you the life you need.'

'How do you know what I need? I have tried to resume my old life in Bath, a social round of parties and concerts and balls, but it all seems so, so *meaningless*.' She clasped her hands together, saying earnestly, 'I was never happier than when we were together, Raoul. I know that now. Remember how we worked together in Flagey? When you were saving the lives of those poor people and I was helping you? For the first time in my life I was doing something useful, not merely giving out alms or delivering a basket of food to the hungry. Let me help you again, Raoul. I have been told that the army allows soldiers' wives to nurse the injured, so why not the wife of a surgeon? There must be *something* I can do.

'It will be hard work, I am not afraid of that, and I know I shall make mistakes because this life is very new to me, but I cannot go back to my old one, the past months have taught me that much.'

'No,' he said, jumping up. 'It is impossible.'

Cassie rose and placed herself before him. She had rehearsed the arguments so often in her head, now she must use them to convince him.

'You say we are too different, Raoul, that we cannot live happily together, but the world is not as it was. The revolution in France has turned the old order on its head. And things are changing in England, too. In marrying you I do not consider I would be marrying beneath me.' She smiled up at him, cupping his dear face with her hands. 'I have no doubt that your colleagues here would think it was you who had the worst end of the bargain.'

He reached up and drew her fingers gently but firmly away.

'No, Cassandra, I cannot do it. I *will not* ask you to marry me.'

'That is why I had to reach you tonight.' She glanced towards the clock ticking quietly on the mantelshelf. 'It is not yet midnight and today is the last day of February. Leap Day. It is an old tradition in this country that on this day a lady may ask a gentleman to marry her and if he should refuse she can demand a forfeit.' She sank to her knees before him. 'And so, Raoul Doulevant, will you do me the very great honour of becoming my husband?'

He drove one hand through his hair as he gazed down at her, consternation in his face.

'Get up, Cassie, you must not kneel to me. You are a lady!'

She smiled up at him. 'You told me once you did not believe my birth made me superior.'

'Not your birth, no.' He reached down and lifted her bodily on to her feet. 'But everything else about you—your bravery, your goodness— you are too far above me, my love. I cannot make you happy.'

His hands were on her shoulders, his grip firm, as if despite his words he could not bear to let her go and it gave her hope.

'How do you know that?' she challenged him. 'Will you not give me the opportunity to show you that I am not the silly, simpering female you think me?'

'That is not how I think of you and you know it!'

She waited patiently, watching the play of emotions in his face. At last he released her and gave a hiss of exasperation.

'And if I refuse, what forfeit will you demand of me?'

Cassie had spent the journey considering that, too, and now she gave her head a tiny shake.

'Why, none, my love, but I shall *"make me a willow cabin at your gate".*' She smiled. 'To be serious, I shall buy myself a house here and use my money to ingratiate myself with the trustees.

I shall help them to expand the hospital here, perhaps I will even invest in their medical school.'

Raoul listened to the reasoned voice, saw the stubborn determination in that beautiful face. His defences were crumbling, but he was not yet ready to give in.

He said dismissively, 'You have no idea how to go about these things.'

'I will learn,' came the calm reply. 'There are always plenty of people ready to advise an heiress how to spend her money. Alternatively, you could marry me, and we could discuss all these matters of an evening.' She put her hands against his chest. His heart reacted immediately, thudding heavily as if it was trying to break out from his ribs and reach her fingers. Her smile told him she was well aware of the effect she was having on him. She stepped closer and murmured, 'When we are in bed, perhaps.'

Raoul's iron control snapped.

'The one thing we will *not* do in bed is discuss business!'

He dragged her into his arms and with something between a laugh and a sob Cassie flung her arms around his neck and turned her face up to receive his kiss. It was hard, demanding and ruthless, everything she had hoped it would be and she responded eagerly. When he broke off and held her away from him she had to stifle a sigh of disappointment.

He frowned at her. 'Are you sure you want this, Cassie?'

'Very sure.' She felt a smile tugging at her lips. 'So sure that I sent the cab away.'

'You are quite shameless.'

Her smile grew. 'Utterly beyond redemption, my darling!'

With a growl he swept her up into his arms and carried her out of the room. Her hands were around his neck and she laughed up at him as he climbed the narrow staircase.

'You are going to marry me, then, Raoul?'

'That depends.'

'Oh? On what?'

He paused, his eyes burning into her in a way that set her pulse racing.

'It depends, *ma chère*, upon what you think of my lovemaking.'

He negotiated the last of the stairs and the doorway into the bedroom. A small fire was burning in the hearth, sufficient for Cassie to see that the room was sparsely furnished, but her only concern was the bed, and that looked wide enough for two. Without ceremony Raoul dropped her on to the covers, but her arms were around his neck and she dragged him down for another deep, passionate kiss.

Raoul could not stop the sense of urgency that overcame him, but it was not just his blood that was heated. Cassie moaned in his arms; she was already plucking at his shirt, as eager as he to feel flesh on flesh. They scrabbled to discard their clothes while all the time those hot, frantic kisses continued. They were consumed with a need to touch, to kiss. At last they fell back together on the bed, a frenzied tangle of limbs. Their coupling was as fierce and urgent as the first time, their cries a mixture of laughter and tears until they collapsed, sated and exhausted, to fall asleep in each other's arms.

Cassie stirred. She did not want to leave this dream, for she was in a comfortable world where she was lying with her lover. Slowly the truth dawned. She was not dreaming, this was not her bed but Raoul's and he was asleep beside her, one arm thrown possessively across her body. It felt so peaceful, so *right*. It was very dark, but she could feel a slight chill on her naked skin and she reached down to the tangle of sheets and blankets they had pushed aside during their fevered lovemaking. Smiling at the memory, she pulled a thin coverlet over them. Raoul stirred, reaching for her, and she went willing back into his arms, kissing the line of his jaw, rough with overnight stubble, before sinking once more into a deep slumber.

When she woke again it was to the delicious sensation of a hand gently caressing her breast. Raoul. She gave a little sigh as she stretched luxuriously. The hand moved down over the curve of her waist. When Raoul's fingers slid through the curls at the apex of her thighs her body arched. She was offering herself to him, inviting him to explore her core. She opened her eyes. It was still dark with a sprinkling of stars shining in through the window.

'Do you have to go to the hospital in the morning?'

Raoul's lips grazed her neck.

'I do, but we have plenty of time yet.'

'Are you sure?' She held him off. 'I want to be

a good wife to you, Raoul. I do not want you to say I am keeping you from your work.'

'I will not let you do that, my love.'

He kissed her mouth and she felt her body liquefying with anticipation. She put her hands on his chest, revelling in the feel of his skin with its covering of crisp hair against her palms. She smoothed over the hard contours, tracing the muscle. She trembled as his fingers began to move again, slipping inside her and slowly, gently stroking until her body began to respond. She moved her own hands down over his torso, exploring his aroused body, watching his reaction and repeating any touch that made him groan with pleasure, sliding her fingers across the silky skin, feeling her own power over him.

His caresses were growing quicker, deeper, rousing her own body to frenzy with the sweet torture of his questing fingers. Suddenly she threw back her head, giving a little scream as she lost control. She shuddered, her whole being rocked with ripples of pleasure evoked by his remorseless stroking. She writhed, arched and cried out as wave after wave of sensual delight coursed through her. And still his gentle inexorable pleasuring continued, until her body was a trembling mass of sensations and she thought her mind would explode. Even when at last his fingers stilled the spasms continued, but she was not afraid because Raoul was holding her close and he continued to hold her until the last shudder of ecstasy died away.

'Oh, Raoul that was…exquisite,' she breathed, when at last she could command her voice.

She heard him laugh softly, felt it rumble deep in his chest.

'I am glad you enjoyed it, milady, but I am not done with you yet.'

She sighed and snuggled closer. 'I think you are. I do not think I could endure anything more.'

Another soft laugh reverberated through him and she felt his hands begin to move again.

'Raoul, no, I cannot…'

She trailed off with a sigh of sheer pleasure. Her body was giving the lie to her words. It was softening, yielding, her skin supremely sensitive to the lightest touch. When he began to kiss her breast she pushed against him and when his kisses moved down over her belly she almost swooned with the delight of it. Gently he eased her thighs apart and she felt the gentle rasp of his stubble as he brought his mouth upon her. Then he was kissing her, his tongue flicking, stroking and setting her body on fire all over again. The swelling wave of excitement was building and she reached for him, driving her fingers through his hair, wanting him to stop, to go on.

He brought her to the crest again, but before she splintered he drew away and shifted his body over hers. She took him into her, wrapped her arms about him and lifted her face to his kiss. Her body flexed and gripped him as they moved together, faster and more urgent until, with a triumphant shout he gave one final thrust and they shuddered against one another, minds and bodies joined as one.

Cassie woke as the first grey fingers of dawn crept into the room. Raoul was lying on his side, watching her.

'What time must you be at the hospital?'

'Not for a few hours yet.'

She snuggled closer.

'Oh, Raoul, it has been five months! I have missed you.'

'And I you,' he muttered, covering her face with kisses. 'How soon can we be married?'

'Within weeks. As soon as the banns are

called.' She felt the familiar knot of desire unfurling again as his hands moved over her body. It was difficult to concentrate. 'Grandmama would like us to be married in Bath, but I told her that would depend upon your work.'

'I am sure I can be spared for a little while.'

'Good.' She sighed with satisfaction as he began to nibble her ear. 'Then Grandmama and I will organise everything.'

'Everything?' Cassie opened her eyes as he stopped his delicious onslaught and held her away from him. He was regarding her with undisguised suspicion. 'It will be a very quiet wedding, I hope.'

She lay back against the pillows, smiling up at him. 'Why, yes, of course,' she murmured, her eyes shining with love and mischief. 'That is, as quiet as a wedding can be for the daughter of a marquess.'

'Cassandra...'

She laughed at him. 'Do not fret, my dearest love, there is not time to arrange a vast ceremony. And once it is over we may return here.' She put a hand up to his face. 'I am impressed with our marital bed. It is extremely comfortable.'

'It is not the bed that is important,' he growled,

rolling on top of her. 'It is how one performs in it, as I am about to demonstrate. Again, if milady is willing?'

'I thought you would never ask me.' She sighed, gazing up at him lovingly. 'Yes, Raoul darling, milady is *very* willing!'

* * * * *

This is the third story in
Sarah Mallory's exciting Regency quartet,
THE INFAMOUS ARRANDALES.

Already available:
THE CHAPERON'S SEDUCTION
TEMPTATION OF A GOVERNESS

And look for the last book in the series,
coming soon!